Counterpointe

Ann Warner

Silky Stone Press

Silky Stone Press

Counterpointe
Copyright 2012 Ann Warner
http://www.AnnWarner.net

ISBN-13 - 978-1497555877
ISBN-10 - 1497555876

Published in the United States of America
Library of Congress Registration: TX7-807-118

Editing by Pam Berehulke, Bulletproof Editing
Cover Art by Ann Warner

Dedication

V.   Always...All ways.

Chapter One

Counterpoint
Multiple melodic lines played at the same time

Clare Eliason escaped the crowded reception and slipped into a deserted studio. Lips curving into a smile, she leaned into an *arabesque penchée*. Her hair, usually tightly controlled for rehearsal and performance, brushed against her cheek. She leaned further still, then slid into fourth and pirouetted, imagining other dancers weaving through the room in response to the *allégro* playing in her head.

"Hiding, are we, Clare?" The sharp words bounced and echoed.

She turned to find Zachary Showalter lounging in the doorway, arms crossed. *Damn!* She thought he'd left already. Usually he couldn't be bothered to spend more than ten minutes at a company get-together.

"I never took you for a coward, Clare, but having Delores make the announcement...that was cold. 'And I have one other bit of news.'" His mimicry of the artistic director's nasal twang was spot-on. "'Clare is leaving us to join Danse Classique. I'm sure I speak for all of us when I say I wish you much success, Clare. We will miss you.'"

He straightened and strolled toward her, moving with what one critic had branded a panther's grace. "Don't you think," the words were spoken in the low purr she used to find appealing but now found ominous, "that, oh, I don't know, you might have told your partner before announcing it to the rest of the world?"

9

He reached for her, but she stepped away. Away from that touch that had once been so welcome, had once been what she lived for.

He dropped his arm, giving her a thoughtful look, and she closed her eyes to block out the sight of him. This man who had once dazzled her with his beauty, his charisma, his unexpected regard.

"You're right to leave, of course." His tone had changed again. Now it was careless, dismissive. "We are too good for Cincinnati. But we're a team. Mannie, you know who Mannie is, don't you, Clare? Manuel Ortega, the artistic director of *the* American Ballet Theater? Mannie is this close," Zach held up two fingers pinched together, "from a contract offer. For both of us. That was my news. News you upstaged with this ridiculous announcement about going to Boston."

Clare lifted her chin and pulled in a slow breath, hoping it would steady her voice. "You have no right to negotiate for me."

"No right? Aren't we being a wee bit precious?" He held out his hands as if balancing two balls. He mimed flipping the balls and catching them. "ABT? Danse Classique?" Then he smiled—a predator's smile. "Why didn't you tell me?"

"Isn't it obvious? I didn't want you to know."

"Oh, ho. Afraid I might change your mind?"

"No."

"Clare, Clare. After what we've shared? Just like that, you walk away?"

"Just like that."

"You said you loved me."

"I was mistaken." It pleased her that she'd managed to pull off a dismissive tone of her own.

A brief expression flitted across his face. Regret? No, the Zach she knew didn't do regret.

"You'll never find another partner like me," he said.

"I certainly hope you're right about that." Standing up to him was getting easier with each exchange.

Zach blinked, his lip curling in irritation. "Lest you forget, I'm the reason you're a principal dancer. You owe me, Clare."

And she'd paid, with pieces of her heart. Still, knowing she'd never dance with him again brought with it an ache. All that power and grace, his sure hands supporting her. The two of them moving together, one perfect entity.

Without the offer from Danse Classique, she would never have found the strength to give that up.

"In actual fact, you're rather ordinary, you know," he said.

The sharp edges of those carelessly tossed words sliced at her composure, and her throat tightened. Carefully, she pulled in another slow breath seeking the discipline that underpinned her every performance. And perhaps if she viewed this as a performance, she could survive it. "Odd you singled me out, then. If you thought me merely ordinary." Good. She'd managed to sound calm, in control.

"You'll see, Clare. Without me, you're nothing."

She straightened her spine and lifted her head, going for a disdainful look. "Wouldn't it be funny if it turned out to be the other way around. That without me, you're nothing."

"How dare you."

Calm settled about her like a cloak. She raised her eyes to meet his angry gaze. Motionless, they stared at each other, dust motes dancing in the space between them. Then with all his trademark elegance, Zach bowed. A surreal moment that left Clare frozen, until carefully, slowly, she stepped past him and through the door, pausing only for a glance back to see he hadn't moved. Then she was running, with quick, light steps, faster and faster, away from the past, toward the future, a smile breaking through.

So T.S. Eliot had it right. It was better to end with a bang than a whimper.

~ ~ ~

You'll see. Without me, you're nothing.

Clare shook herself, trying to dislodge the echo of Zachary Showalter's words as she climbed out of a taxi in front of the Danse Classique practice center. The building's facade, slices of glass caught between columns of concrete, was an anomaly in this neighborhood with its tired row of storefronts and triple-decker houses.

She walked through the main door and into an atrium ringed with greenery. Her pulse picked up as she tiptoed down the hall to the right, peering into studios both large and small.

Nothing...you're nothing.

Annoyed she couldn't keep Zach from intruding on this her first day with her new company, she stopped short of the doorway to the last studio. The music in her head switched to pizzicato, as did her nerves. Like every dance studio she'd ever known, this one was bare and workmanlike—its beauty residing in the possibility of what would be created within its walls.

A flow of light through clerestory windows banded the floor and illuminated a piano, which sat casually pushed into one corner. The portable *barres* and rosin boxes needed for company class were clustered in the back, and dancers were scattered around the room, multiplied into a daunting number by the mirrored walls.

Joining in would be like stepping into the territory of a pack of dogs without knowing if their greetings would be wagging tails or snarls and snaps.

She hesitated one last moment on the brink of that discovery. *Okay, Eliason. Enough dithering. Just go for it. The petite blonde in mid-stretch? Think Pomeranian. The redhead with the thick orange leg warmers? Irish setter. As for the two guys by the piano... definitely golden retrievers.*

So...perhaps a *grand jeté* followed by a series of *fouettés*?

Indeed. And wouldn't that make the perfect first impression. Laughter bubbled up, but in an instant, nerves snuffed it out. Okay, no *jetés* or *fouettés*. Instead, she would simply walk in and take her place in the center of the room in the space reserved for principal dancers.

"Clare. Wow! We heard you were coming. Welcome to Boston."

She turned to find Denise Ross, who'd been in the Atlanta company with her.

"It's terrific you're joining us."

Clare returned Denise's enthusiastic hug feeling a wave of giddiness at reconnecting with someone she knew and liked.

"Hey, people, this is Clare Eliason. Just wait until you see her dance. She's amazing."

The pack rearranged itself into individuals, most dressed in the drab garments reserved for company class and rehearsal. Some were beautiful, some plain, but all had the lean, muscular physiques that were the dancer's hallmark. Each greeted Clare with outward graciousness, but she could see the wariness in the eyes of the women who were principals or soloists. She was the competition, after all. The one whose coming would affect their opportunities to advance or to dance the best roles.

With the social niceties satisfied, everyone except Denise drifted away to take their chosen places.

"I saw you on television, the night you and Zachary Showalter danced at the Kennedy Center Honors," Denise said, holding the *barre* and stretching out her other arm. "You two were amazing together."

"That was a special night."

"A dream partnership like that...how could you give it up?"

"It was easy, after he turned into a nightmare."

Denise, straightening out of a *plié*, looked startled. "Really?"

Uh-oh. "Well, no question, he's a marvelous dancer." And she'd once thought him the answer to her dreams—at least in the beginning when he was determined to charm her. She did a *plié* of her own, holding it, avoiding Denise's gaze, but when she checked, Denise was still eyeing her.

"So is he the reason you left Cincinnati?"

Although Denise's unruly brown curls suggested poodle, she was in reality more terrier, for let Denise get her teeth into a scrap of information that interested her, and she would hold on and shake it until she was satisfied she had all the details.

"I left for a number of reasons, the main one being I couldn't pass up a chance to join a company that had a more classic repertoire." She moved her arm into second position, going for nonchalance. "Why don't you tell me something about Stephan Orsini." Orsini was the most senior of Danse Classique's male principals. Even better, he was a change of subject.

"He's a terrific dancer. Not as charismatic as Zachary Showalter, but close. Has a very classical approach. Good stage presence, tremendously athletic. Lisa," Denise gestured toward the petite blonde stretching across the room from them, "claims he's the perfect partner. You'll want to watch your back with that one, by the way. The Wicked Witch of the West could take lessons."

Clare exchanged a grin with Denise. "I was thinking Pomeranian."

Denise shook her head. "Don't you believe it. There's absolutely nothing warm and fuzzy about Lisa. You'll see. Sooner rather than later, probably."

~ ~ ~

Lisa waited until the end of the day when most of the women had gathered in the changing room before addressing Clare directly. "We did think it a bit strange. You know, that Justin would hire someone so...senior? Usually he brings in young dancers and develops them himself." Definitely a Pomeranian-type snap, and with a bit of tooth in it.

Clare straightened from tying her shoe. *I'll just see your snap and raise you a tooth.* "Perhaps he didn't find that approach as successful as he'd hoped."

Denise grinned in appreciation while two other women suppressed smiles.

"Our schedule is much more rigorous than Cincinnati's." Lisa's tone was condescending. "I do hope you won't find it too difficult to keep up with us."

Clare forced her lips into a smile. "From what Justin told me about his plans for the season, I expect we'll all be kept on our toes."

One of the women snickered, which earned her a glare from Lisa.

"Didn't I tell you," Denise said, as they walked to the trolley stop afterward. "Lisa, principal witch of Danse Classique. You handled her perfectly. I'd forgotten that about you."

"What?"

"You can put someone down so gently, they don't even realize you've done it until they find they're flat on their tush."

Clare placed an arm around Denise's waist and gave her a brief hug. "Did I happen to mention how glad I am we're dancing together again?"

Denise giggled. "Little old *moi?*"

"Still a fan of Miss Piggy, I see."

"Hey, you know me. I like what I like."

"Of course you do." Definitely a terrier.

Chapter Two

Relevé sur les pointes
Rising to the tips of the toes

The company gathered in one of the smaller studios for the meet-and-greet with the stager for the season's opening ballet. Colin O'Connor, on loan from Toronto, entered and took a seat on a folding chair, and dancers settled on the floor around him—rather like children waiting for story time.

"I expect you think this ballet is old hat, hmm?" With his balding head and spectacles, O'Connor appeared mild and unassuming, avuncular even, but he had a reputation for pushing dancers to their artistic and emotional limits.

"You all know the story, of course. Peasant girl falls for peasant boy, but when she discovers he's an aristocrat in disguise, not to mention already engaged, she goes mad." He placed his hands over his heart and tipped the chair. "And dies."

Laughter gusted through the room.

"So the guy in the piece is simply another sterling example of your garden variety frog," Clare whispered to Denise, who chuckled in response.

"Ah, but what are we to make of this woman, this Giselle, who would die for mere love?" O'Connor leaned forward, his arms on his thighs. "Are we sympathetic? More important, will our audience be?" He paused dramatically. "You, my dear." He pointed. "What's your name?"

"Lisa."

"What makes you care about Giselle, Lisa? You do care about her, right?"

"Well...sure. I suppose because she was treated so badly, and...her heart was...broken."

"How many of you have had your hearts broken? No. No, that's all right." He lifted both hands in a stopping motion. "No need to confess your sins."

Laughter again.

He stood and gestured as if he were conducting an invisible orchestra. "You see, my dears, you know how it feels to love and to lose. To be joyful, to be anguished, to be conflicted."

One of the men rolled his eyes. "Yeah. But we don't go bonkers."

"Ah, perhaps not. We're too civilized, eh? But loving deeply and losing...we do go a bit mad, hmm? Giselle only a more dramatic example."

Clare looked down as O'Connor's gaze swept over them. Mad indeed. Certainly, it was one way of viewing what had happened with Zach. The mad excitement when he'd singled her out. Falling madly in love—or so she'd thought. All that madness...it had blinded her to his essential nature.

"You okay, Clare?" Denise whispered.

She shook herself and gave Denise a distracted smile before focusing her attention back on O'Connor's introduction.

"You will see, my dears. You have that inside you. And for this ballet, you will tap into that emotion. For this ballet, I will not tolerate merely pretty dancing. Or, indeed, any halfhearted efforts."

Again, he looked from one face to the next. This time Clare managed to meet his gaze. Then he turned and picked up the clipboard he'd leaned against the mirror when he first entered the room. "All right then, let us begin. Clare, Ramon, Stephan, and Lisa, to the front please. The rest of you may go."

As the other dancers trickled from the room, O'Connor pinched his lips with one hand and peered at the four of them. Two of them blonde—Lisa and Stephan-two brunette—Ramon and Clare. So, would O'Connor mix or match?

While he pondered, Clare examined Ramon and Stephan's reflections. Ramon, dark and intense, had impressed her in company class with his explosive athleticism. Stephan was a more elegant dancer, with a style reminiscent of Zach's, actually. In fact, Stephan and Zach were men who physically mirrored each other. Both tall and lean. Both with the regular features prized in romantic leads—Zach the black prince, Stephan the golden one.

"Lisa, next to Ramon, please."

At O'Connor's crisp command, Lisa's face registered shock that quickly morphed into a mulish expression. "Stephan and I are partners."

"My dear, perhaps it has escaped your notice that I am the one in charge, eh?"

Lisa took the place by Ramon looking angry, but with the four of them standing in the new arrangement it was clear, at least on an objective level, O'Connor had it right. The petite Lisa was the perfect size to partner with Ramon, while Clare was a better match for the taller Stephan. That wouldn't help Lisa to accept it, of course, and Clare already knew that when Lisa didn't like the way things were going, she channeled her "inner evil stepsister," as Denise put it. A shame it seemed to be a law of the universe that every company have at least one Lisa.

Good, though, that O'Connor had been firm with her, and good, that his approach was to seek out the emotion in this piece. For despite its bizarre storyline, *Giselle* was an emotional piece and one of Clare's favorite ballets. She especially loved the part when Giselle and her ghostly sisters sought out the men who'd deceived them in order to dance them to their deaths. With the right staging, the lyrical, delicate choreography could be magical.

~ ~ ~

"Bitch!"

Like an anonymously honking horn, the word, laden with venom, drifted by Clare's ear as she pulled on a skirt. She turned her head to find Lisa glaring at her.

"Don't think you can just waltz in here and take over."

Clare turned away and continued to change into street clothes.

"Did you hear me? Stephan is off-limits."

"I'm only intend to dance with him."

Lisa snorted, the sound, full of disbelief. "Like you danced with Zach Showalter?"

Clare's heart rate kicked up a notch, and her mouth went dry.

"I heard all about it from a friend of mine." Lisa's tone was the taunting one children use in the schoolyard. "She said you and he were an item. Except Zach couldn't keep his dance belt on, and it pissed you off."

Clare took a calming breath, not that it did any good. Slowly she turned to face Lisa, aware that other dancers had halted what they were doing to watch. It meant her response would affect not only her ongoing relationship with Lisa, but her standing with the other dancers.

She sucked in a quick breath and prayed her voice wouldn't shake the way the rest of her was. "You know, that's quite a clever way of putting it. But I fail to see your point in bringing it up."

"My point is you keep your grubby hands off Stephan."

Clare almost sagged with relief that Lisa's focus had shifted away from Zach. "I've already assured you of that." She zipped her duffel and swung it onto her shoulder. "Now you'll have to excuse me. Places to go, things to do, you know."

Lisa's chest heaved. She started to speak, stopped, huffed out another breath and narrowed her eyes. "You. You—"

"Bitch? I know, I heard you the first time. You really do anger outstandingly well. It'll be fascinating to see if you can also manage pathos. I'm guessing not." She waited a beat, then, as if this were a simple stage-right exit, left the locker room, head high, steps unhurried, trying to give no hint of the agitation she was feeling at Lisa's easy and unexpected breach of her defenses.

She slipped into the first room she came to, pulled the door shut, and sank to the floor. Then she buried her face in her hands and waited. Waited until her racing heart slowed and the trembling eased. Waited until both Lisa's and Zach's words stopped playing in an endless loop. Waited until everyone had to be gone for the day.

~ ~ ~

"Do you ever think about what you're going to do after...you know, after you can't perform anymore?" Denise posed the question as she and Clare sat waiting for a rehearsal to begin.

"Of course. Doesn't everyone?" Actually, Clare avoided thinking about it, even though she knew her time as a principal was limited to another five to seven years max—if she stayed healthy. But right now any ending still seemed too distant to give it serious consideration.

"And..." Denise waved a hand. "What conclusions have you reached?"

"I want to stay involved with the dance world. I simply can't imagine my life without it." After all, the ballet had been her focus since age seven, and it had replaced all the ordinary, everyday experiences of being young and silly with friends, falling in love with the captain of the football team, running out the door to go on class trips or to the prom.

She wouldn't change any of that, although she did occasionally awaken in the middle of the night to find niggles of regret keeping her company. Regret that she'd not managed to fit in more. More relationships that were about something other than dance. More time to read or sew or garden, or whatever it was other people did in their leisure hours. Just...more.

Denise sighed as if Clare had spoken aloud. "I've already been a soloist six years. I don't think I'm ever going to make principal."

Clare rested a hand on Denise's arm. "You're a wonderful dancer. Don't even think about it not happening. You do know there's a possibility Justin will add another principal next year. It could be your shot."

"You're not just saying that?"

"What? You think I'd pander so I can spend the night occasionally? No way. Please, promise me...promise yourself you won't give up. Not yet."

"I've decided if I don't get promoted this spring, I'll stay one more year. Then that's it."

Clare felt relieved, although she was uncertain exactly why it seemed so important that Denise not quit anytime soon.

"What I'd really like to do is get married," Denise continued. "Have a couple of kids, do the mommy thing for a few years." Her tone was wistful.

"You have a daddy in mind?"

"Doesn't look like that's going to work out either." She shook herself. "Sorry. Enough of the doom and gloom, okay?"

Clare watched Denise more closely after that. It didn't take long to figure out that the man Denise didn't expect it to work out with, but wished it would, was Stephan Orsini.

~ ~ ~

"Excellent work, Clare, Stephan. Go ahead and take a break."

As they walked to the corner of the room, O'Connor motioned to Lisa and Ramon. Clare sat on the floor and wiped her face with a towel. Then she shook out her hair before pulling it back and refastening it at the nape of her neck. Stephan sat next to her, taking a long pull from a water bottle.

19

They were both sweaty, but thank God Stephan wasn't a smoker. She'd once had a partner who smoked, both pot and tobacco, and his breath and body odor had been nauseating.

"How're you doing?" Stephan asked.

"Fine. I was ready for a break, though."

"Yeah. These first weeks are brutal." He took another swig of water, then wiped his mouth. "You know, there's something I've been wanting to ask you."

She glanced at him, taking a drink of her own.

"What color do you call your eyes?"

"What?"

"They aren't exactly either green or blue. So I'm wondering what you call them."

"According to the State of Massachusetts, they're gray."

"Gray, hmm. But with a bit of jade swirled in."

Oh, no! Stephan was hitting on her. "My goodness, we're poetic today."

"That was good, wasn't it?" His voice was smug.

"Weird, though."

"I'm taking a creative writing class." He sounded hurt. "We're being encouraged to think poetically."

She bit the inside of her cheek to keep from smiling and nodded toward Lisa and Ramon. "You know, I think those two could be something special."

"Too bad Lisa is determined not to let it work."

She looked at Stephan in surprise. "Is she?"

"See that?"

Clare looked back as Ramon lifted Lisa. Lisa's lips pinched together.

Frowning, O'Connor signaled a halt. "I want to see that lift again." He moved to the side and watched as Ramon lifted a wincing Lisa.

"Stephan, to me." O'Connor spoke in a quick staccato. "If you would, please, the lift sequence with Lisa." He nodded at the accompanist as Stephan took Ramon's place.

Clare watched Lisa and Stephan go through the steps—two beautiful people moving beautifully together. They turned in unison, arms and legs in perfect alignment, and the lift, when it came, was executed flawlessly. Misgivings about how well her own partnership with Stephan was going nudged at her.

"All right, good. Now, Clare and Ramon. Same sequence."

Ramon wasn't as tall as Stephan, but he was powerful. After a run-through to adjust to each other, the second time they moved more in sync, and the lift felt good. Ramon had gentle hands that tightened on Clare's waist only enough to make the lift appear effortless, but without any of the pinching or rough handling Lisa's grimacing had hinted at.

O'Connor pursed his lips and looked them over, as he had the first day.

Lisa cocked her head and gave O'Connor a satisfied look.

"You, my dear, have been trying to fool me." O'Connor's expression hardened. "I suggest you not do it again. Now, with Ramon again, if you please."

Lisa looked stricken.

Clare retreated to the corner, and Stephan joined her.

"I wish we didn't have to be part of that," she said. In order not to watch the drama in the middle of the room, she pulled a new pointe shoe out of her bag and began working with it. She couldn't block out the sounds, though. The music starting then stopping, interspersed with O'Connor's crisp commands as he corrected an arm placement here, a leg position there. "Lisa hates me enough already."

"Trust me, that's better than if she likes you."

She glanced at Stephan, to see if he was joking. He didn't appear to be.

"I slept with her because she said it would make us better partners, more physically attuned to each other. That part worked, as a matter of fact. Girl can dance, that's for sure. You know, we could try that."

"Absolutely not. I do not sleep with men to improve my dancing." Despite how it might have appeared with Zach.

"Oh, well, worth a shot." He shrugged, with a sheepish look. "Hey, if you won't sleep with me, will you at least have dinner with me?"

She shook her head, relieved Stephan was proving to have such a sunny personality she could turn him down without making an enemy of him. "Look, let's just agree we'll work as hard as we can during rehearsals to improve our technique."

He started to grin.

"Our *dancing* technique."

"And outside of rehearsals? Am I supposed to ignore you?"

"Of course not. You can be...friendly." She finished fussing with the shoe, debating. Then decided, why not. "Would you rather be Lisa's partner?"

"God, no. Dancing with Lisa, it's got to be all about her, all the time." He shuddered. "It's exhausting. But enough Lisa. About that dinner. Saturday work for you?"

"Sorry. No."

"What? Ah, come on. We can't let one bitchy ballerina dictate what we do."

"That bitchy ballerina can make life miserable for us both. I say we cool it."

"As long as that wasn't your final answer."

She smiled, going for an inscrutable look, because of course it was. Final. No way would she allow for even the slimmest chance of reprising her relationship with Zach, and especially not when a friend's heart was also in the mix.

~ ~ ~

> *Boston Globe*: Danse Classique opened their twenty-fourth season last night with *Giselle*. First performed in 1841, *Giselle* has none of the splashy choreography that is the hallmark of more modern ballets. What carries this piece is subtlety, and in the hands of artist-in-residence, Colin O'Connor, and his principal dancer, Clare Eliason, this version is dark and devastating. Ms. Eliason, in her first appearance with Danse Classique, danced an incandescent Giselle with a tenderness that was heartbreaking in its intensity. It was a performance that brought tears to the eyes of many seasoned balletomanes, including this one, and it earned Ms. Eliason a rare standing ovation.

Abruptly, Clare stopped reading. It had loomed so large for so long—her first performance and how it would be received. Now it was done, and the review was...fantastic! Zach was wrong. Without him she was something. Something special.

Her butterflies last night had been world class, and the performance had required her to tap into the anguish of Zach's treachery, which had been exhausting. Afterward, she'd endured the reception for donors in a fog of fatigue. As further proof of her weakened state, she'd even let Stephan drive her home, and here he still was, drinking coffee and waving the newspaper at her when she came downstairs.

"You haven't finished, have you?" He poked at the paper. "Go on, read the part about us."

> Worthy of mention, as well, is the felicitous pairing of Ms. Eliason and Stephan Orsini. In the past, Orsini has given only hints of the proficiency, depth, and élan on display as he partnered Ms. Eliason. It will be fascinating to watch as these two challenge each other to even greater heights.

Fascinating indeed.

He'd insisted she shouldn't be alone when the newspaper and its review arrived. Ultimately, she'd judged it easier to hand him a pillow and blanket than to argue with him.

"It's you and me, girl," he said. "The next Baryshnikov and Farrell."

"You do realize they never danced together." She put the paper down and stuck her head in the refrigerator.

"Just think if they had."

"How about I scramble you some eggs before you go home?"

"I figured I'd stick around, drive you to company class."

"No thanks." Bad enough she'd accepted a ride last night. "I have an errand I need to run first."

"I don't mind taking you."

Good Lord, the man was dense. She tried again. "Don't you need to get home and shower, change clothes first?"

"Okay. I got it the first time. But you can't blame a guy, especially one with élan, for trying, can you?"

She rolled her eyes. "Tell you what. Why don't you join Denise and me for dinner after Saturday's performance?"

He stood for a moment with a thoughtful look. "Okay. Sometimes a guy has to take what he can get."

"Well, that was certainly gracious."

He grinned. "I'd be thrilled and honored to escort two such beautiful ladies to dinner."

"Good. So, eggs before you leave?"

"Naw, I'll just pick up something on the way."

"I do appreciate the ride home last night."

"My pleasure. Anytime."

Nope. Never again. And that was her final answer. He might not know it yet, but Stephan was taken.

~ ~ ~

Although they had one ballet left to close out the season, the artistic director had begun conducting annual reviews, and today was Clare's turn.

Justin sat back rubbing his hands together. "An excellent first season, Clare."

She sighed with relief. *Justin always gives it away,* Denise told her in preparation for the review and, hopefully, contract renewal meeting. *If he rubs his hands together, you're golden, but if he peers at you over steepled hands, you're toast.*

"You and Stephan are progressing nicely."

Clare started to respond then, remembering the rest of Denise's advice—*don't babble, whatever you do, Justin hates babbling*—let her breath out without speaking.

"I've been waiting for a dancer with just the right combination of artistry and emotional fearlessness to dance *Swan Lake* the way it should be danced. You are that dancer, Clare. I've known since I saw your Giselle that you had to be my next Odette/Odile."

Justin propped his head on his hands and grinned. "You may want to start breathing again."

Startled, she realized she'd stopped when he said the words "Swan Lake." It was every dancer's dream, or at least it was hers, to dance the dual role of Odette, the white swan, fragile and vulnerable, and Odile, the black swan, strong and seductive.

"You will be returning to us next year?" Justin said. "Because if you have other plans, I need to know now. Before I make the announcement."

She straightened and looked Justin in the eye. "There's no place I'd rather be than Boston."

And nothing she wanted more than this role.

Chapter Three

I am among those who think that science has great beauty.
Marie Curie

Rob Chapin pulled off his glasses and rubbed his eyes. He'd been working on a grant application for the last three hours in his office at Northeastern University, and when the phone rang, he debated answering. The rest of the faculty and office staff had left some time ago. That meant it wouldn't be a colleague. More likely to be either his mother or his sister, Lynne.

"So, I was right, *Professor* Chapin," Lynne said when he picked up the receiver. "I called your apartment, but when you didn't answer, I figured this was where you'd be. For Pete's sake, Rob, you need a life."

"I have a life. A perfectly good one, as a matter of fact."

"Sure you do. Seven days a week at the university? You're going to turn into Dr. Frankenstein."

"Odd. Not one student has remarked on any peculiar tendencies."

"They wouldn't. They're sucking up to protect their grades. Listen, the reason I'm calling...I have a favor to ask."

"Of course you do."

Lynne huffed, but he knew she was faking.

"Jim will be out of town this weekend, and Saturday is the last ballet performance this season. I'm hoping you'll take me. That is, if you can tear yourself away from your molecules for an evening?"

"You know I'm not into ballet."

"It'll do you good. Expand your horizons."

"My horizons suit me just fine."

"Right. You already know what I think about that. So, will you take me?"

When his sister decided she wanted him to do something, it was always easier to give in sooner rather than later. "What time do you want me to pick you up?"

~ ~ ~

Rob watched the opening moments of *Romeo and Juliet*, impatient at the loss of an evening better spent doing research, preparing a lecture, or finishing the grant application. Then his attention was snagged, by the dancer in the leading role. Even to his untutored eye, it was obvious why she'd been chosen. Elegant and fine-boned, she danced as if she were floating an inch above the stage, her face alive with emotion.

When the lights came up for the interval, Lynne touched his arm. "I'm going to get a drink. Do you want anything?"

"No thanks."

Lynne left, and he opened the program, searching for the dancer's name. Clare Eliason. In her first year in Boston. Previously, she'd been with companies in Atlanta and Cincinnati.

Lynne returned and slipped back into her seat. "Do I dare ask what you think?"

"As a matter of fact, I'm rather enjoying it."

"Maybe you should come more often."

"Don't push it."

She pulled a face, looking as smart-alecky as she had at twelve. "There's a reception afterwards. I'd like to stop by for a few minutes."

So much for his plan to get some work done yet this evening. But as he and Lynne moved around the room, speaking to people his sister knew, he was glad he'd agreed to the reception, since it gave him a chance to see more of Clare Eliason.

She wore a simple green dress that flattered her slender figure, and her hair, tightly styled during the performance, was now a silken fall of rich brown that reached the middle of her back. Her eyes, a color he could not quite name from across the room, were an arresting contrast to the dark hair. The vividness she'd projected onstage was muted, as if a light had been dimmed inside her, but her serene, self-possessed manner still made her the most compelling woman in the room.

Lynne nodded in Clare's direction. "I see Justin is taking care of his star."

"Justin?"

"The artistic director. Would you like to meet Ms. Eliason?"

Rob shook his head, although he felt a totally absurd relief to discover the man with Clare was there in an official, not personal, capacity.

"Oh, come on, big brother. I saw that look. Besides, I owe you one." Lynne pulled on his arm, and he gave in, letting her tow him across the room.

~ ~ ~

Easing down from her performance high, Clare responded to compliments and comments as Justin introduced her to one elderly matron after another. These were the angels responsible for the donations critical to the company's financial health.

"Lynne, it's good to see you here." Justin embraced a woman who was much too young to be labeled a matron. He also kissed her cheek, a gesture he granted only a select few. "Clare, allow me to present Lynne Galt, one of our most generous supporters."

Translation: Major angel alert. Be very, very nice to this person.

Lynne took Clare's hand between hers. "We met last fall, right after *Giselle*, but I don't expect you to remember. You have been simply amazing this year."

It was an excellent thing, of course, for a first-tier angel to gush over your performances. "Thank you...so much. For your support. It means the world to me...to us." Ugh. That support line sounded like something from an insurance company ad, but she was too tired to come up with more gracious phrasing.

"I can hardly wait to see you in *Swan Lake* next year." Lynne released her hand and tapped Justin on the arm. "And shame on you, making us wait until the end of the season for that."

Justin chuckled. "It's a rule. Always save the best for last."

"Indeed." Lynne Galt shook her head in mock reproach before nodding her head to include her companion. "Ms. Eliason, Justin, this is my brother, Rob Chapin. Rob's a terrible philistine, but he had to admit he enjoyed your performance."

The brother, whose studious appearance was enhanced by wire-rim glasses and rumpled hair, shook Justin's hand before turning his attention to Clare. "Cincinnati's loss is clearly Boston's gain."

The voice was good and Clare had always been a sucker for a good voice. She smiled, a safer response than more of the claptrap that had come out of her mouth earlier. Lord, she hated these affairs, necessary though they might be.

Lynne and Justin stepped to one side, to speak privately, marooning Clare with the serious brother.

"I'm wondering what you think of Boston so far?" he said.

"I've been so busy since I arrived, I haven't really had time to form an opinion."

"That's a shame. Boston has so much to offer. I'd be honored if you'd allow me to introduce you."

"That's nice of you, but it's too much trou—"

"Not at all. One of my chief pleasures in life is introducing people to Boston."

"And," Justin said, breaking in, "you won't find anyone more qualified to show you around than a member of Lynne's family."

The sister, the angel, appeared bemused.

"How about it, Ms. Eliason? Would Saturday morning be convenient?"

How could she turn down an invitation delivered by a close relative of a major donor in front of that donor, not to mention endorsed by her artistic director? Answer: she couldn't. "That would be lovely."

Rob Chapin pulled a pen and a copy of the program out of his pocket and wrote down her number. But when he called to confirm, she had every intention of employing the polite, firm refusal she was biting on for the good of the company.

Well, that was her plan until she made the mistake of mentioning the invitation to her mother on her next phone call home.

"Oh, what fun, Clare. You've been complaining for months you've barely had time to see anything besides the practice center. And someone you met at a donor reception? That sounds promising. Is he good looking?"

"In an Atticus Finch-ish sort of way." As she spoke, she recalled the meeting with Rob. Her immediate impression as he shook her hand? That he was appealing. Not because he was classically handsome. He wasn't. But because of the intelligence and good humor in his expression as he smiled at her.

"Even more promising. Come on, hon, you need to jump back in sometime. I know Zach treated you badly, but he isn't every man, and I like the sound of this one."

Clearly, if she still intended to turn the invitation down, which she did, she should have kept her mouth shut, particularly about the man's resemblance to Gregory Peck, her retro mom's favorite movie star.

~ ~ ~

As he wrote down Clare's number, Rob felt like a man transported to the top of Everest, and he was still feeling high when he arrived at her house in Marblehead Saturday morning.

Clare opened the door, obviously not prepared to go out. "Oh, it's you."

His heart sank.

Then she smiled. "Sorry. I was assured Bostonians always ran a half hour late."

"Someone was pulling your leg. In fact, we're often fifteen minutes early."

"How about coffee? I need to finish getting ready."

Relieved that her appearance was a matter of poor timing rather than part of a plan to turn him away, he followed her into the small house and up one flight of stairs to the kitchen. She left him there with a full pot of coffee and an empty cup. He filled the cup then looked around at his surroundings.

Principal dancers must be paid considerably more than university professors, for no way could he afford a four-story house in Marblehead, even one as small as this one, where each level was the size of a single room. On this floor that modest space was divided between a galley-sized kitchen and a dining area. Not unlike the arrangement of those two areas in his apartment.

However, unlike his apartment, Clare's home featured elegant furniture paired with surprising swaths of color—a deep blue wall at one end of the room, a tangerine backsplash in the kitchen, a turquoise wall next to the stairs. The colors picked up the jewel tones in the Oriental rug that lay beneath a teak dining table, and on that table sat a bowl of lilacs.

It was a perfect setting for a ballerina, except for one discrepant note—a brown floppy cushion lying in the corner by the window. And lying on the cushion was a small, odd-looking dog with stubby legs and floppy ears. Not at all the sleek, aloof sort of dog he expected a ballerina to choose.

Solemn eyes met his as he walked over to offer knuckles for a sniff. The dog licked his hand before dropping its head back on its paws. Rob rubbed silky ears and patted the odd tuft on the top of its head—a hippie dog—before standing to look out the window at the harbor sparkling in the morning sun.

"That is a terrific view, isn't it." Clare came down the stairs wearing a gauzy skirt that fluttered around slender legs. Her hair was smooth and tied back with a blue scarf and she no longer had dark circles under her eyes. Circles he suspected that had been deliberately applied. As part of a plan to blow him off?

"Is that what sold you on the house?"

"Oh, I'm not the owner. I'm house-sitting for friends. It's the only way I could afford to live here, although that view did make me lose my common sense."

"Why do you say that?"

"How long did it take you to get here?"

He glanced at his watch. "An hour and ten, no make that fifteen, minutes."

"See? I take the bus, and that lets me nap or read. But it's still over two hours of travel a day."

He gestured toward the harbor. "Do you like to sail?"

"Hmm. I don't know, actually. I've never been."

He almost said his sister and her husband had a sailboat he could borrow, but that was moving too fast, and something about her warned him it would be best to go slow.

"I like your friends' color scheme."

She smiled. "Oh, I'm glad to hear you say that. They asked me if I'd add some color. They were getting tired of white walls."

That described how he felt about his apartment, although he had no intention of doing something about it.

She stooped to pick up the dog. "Did you and Miss Margarita get acquainted?"

"That's a pretty heavy-duty name for such an unprepossessing dog."

"Unprepossessing, hmm? Actually, that's what the shelter named her. I call her Margo. We only get formal when she's first introduced." Clare moved closer, bringing with her the fresh smell of soap and something pleasantly herbal.

"I got a lick."

"Oh, that's a very good sign. Margo doesn't lick just anybody."

Foolish to feel so pleased about a tongue swipe, yet he did. "So what kind of dog is she?"

Clare shrugged, stroking the small animal, running slender fingers through that absurd tuft on its head. "The vet thought miniature poodle with a bit of terrier and possibly dachshund thrown in."

"Is she always so quiet? I thought most dogs jumped around and barked at strangers." Especially little ones. In his experience, they were always yippy.

Clare frowned, as if he'd told her she had an ugly baby.

"I just meant, she's not much of a watchdog."

"Oh, I beg to differ," Clare said. "Margo watches everything. But she's conserving energy. She's very, very old, you see."

"You've had her a long time?"

"Not so long. Three months is all."

He blinked in surprise.

"Right. I know. You see, I went to the shelter to help a friend choose a cat. And Margo was there." She shrugged, rubbing her cheek against the little dog's shaggy head. "They were going to put her down, and she looked at me, as if to say, 'Can't you please do something about this?' And well, I couldn't just leave her there."

Margo licked Clare's cheek.

It gave Rob hope. Clare rescuing an elderly, unlovely dog. Because otherwise, what chance did he have with a woman like her? He was just an ordinary, garden-variety guy, while she was...amazing. Not that he didn't have talent, but it was of such an esoteric nature he certainly couldn't depend on it to dazzle Clare the way she dazzled him.

~ ~ ~

In the car, as Rob drove, he asked Clare a series of questions about the ballet and her career, questions that made it obvious he knew nothing about dance. As they continued to chat, Rob turned onto the turnpike, and they left the city behind. That surprised her. Weren't most of Boston's sights near downtown?

Instead, when he finally exited, they were driving through a residential area of stately homes with expansive yards shaded by huge trees. After several minutes, he pulled to the side of the road in an area without any houses.

"So are we there yet?" she asked feeling a touch of nerves, until she noticed a couple with a baby getting out of their nearby car.

"We are." Rob said.

As he led the way into the wooded area, it seemed improbable that they could be in the middle of a large city, for here traffic sounds were replaced with birdsong, and the cool air carried a delicious scent.

Clare stopped walking and closed her eyes to breathe it in. "This has got to be what heaven smells like."

She opened her eyes to find Rob grinning at her. "Do you know what it is?"

"Of course. It's lilac." She concentrated, taking in small puffs of air, then one deep breath. "It's amazing. Where is it coming from?"

"There, see." He pointed toward a grouping of large bushes.

Drawing near, she saw each had clusters of blossoms—pale lavender, pink, white, purple. Her internal music offered a bright glissando as accompaniment.

"You had a bowl of lilacs on your table," Rob said. "It made me think of this." He stood with his hands in his pockets, looking pleased as she went from bush to bush, sticking her nose into blossoms, trying to detect that particular flower's contribution to the overall bouquet.

"It's wonderful. What is this?"

"Arnold Arboretum. It belongs to Harvard University, and lucky for us they're willing to share. Next we'll go where I originally planned to take you."

"I bet it can't top this."

"You're probably right, but you still need to get your historical ticket punched."

Back in the car, Rob retraced their route, heading back toward downtown Boston. "Are you a fan of 'The Landlord's Tale,' by any chance?" he asked.

"I don't think I know it."

"'One if by land, two if by sea?'"

"Of course. But it's called, 'The Midnight Ride of Paul Revere,' isn't it?"

"That's what everybody thinks." Rob maneuvered his elderly Buick into the last bit of open curb adjacent to a No Parking sign. "I hope you don't mind if we walk from here?"

"Absolutely not. Snagging this spot was practically miraculous. I do know that much about Boston."

When he helped her out of the car, she stood for a moment with her eyes closed, sampling the rich mix of odors—baking bread, garlic, and something green, with a faint, sour undertone of garbage. The bread and garlic scents made her mouth water.

"I think you could blindfold me and bring me back here or to the Arboretum and I'd know exactly where I was each time." She opened her eyes to find he was studying her. She spoke quickly to cover a frisson of nerves at the look on his face. "So where to first?"

"I thought we'd start with Paul Revere's house." He pointed toward a dark gray structure then looked at her as if gauging her interest. "That's only its conjectured appearance, of course."

"Conjectured?"

"Would you prefer purported?"

"I rather like conjectured. I'm just not sure what you mean by it." What an interesting, unusual companion he was turning out to be.

"Well, Revere owned it from 1770 to 1800. After that it was used for shops and apartments and who knows what. A hundred years later, when someone finally had the idea to save it for posterity, there was nobody left who knew what it looked like originally."

"So you're saying all it is, is someone's best guess."

"That's right. You want to take the tour?"

"You know, it's really too pretty a day to spend it inside examining purports and conjectures."

Smiling, he nodded in acknowledgement. "Done. Do you prefer the sunny or the shady side of the street?"

"Oh, most definitely the sunny."

He offered his arm as they crossed the uneven cobbles. "Do you happen to know what Paul Revere yelled as he banged on all those doors?"

"I take it from your manner it was definitely not, 'The British are coming.'"

"Definitely. That would have simply confused everyone, since they were, after all, still British themselves. They might have decided the local pub had just closed and gone back to sleep, and then where would we be? More than likely he said, 'The Regulars are on the move.'"

"It simply doesn't have the same panache."

"Panache. I like that. No doubt why Longfellow invoked artistic license."

At the least, the man had an interesting vocabulary, and it seemed to be catching.

"See that shop?" he said. "They make the best macaroons in the city. Light, chewy, delectable."

Delectable? "You're making my mouth water."

"All part of the plan."

Definitely harmless. Probably.

They walked into the shop and five minutes later walked out carrying a bag containing a half dozen warm macaroons. Rob handed her one, and Clare took a bite to find that, indeed, the crisp outside gave way to a moist, chewy, and—there was no other word for it—delectable center. "Oh my, is that ever good."

He took a bite of his own cookie, his expression one of such pure enjoyment, any remaining hesitation about having agreed to go out with him evaporated.

As they continued to stroll, he pointed with his cookie at a pocket garden she would have walked by without noticing. "See those flowers?"

"The tulips, you mean?"

"Umm. That color would suit you. Rose. Like the color in your cheeks." His gaze held hers for a questioning instant.

Her heart skipped in surprised response.

"You ready for another cookie?" he said.

"Maybe later."

"Maybe?"

"Definitely later."

"I share only with people I like, you know."

"So you're saying I'd better take one now, before I fall out of your good graces?" As she concentrated on matching his banter, something else was beginning to happen. A shimmer of...awareness.

"Or before I eat them all. There we are. The Old North Church."

Halfway down the narrow street, a steeple rose above the jumble of buildings.

"Is that also conjectured?"

"You know, it may be, more or less, since the weather vane is the only original part left. The steeple's been destroyed by storms not once, but twice."

"Ah, the wrath of God."

"Now that's an interesting interpretation."

"What about the inside?" she asked.

"I believe it's authentic, and it's quite nice."

"Perhaps I'd better see it, then."

He bought tickets, and they were ushered into the church. As the guide started her spiel, Clare gazed at the plain interior—the white of the walls and pews contrasting with the scarlet seat cushions. Clearly, a space to bring a troubled spirit to, or even an untroubled spirit. Rob stood beside her, in silence, and she appreciated his not distracting her from her contemplations. Slowly, the sense that he was someone worth knowing grew.

"That was nice," she said when they were back outside. "Very peaceful."

He pursed his lips, nodding. "It's my favorite historical building. Although, there's another one near here I think you'll find interesting." He led the way, finally stopping and pointing toward a narrow house.

"Anorexia House?"

"Good one. Your house reminded me of this one."

"Oh, mine's bigger." But perhaps not by much.

"You're right. This is officially the skinniest house in Boston. It's ten point four feet wide."

Clare stared at the house trying to decide how to frame the question she'd been wanting to ask him ever since they stopped by the garden. But why shilly-shally around? After all, she'd shared macaroons with this man.

"History buff, cookie lover, flower connoisseur, ballet fan. So what else are you, Rob Chapin?"

He gave her a rueful look. "Nothing very exciting, I'm afraid. I'm a professor of medicinal chemistry at Northeastern University."

With his glasses and mostly serious demeanor, he certainly fit the part.

"Medicinal chemistry?"

"Design, structure elucidation, and synthesis of drugs. Therapeutic ones, of course."

"Of course. Structure elucidation?"

"Sorry. I spend so much time in the lab, I sometimes forget to translate."

"I doubt a translation would help. The only chemistry I'm acquainted with is personal chemistry."

"Personal chemistry?"

"You know, between two people."

"Of course. Pheromones, vasopressin, and oxytocin."

Clare rolled her eyes. "Do I want that translation?"

"Probably not."

"You know, you carry that off pretty well."

"What's that?"

"Sounding scholarly without being too stuffy about it."

"Are you saying I'm stuffy?"

"Just a bit."

"Hey, we guys can take only so much honesty."

She looked at him, liking what she was seeing. Enjoying the banter.

Then his expression sobered. "As long as we're doing the honesty bit, I have a confession. I'm not a ballet fan. I was just filling in as Lynne's escort. She dragged me there." His mouth quirked. "Although, I have to admit, I'm glad she did."

"Do you think you could like it?" Might as well get that out of the way, although she was unsure how the clarification would affect her growing pleasure in his company.

His expression once again turned solemn. "Definitely. If you're the one dancing."

She could work with that. Probably. At least his honesty was a nice change from the lines most men tried on her. Or it might simply be a different kind of line.

"A professor, hmm? Your family must be pleased."

"They're mostly relieved I'm no longer brewing stinks in the basement."

"Uh-oh."

"Their own fault. They should have known better than to give a twelve-year-old boy a chemistry set." He touched her elbow, and they began walking again. Before long they reached a small square with a vacant bench. "All right if we sit?"

She nodded, relieved for the respite, as she was still recovering from the rigors of the season. If necessary, she could no doubt manage six hours of rehearsal, but only with a ballet master pushing her.

Rob sat next to her and pulled out another cookie, broke it, and offered her half. "My sister says that Mom's only revenge is if I have a child exactly like me."

Accepting the cookie, Clare pictured him as a small boy with a sooty face, wearing glasses no doubt held together with tape. The thought made her smile.

"What?"

She shook her head. "How's that revenge coming?"

"Not so good. I kind of need a wife first."

"You've never been married?"

He leaned over and flicked a crumb off his pants leg toward a sparrow. "Not so far."

"How come?"

He shrugged and sat back. "Oh, I don't know. Bad timing maybe, never met the right woman. How about you?"

"Never married. Bad timing. Wrong man." *Really wrong man.* "See? Doesn't tell you a thing."

"You're right. Maybe that's a subject for when we know each other better."

"Are we going to know each other better?"

"If we get past today."

"And in order for us to get past today...?" She flapped the hand holding the last bite of cookie.

He met her gaze and held up his hand. "Let's see what we've got so far. A fellow lilac lover. Check." He bent his thumb. "Someone who's willing to walk substantial distances without whining. Check. Able to look interested as I expound on the historical facts about Boston I've gleaned from *Reader's Digest*. Check. Able to continue to look interested when confronted with scientific jargon and stories of a benighted childhood. Check." He wiggled his small finger. "The only thing left is table manners."

Amused, she cocked her head. "So, as long as I don't slurp or chew with my mouth open, I'm set?"

"More or less, although I do intend to keep an eye on things like napkin handling and proper utensil choice."

Good lord, the man was a stitch. "Are you trying to make me nervous?"

"I'm the one who's nervous." He continued to look solemn. "Working to impress someone who can dance on the tips of her toes in front of hundreds of people without turning a hair. It's a tough go."

"Good job of hiding it. You read *Reader's Digest*?"

"My grandmother was a fan."

"So how old are you?"

"Thirty-eight. How old are you?"

"You're never supposed to ask a woman her age. It's impolite."

"Also impolitic, I imagine. So what year were you born?"

"You're a persistent bugger, aren't you. Nineteen fifty-two."

"An auspicious year indeed." He pretended to count on his fingers. "Let's see, that makes you—"

"Thirty-three."

"A mere babe."

"That's also impolitic of you. Calling me a babe."

"Well, you called me a bugger."

"I guess we're even then."

"Even. You ready for lunch?"

How could he think about lunch after eating two and a half, no make that three and a half, macaroons? But then, she was hungry herself, in spite of sharing the cookies with him—a rare indulgence.

They walked back to a tiny restaurant two doors from the macaroon shop, where they sat on an even tinier back terrace and ate a heavenly chicken scallopini. The spaghetti side was smothered in the best red sauce Clare had ever eaten.

On the drive back to Marblehead, Rob invited her to dinner the next Friday. She accepted, deciding it was worth investing more time to see if this man might turn out to be as nice as he seemed. Unlikely, of course, but how lovely if he was.

Chapter Four

Grand pas de deux - Entrée
Grand dance for two in five parts:
The beginning

After Clare accepted his second invitation, Rob knew he could no longer put off talking to Joyce Willette, the woman he'd been casually dating for the past six months. Although Joyce had initiated the relationship, he hadn't objected. But Joyce caught a cold and was missing from work all week, delaying a meeting. He'd even had to give a lecture for her. On Thursday, he finally called to ask if he could stop by.

"I may still be contagious." Her voice sounded waterlogged.

"That's okay. I'll chance it. I'll bring food."

She answered the door wearing a caftan and sandals, although he suspected she'd rather be wearing the flannel robe and lamb's wool slippers he knew were stashed in her closet. Her nose was red, but otherwise, she looked good. Her hair, which she wore in a bun at work, was a loose cloud of gold.

Seeing the effort she'd made for his visit, Rob felt the first stirrings of discomfort. Joyce was bright and attractive, and he'd recently begun to think she might make him a good wife. The only thing stopping him from broaching the idea to her was the silly romantic notion that falling in love ought to involve more than a ticking off a list of positive attributes.

He moved around Joyce's kitchen setting out dishes and silverware and opening the cartons of food he'd brought along to help ease him into what he needed to say. Finally, he uncorked a bottle of wine and took two glasses out of the cupboard. "There you go. Thai. Had them make it extra hot. To help clear your sinuses."

Joyce kissed his cheek as she picked up her wineglass. "Only a scientist could be so incredibly romantic."

He smiled at her, distracted by a deepening disquiet. Maybe this wasn't the best way to do this, although that was difficult for him to assess since he'd had no previous experience with this kind of thing. Still, he and Joyce had agreed on a casual relationship. Except, now he was feeling as though he had violated an ethical standard by taking Clare out. Not that he regretted it, but sharing this meal with Joyce, he found he had to force himself to eat and to make conversation about how things were going at the university.

When they finished eating, Joyce suggested they move to the living room with cups of hot tea. She patted the spot beside her on the sofa, and he sat.

"Is it starve a cold and feed a fever or the other way around?" she asked.

"Does it matter? You feel better, don't you?"

"I do." She stretched, then leaned against him. "This is really nice of you, Robbie. To spend the evening with a sick woman like this."

He shifted but didn't pull completely away. This was turning out to be trickier than he expected, especially given Joyce's status as a senior colleague.

"There's something I need to tell you."

"It must be important for you to go all out and bring in a fancy dinner."

"Yes. Well—"

"You okay, Robbie? You don't usually let me get away with a jibe like that." She pulled away to look at him.

"I, ah, met someone."

"What does that mean, exactly?"

"A woman."

Joyce straightened and stared at him. Seeing her expression, his mouth dried out, and his hands went clammy.

"You and I. We did agree we'd keep it casual." Although it now appeared his definition of casual might be different from hers.

"Someone I know?"

"No."

"But, I thought we... Is she a scientist?"

"No."

"What then?"

"She's a principal dancer for Danse Classique."

40

There was a beat of silence, then Joyce started laughing. "Good God, Robbie. A dancer?" She blew her nose. "How quaint. You have got to be kidding."

"No. I assure you, I'm not."

Several expressions flitted across her face. She started to speak, stopped, took another anticipatory breath, then turned away as a sneeze overtook her. And he would give up his grant funding if he could just leave before she finished blowing her nose.

"But you told me you liked that we had so much in common," she said.

"I'm sorry." Sorry he'd misled her. Sorry he'd compromised himself, he now saw, because it had been a convenient companionship and he'd been flattered by her interest.

Joyce stared at him for a moment then spoke in a toneless voice. "You men are all alike, aren't you. Young and sexy trumps mature and intelligent every time." She wiped her nose and her lips thinned. "I want you to go. And forget about us being friends. Lucky for you, you already have tenure, or I'd make damn sure you didn't get it."

~ ~ ~

Rob stood in the doorway of the department secretary's office. Donna, middle-aged and resolutely plain, greeted him, as she always did, with a warm smile. "Dr. Chapin, what can I do for you?"

"Just checking to see if my grant paperwork is ready yet."

"It's on its way to the dean. Dr. Willette said she would drop it off."

Damn it. No way! He pulled in a breath and struggled to sound normal. "How long ago?"

"Umm, maybe an hour?"

When, as expected, the dean's assistant had no record of receiving the paperwork, Rob's next stop was Joyce's office. "Donna said you took my grant application to give to the dean."

"That's right. I was going that way."

"He said he hasn't seen it."

"Perhaps his assistant misplaced it. Sorry, Rob. I was just trying to do you a favor." She gave him a satisfied look. He wondered which trash can she'd pitched it in.

He returned to Donna's office. "Dr. Willette lost the paperwork. That means it has to be retyped and re-signed. Unfortunately, it has to go out today."

Donna frowned. "She lost it? How did she manage that?"

A tricky question to answer. Still, he'd worked with Donna nine years and their relationship had always been a good one. He just hoped it was good enough. "She did it deliberately, I'm afraid. She's angry with me."

"What did you do to her?" Donna's eyes, behind round glasses that made her appear perpetually surprised, were bright with interest.

"I'd rather not to go into it. But, please, keep my work out of sight from now on."

"I may have a word with her myself. After all, I'm the one with the increased workload."

"Please don't. It would simply make matters worse."

Donna rolled her eyes. "Likely, you've got that right. She can be a real pain unless every T is crossed and I dotted to her satisfaction. Well, today she'll just have to wait on her exam while I redo your grant." She sighed. "Come back at two. I'll have it ready for you."

Rob was both surprised and relieved at Donna's reaction. Surprised to learn Joyce hadn't treated Donna particularly well; relieved to be able to count Donna on his side since she was more important to his day-to-day well-being than was Joyce.

He went off to teach his class, hoping this wasn't the opening salvo in a war, but suspecting it might be.

~ ~ ~

Although Rob had arrived a few minutes early for their third date, to take Clare sailing, she had been ready as she had been the previous Friday, with no resorting to dark circles or unkempt hair.

"Are you always so prompt for everything?" she asked as he held the car door for her.

"I try to be. I hope it's okay?"

"Actually, it's a quality I appreciate in a man."

"Is that on your checklist then?" he asked, beginning to maneuver through the narrow Marblehead streets. "Punctuality?"

"Checklist?"

"For the perfect man. You've heard mine for the perfect woman—physically fit, excellent table manners, attentive to my every utterance. I thought you might be willing to share."

His tone was teasing, but she sensed it was a serious question. She could blow him off, of course. Give him a stock answer, like the one they'd given each other to the how-come-you-never-married question. But he'd made her think. Did she have a checklist for the perfect man?

Well, for starters, someone who wasn't Zach. Zach who had been lacking in every way except one—his absolute passion for dance. And could she ever be involved with someone who had little or no interest in the ballet?

"It's okay." Rob's voice startled her. "You don't have to share."

"I don't mind sharing. It's just not something I've thought about."

"I thought most women started working on their lists in kindergarten."

She shook her head, amused. "As a little girl, I guess I planned to marry a prince."

"You ever notice how princesses are mostly blonde but princes usually have black hair? Kind of makes a body wonder how royal families manage to defy genetics that way."

What an odd sense of humor he had. Because he was a scientist? Whatever the reason, he made her laugh more easily than...well, certainly more than Zach ever had.

Rob fiddled with the knob on the car's tape player. "I thought you'd get a kick of this."

The music had a lively beat, and the song, sung by a man with a slightly nasal voice, was "Margaritaville."

Oh, too funny. "Jimmy Buffett, right?"

"Are you a fan?" Rob sounded pleased.

"Not exactly. But since Cincinnati considers itself Parrothead Central, exposure was unavoidable. How about you?"

"Definitely a fan, although I draw the line at wearing a parrot on my head."

He played the rest of the tape, and by the time they reached Falmouth, they were both singing along, amply demonstrating that neither of them had been endowed with singing talent. It was the most silly fun Clare remembered having in a long time.

When they arrived at the harbor, Rob pointed out his sister's yacht. "She's a forty-foot Morgan sloop. Jim bought her used, which is how he explains her name."

When Rob issued the invitation, Clare had pictured a tiny sailboat like the ones on the Charles River, so the *Ariadne* was a pleasant and welcome surprise.

They motored out to the yacht in a Zodiac. Rob helped her aboard, and after securing the Zodiac, he unlocked the door leading belowdecks. She descended the ladder-like steps to find herself in a main cabin that was far roomier than she expected. The ceiling was a comfortable height for even a six-footer like Rob. The bow area was closed off by a door. She slid it partially open to find a stateroom containing a queen-sized bed. She closed the door and turned back to the main cabin as Rob came down the steps carrying a cooler. He pointed out the head and gave her a quick lesson on the proper use of a marine toilet, followed by safety instructions and a life vest fitting. Then they climbed topside.

After they cleared the harbor, Rob had her take the helm while he turned various cranks to pull the sails into position. Although he had a rangier build than most dancers, he moved on the slanted deck with a competent assurance that was a pleasure to watch.

That was definitely on her list, Clare decided. To attract her, a man didn't have to be a dancer but he couldn't be physically awkward.

Work on the sails complete, Rob came and stood beside her, letting her continue to steer. After several minutes, he leaned closer and adjusted the wheel slightly, saying "Keep us lined up with that spit of land." Then he fell silent again. It was one of the things she liked about him—that he didn't try to fill every quiet moment with words.

The boat skimmed along, responding to wind and current, that responsiveness transferring through deck and wheel into Clare's arms, hands, body. It was enough to concentrate on, to savor, without the distraction of speech.

Most days, her life was saturated with sound. The ballet master counting out the steps for company class, her voice echoing off the mirrors in the big studio. The controlled chaos of rehearsal, the stopping, starting, stopping. The constant chatter in the dressing rooms, the deeper mutter from the male dancers waiting out a break.

"Can you teach me how to do this. To sail?" she asked the silent man standing by her side.

~ ~ ~

"So when were you going to tell me?" Denise asked as she and Clare lay stretched on lounges on the roof of the Marblehead house soaking up the weak spring sun.

"Tell you what?"

"About you and Stephan."

"What about me and Stephan?"

"That you're a couple."

"What on earth makes you think that?"

"It's...well, you've been too busy for us to get together lately, even though it's off-season, and I thought..."

"Oh, Denise. I know you like Stephan. I would never go behind your back. Besides, he's my dance partner. Been there, done that." Clare shuddered and spoke reluctantly. "I am seeing someone, but it isn't Stephan."

"Who? Come on, Clare. Spill."

"He's a professor of medicinal chemistry at Northeastern."

"Okay. Tell me something believable."

"No. Really. His name is Rob Chapin."

"Is it serious?"

"We've only gone out a few times."

"Which doesn't answer the question, Eliason."

"It isn't yet." *But maybe...*

~ ~ ~

The *Ariadne* swung at anchor a short distance off a rocky beach. Clare sat in the shade of the cockpit, her arms around her knees, watching Rob tend a fishing line. Margo sat beside Clare, head up, eyes bright and alert.

In the past month, she and Rob had been sailing twice, and they'd gone to dinner together four times.

Okay, Eliason. Enough dithering. Go for it, already. Ask the man. "So...here's what I've been wondering, Rob. Why do you want to spend so much time with me? I know nothing about chemistry. In fact, compared to you, I'm barely educated."

"Why do you accept?" He reeled in the line, sprinkling drops of water on the deck, and propped the rod on the rail before coming over and sitting on the bench seat facing Clare. Margo crawled onto his lap, and he rubbed the little dog's head without moving his gaze from Clare's face.

"I asked first," she said.

He glanced down at Margo before meeting her eyes. "You're so...alive." He shook his head and the hand rubbing Margo's ears stilled. "Sometimes, I get caught up at work, and I forget to...stop and smell the roses. You remind me."

It was a graceful compliment but not what she wanted to know...which was, why had he done nothing more than hold her hand briefly or kiss her on the cheek? That had been all right in the beginning, of course, when Rob, in his slightly dorky professor mode, seemed a safe choice as a sometime companion. But now, although it was scary to admit it, the no-strings relationship she thought she wanted was no longer enough. She was ready for a string or two, but the question remained. Was Rob?

"Smell, but don't touch, is that it?"

His look quizzed her.

"The roses. You stop, you smell, but you don't touch."

He continued to appear puzzled.

Enough already. Better to know than not know, and sooner was better than later. She lifted Margo off his lap and set the small dog, who whined in protest, on her pillow out of harm's way. "I see a demonstration is in order."

Frowning, Rob let her take his hand. His palm, soft and smooth, was obviously that of a man whose work involved brains, not brawn. She examined it to find his head line indicated he was a logical thinker. Not a surprise. And it was parallel to his heart line, which was straight, although even without that confirmation, she knew he had excellent control of his emotions. Unless... did he really see her as only a casual friend?

She linked her fingers with his. His hand was larger, his fingers longer than hers, but their hands fit comfortably together. "This, Professor Chapin, is called holding hands. A *Reader's Digest*, and grandmother-approved activity." She glanced at him to see the beginning of a smile. She ignored it and settled his hand in her lap, then she ran a fingertip up the inside of his forearm. The skin smooth, pale, and soft, dimpled with gooseflesh.

Satisfied, she lifted her finger from his arm, to trace the curve of his cheek. He'd obviously shaved that morning but she could feel the faint rasp of beard beginning to emerge. "Now, this is a more advanced form of touching. It depends on location and intent as to what level of approval it attains." Her finger traced his lips.

As she conducted her explorations, he sat without moving, but he had a dazed look. *Thank God.*

"And finally, there's this." She leaned in and pressed her lips briefly against his. "It's called kissing. I've heard it's quite popular. Men and women have been doing it for centuries."

She sat back and he shuddered and blinked, as if he'd just awakened. A sleeping prince. Now that was an interesting thought.

"As a matter of fact." He stopped and cleared his throat. "I doubt kissing came into vogue until dental hygiene improved in the 1900s or so."

She debated for a moment before deciding to play along. "A truly dedicated student does not sidetrack a lesson with irrelevant information."

"Sorry."

She pulled out a haughty expression and put it on. "You should be. Smart alecks rarely make good students. They tend not to pay attention, and their technique invariably fails to enchant as a result."

"Really sorry. It won't happen again, ma'am." His eyes held a delighted glint. "Could we perhaps go over the bit with the lips again?"

"I do not repeat lessons for people who ma'am me."

His lips moved into a grin. "Then allow me." He pulled her close, bent his head, and kissed her. Thoroughly.

His mouth felt every bit as good as it looked, and wow, the man knew how to kiss. After a time, dazed and dizzy, Clare leaned her head on his shoulder and buried her nose in his neck. His skin was sun-warm and smelled of aftershave and the exertions of the day. A smell as good as baking bread or apples and cinnamon. "You keep this up and you may turn out to be one of my better students."

"That's certainly my intention." He bent his head, smiling at her. "It so happens there's a comfortable bed downstairs, if you would care to conduct an advanced seminar?"

Uh-oh. But after all, she was the one who opened the door to the possibility. "I need to make sure you've fully mastered this material first." Although, no question he had.

He leaned further back and grinned at her. "Indeed, and would you perhaps give me a critique? So I can make the necessary corrections."

She tried to appear stern, but it wasn't easy. He had such a loopy look on his face, and she was feeling a swoop of giddiness herself. "Well..." But there was nothing to correct in his technique. Besides, it was time to stop teasing. Past time, actually, for them to share their real thoughts and feelings without the camouflage of humor.

She straightened, pulling away, because cuddling against him made thinking a definite no-go. "You seem to enjoy kissing me. So why didn't you...before?"

"*Seem* to enjoy. My God, woman. There's no seem-to about it."

"So...why?"

He glanced at her, then away. "When you agreed to go out with me, I couldn't believe my luck, and I didn't want to do anything to mess it up." When he spoke again, it was with his lips brushing against hers. "Ever since we met, I've wanted not only to kiss you, Clare, but to make love to you."

"But you've done nothing about it."

"Of course I have. I've been doing everything I can think of to get you to fall in like with me."

"Well, clearly I do. Like you, I mean."

"What about that eye-shadow-under-the-eyes trick you pulled the first day?"

She had to be blushing. "Well, that's embarrassing."

"Never try to fool a guy who has a sister. You changed your mind, though."

"I guess I decided you were harmless. And a tour of Boston on such a lovely morning was...appealing."

A chuckle made his chest vibrate against her hand. "Oh, that works. It's every man's dream to be told he seems harmless by the woman he wants to take to bed."

"You shouldn't knock it. Why do you think I keep going out with you?"

"Because I'm safe?"

"You don't exactly seem safe at the moment."

"You brought that on yourself. So about the bed?"

"I don't have casual sex."

"It wouldn't be casual. And it wouldn't just be sex." He pulled her back into his arms and for a time the only sounds were the slapping of waves along the sailboat's hull, the creak of rigging, and the calls of seabirds carried past by a sudden breeze.

She pulled away. "Please. Can't we just...go on this way for a while? I like kissing you. A lot. And being with you. We can take our time...see how it goes."

He leaned his forehead against hers and rubbed her nose with his. "If that's what you want, Clare, you've got it."

~ ~ ~

On Labor Day, Rob took Clare to his sister's for a family picnic. "It's wonderful to see Rob so happy," Lynne told Clare as they worked together in the kitchen. Rob's parents were the other invitees, and Clare was shredding lettuce because she was too nervous to be trusted with a knife.

The house, a large colonial in Wellesley, had a kitchen that would make a professional chef drool, although Lynne had softened the industrial look of stainless steel appliances, large gas cooktop, and solid countertops by painting the walls apple-green.

This was the first time Clare had been at the Galts' home, but she knew Lynne and Jim reasonably well, since the four of them had gone sailing together during the summer.

"Sometimes he's real hard to figure." Lynne paused from peeling the hard-boiled eggs for the potato salad and looked out the window to the backyard where her husband and Rob were firing up the grill.

"How's that?" Clare asked.

"Rob's one of the smartest men I know. Not to mention sweet, even if he is my brother, but he's never dated much. In fact, you're the first woman he's brought to meet our folks since high school."

"Absolutely no pressure, I see."

"Oh, sorry. I didn't mean to make you nervous. I'm just so pleased he's finally realizing there's more to life than living in that dreary apartment at the Prudential Center and spending every waking hour at Northeastern." She sighed. "We've all worried about him. That's why we're so glad he has you."

Except, he didn't "have" her in at least one important sense of the word. It wasn't likely that was what Lynne meant, of course.

"Mom used to worry Rob was gay and not telling her. You'll find Mom can be not terribly subtle at times. Especially when it comes to..."

Or perhaps it was precisely what Lynne meant.

So what am I trying to prove by not sleeping with him? That she could hold onto a man without sex? Indeed, maybe that was exactly what she was trying to prove. For sure, she'd failed to hang onto one with sex. She glanced at Lynne to find an odd expression on her face. "What is it?"

"Oh." Lynne shook herself and rubbed her eyes with the back of her hand. "It's...damn it. I wish..."

Seeing the pain in Lynne's eyes, Clare spoke gently. "What do you wish?"

"My period. It started this morning. It's...it was late, and we were really hoping this time... Sorry." The words trailed off, and she turned her head away.

Clare waited for Lynne to regain her composure, thinking how impossible it was to know all the pain another person carried inside them.

~ ~ ~

"Mom, Dad, I'd like you to meet Clare Eliason," Rob said.

Mrs. Chapin gripped Clare's hand between both of hers. "Lynne told us you were coming, of course. We are so thrilled to meet you." Justin had dubbed Lynne's family Boston royalty, and Clare, greeting the two formally dressed senior Chapins, could see what he meant.

After the flurry of arrival, the men repaired to the backyard leaving the women to return to the kitchen.

"Good. I was hoping we'd have a chance to chat." Mrs. Chapin helped herself to an apron. It made her appear a bit more everyday, although the stiff hairstyle and careful makeup were difficult for a mere apron to overcome.

"Now, I want to know everything about you and my son, Clare, starting with how you met."

Lynne raised her eyebrows at Clare. *See what I mean?* the look conveyed.

Clare smiled back. *Indeed I do.*

"We met at the donor reception at the end of the ballet season last spring."

That clearly caught Mrs. Chapin by surprise, and Clare had to bite her lip to hold in a laugh.

"Clare's a principal dancer with Danse Classique, Mom. As a matter of fact, I'm responsible for them meeting. I talked Rob into taking me when Jim was out of town."

The obvious relief was almost as comical as the startlement had been. "Well, of course, I know Rob wouldn't go to the ballet unless someone dragged him. Don't you remember when we took you children to *The Nutcracker,* and afterward he asked if we were going again next Christmas. I said, of course, would he like that? He said, 'no.' Very emphatically, I might add."

"Rob was ten, I was six." Lynne directed the comment with a smile at Clare. "I don't remember the actual event but I've heard the story enough times I feel like I do."

Clare struggled to hide her dismay.

"*The Nutcracker* had the opposite effect on Lynne. She took lessons and now she goes to practically every ballet performance."

"You were a dancer?"

Lynne shook her head. "I discovered rather quickly I had more talent for appreciating than for performing."

Listening for a wistful nuance, Clare didn't hear one. A relief after Lynne's earlier revelation about dashed pregnancy hopes. "The ballet wouldn't survive without both."

"No, I don't suppose it would."

"You know," Mrs. Chapin said. "I haven't been to *The Nutcracker* in years. I do believe it's something best enjoyed in the company of a child. Perhaps when I have grandchildren—"

"Should I go ahead and put dressing on the salad now?" Clare said.

Lynne mouthed a silent *thank you*.

Mrs. Chapin appeared annoyed but recovered quickly. "Lynne, don't forget, your father takes his salad without dressing. Now, Clare, I want to hear more about you and Rob."

"What do you want to know?"

"You met each other, four months ago, you say?"

"That's right."

"Hmm. He must like you."

"I hope so, since I like him."

"Are the two of you...you know, it's such a modern thing, these days. Cohabiting?" Mrs. Chapin finished off with a tight smile.

Clare drew in a breath to catch her conversational balance and covered her surprise at the bald question by getting out a bowl to set aside a serving of the salad for Rob's father. "I've never heard it called that before." Outside of Jane Austen.

Was that where Rob got his peculiar vocabulary, his mother, not the Reader's-Digest-reading grandmother? "Certainly, in a sense you could say we cohabit, since we both live in Massachusetts, although Rob lives in Boston, while I live in Marblehead." She took a quick breath and kept the words coming. "I'm renting a house from this couple I know while they're in Europe. I keep an eye on everything, and in return, I pay a reasonable rent. Not low, you understand, but definitely affordable for the area. It's terribly inconvenient, of course. Sometimes after a late performance, I cohabit with one of the other dancers instead of going all the way home." A glance at Mrs. Chapin confirmed that the steady flow of irrelevant information was having the desired effect.

Lynne appeared to be amused, Mrs. Chapin not so much.

"How nice for you, dear. Marblehead is lovely, although I haven't been in years. Now, Lynne, do you want me to take the meat out to the men?"

"Game, set, match, rout," Lynne whispered as her mother swept out of the kitchen bearing a platter of hamburger patties. "You must teach me how to do that."

"It's simple, really. Deflect the question, then keep talking boring nonsense until the person is sorry they ever spoke to you."

"That's all well and good. Unfortunately, Mom can be very persistent. She considers it her duty to check our friends out. That's no doubt why Rob keeps most of his under wraps."

Mrs. Chapin, obviously a strategic thinker, waited until they were all sitting around the picnic table in the back yard before launching her next foray. "I think it's so interesting you're dating a dancer, Rob. Somehow, I always pictured you with a professional woman."

"Clare is a professional woman, Mom."

"I didn't mean to imply she isn't. She just doesn't, well, do something...usual."

Had she wanted to say *useful* and pulled back? Smiling, Clare waited to see who would outwit whom.

"It's one of the many things that makes her interesting." Rob placed a hand over Clare's on the tabletop where his mother could see.

"It must be difficult, though. It isn't a career that's exactly conducive to family life." Clearly, Mrs. Chapin didn't give up easily.

"Family life comes in all shapes and sizes, Mom. I expect every family has to work out its own peculiarities. Personally, I've always thought those corporate types, the ones who jet around the world at a moment's notice, have the least conducive careers for family life. I don't have any hard evidence to support that hypothesis, and it isn't good science to generalize without data, of course, but sometimes temptation overcomes even the most virtuous."

~ ~ ~

As the senior Chapins pulled out of the driveway at the end of the day, Lynne bent over in mirth. "Did you see her face? Did you teach Rob how to do that?"

"No. Of course not."

"Yes, you did," Rob said. "When I came in to get the salt, I heard you and Lynne talking. Then when the opportunity presented itself, I simply couldn't resist. It worked great. We owe you big-time, Clare." He dropped a kiss on her cheek.

She smiled at him. *Fall in like,* wasn't that how he'd put it?

She appeared to be well on her way.

Chapter Five

Grand pas de deux - Adage
Dance for two - slow sustained work

In the fall, neither Clare nor Rob had as much time together—she was busy with rehearsals, he with teaching. But he found a way to spend time with her after he attended the first ballet of the new season.

"What do you usually do after performances?"

"You mean, when a certain professor doesn't show up to drive me home?" She linked her hand with his across the car's console. "If it's a matinee, I take the bus home. If it's late, I spend the night with Denise. Either way, the first order of business is food, because I'm always starving."

"Do you want to stop somewhere?"

"No, better if you just take me home. I'll find something to heat up."

"Why don't you let me cook?"

"You cook?"

"It's not very flattering to sound so surprised. If I didn't cook, I'd starve. In case it's escaped your notice, I do live alone."

"Okay. I accept."

While she showered, he assessed the contents of her refrigerator and ended up making his late-night specialty-fried egg sandwiches.

Clare came downstairs, wearing a terry cloth robe, her face pink and scrubbed. They ate and talked quietly until Clare stretched and yawned. "You know, I'm sleepy, which is amazing. Usually, it takes me hours to relax after a performance."

"It's my gift. Making women sleepy."

"It's a wonderful gift."

"What were you thinking, just then?"

She shook her head. "Oh, nothing."

"You seemed sad."

She sighed. "I was remembering...oh, it isn't important."

"Not a good memory?"

"Parts were good. Once upon a time." Her hands plucked at a loose thread on the robe. Rob doubted she realized she was doing it.

He'd never hunted but perhaps it would be like this. Watching, catching a glimpse, a flash of movement, and freezing in place, so you didn't startle whatever wild thing was there. He waited, silent and still.

"It's just...sometimes, when the dancing goes really well, it's easy to forget it isn't real. That closeness to a partner. And after a performance..." Her words trailed off, her gaze focused inward.

Was she trying to tell him she was in love with Stephan Orsini? Rob's chest tightened.

"Oh, damn. I'm just being maudlin." Clare shook her head. "Ridiculous. It's in the past, after all."

Although he wasn't completely reassured, Rob's breathing eased. She stood and began clearing the table, which meant no more confidences tonight.

"I guess I better get going."

Clare halted halfway to the kitchen with her empty plate and turned to face him. "Would you like to stay?"

It seemed to take forever to drag the breath back into his lungs. While he did, he stared at Clare across the length of the room.

Her expression became tentative. "It wasn't a trick question, you know."

"God, yes, I want to stay."

She set the plate down and reached out a hand to him. Although, he felt light enough to leap over the table, he approached her cautiously, reality unspooling, spinning away, as he placed his hand in hers.

~ ~ ~

Clare stepped into Rob's embrace, as surprised by her invitation as he'd obviously been. But with the words spoken, she found she had no wish to take them back.

55

One of Rob's hands slid through her hair, smoothing it, massaging her scalp. "I love your hair. I wanted to do this the first night we met."

She bit down on the temptation to counter with a smart remark. Instead, she relaxed, letting her thoughts slow to the pace of his stroking. Safe. She was safe with Rob. She settled against him, using her lips to taste and touch. Letting everything else fall away—memories, fears, doubts.

~ ~ ~

Rob's desire for Clare had become a deep, stubborn ache. What an enormous relief when she took his hand and led him upstairs to her bedroom. There, she unwrapped him with a slow, solemn deliberation he then turned on her.

Naked, she was even lovelier than he imagined she'd be. The elegant definition of muscle in leg, shoulder, and arm now fully revealed—tensile strength, tempered by delicacy. The silken slide of her skin, rosy with arousal against his fingertips. Her lovely dancer's body, moving in a rhythm, finally, of his devising.

Before he met Clare, the thought he might be missing something had been vague, formless. Now she had brought shape and weight, sound and touch, taste and smell into his life. Thank God he hadn't settled for less.

"Tell me," he said, holding her close. "What it's like when you dance."

"It's..."

He waited.

"Always before a performance, it's a madhouse backstage. Everyone rushing around until this moment when everything goes still, and we all stop moving, speaking. As if we've been frozen by the casting of a spell. Then the music begins, and when I step onstage, it's like stepping into a different dimension. As if I'm dreaming it. And everything is effortless, even the bits I've had trouble with. And nothing hurts. It's the most amazing, fantastic feeling. There's really no word that can quite describe it."

For him, it was what making love to her was like.

~ ~ ~

Rob tucked Clare's body into his and drifted off to sleep.

Wide awake, she lay beside him, trying to outwit the uninvited memories of the last time she'd slept with a man.

Zach. He'd been a demanding lover, especially when he was on a performance high. Those nights, he'd stripped off her clothes as soon as they entered his apartment, expecting her to be ready as quickly as he was. Impatient if she was not.

When she'd matched his passion, it was like falling off the edge of the earth. At least, in the beginning. Her body stiffened at the memory of that later time.

"You okay, Clare?" Rob slid a hand gently along the curve of her hip.

"Umm. Didn't realize you were awake."

He turned her until she lay facing him. "A penny."

"You'd be overpaying."

"Try me."

She'd read somewhere it was in lovemaking that a person's character was most fully revealed. So why did it take her so long to see Zach clearly? Zach, who danced like an angel but made love with a careless ferocity. In contrast, making love to Rob was like curling up with cookies and milk when she was hungry, or snuggling into a quilt in front of a warm fire when she was cold.

"I was thinking you're one of the gentlest men I've ever known."

"Is that a good thing or a bad thing? Because I can be ungentle if that's a requirement."

How easily he could make her smile, this man whose lovemaking had soothed her Zach wounds.

"No, it's a good thing." *A terrific, amazing thing.*

Chapter Six

Divertissement
A short dance offered as entertainment
between the main parts

Rob had begun to dread faculty meetings since they afforded
Joyce, who was still angry, such rich opportunities to snipe at
him, although she was subtle enough that he appeared to be
the only one aware of her tactics. They included comments
veiled with apparent admiration as she proposed him for the
most onerous and time-consuming duties.

"It's obvious the best person to head the curriculum review
is Rob." Joyce smirked at him. "He has such an excellent
understanding of academic requirements, not to mention,
great rapport with the students."

"Rob has a full plate right now, Joyce, with his grant
renewal being approved." The department chairman gave them
both a thoughtful look. "I believe I'll table that assignment for
the moment."

Rob, relieved, didn't even glance in Joyce's direction,
knowing it would only encourage her to try harder next time.

~ ~ ~

"Dr. Chapin?"

Rob looked up to find his Japanese graduate student
standing in the doorway of his office. "What is it, Hatsume?"

"A small problem. I don't like I have to bother you."

"No bother. Please, tell me what it is."

With head bowed, the girl came and perched on the edge of
the chair next to his desk. "Is what Dr. Willette say."

58

"And what was that?" His hands clenched. He was damn tired of Joyce's sniping.

"She say the IR bought with her money. I no can use without asking her permission."

The IR, infrared spectrometer, was located in a room with other equipment various faculty, including Rob, had purchased with grant funds. Only the most sensitive instruments were restricted. The IR was one of the workhorses. Even undergraduates used it.

He could retaliate, of course. Require Joyce's students to seek his permission to use the instruments his grants had supplied, but it would only make the situation both more uncomfortable and more public.

"I'm sorry, Hatsume. But if Dr. Willette wishes to restrict access, it's her prerogative."

Against his better judgment, Rob went to see Joyce. He stood in her doorway waiting for her to acknowledge his presence.

"Well, well, Robbie. This is a surprise. To what do I owe the pleasure?" She didn't invite him in, not that he had any intention of getting closer.

"Hatsume tells me you've restricted access to the IR."

"That's right."

"You're angry with me, Joyce. Why take it out on a student?"

"It's *Doctor* Willette."

He'd once thought her both attractive and accomplished, failing to see below the thin surface coating to her true nature. Now it was all he did see. Intelligence in the service of vindictiveness. A lovely face masking an ugly disposition.

"I'm not playing your game, Joyce. Attack me if you must, but lay off the students."

"So, report me, why don't you?" Her smile was that of a crocodile getting ready to feed.

"I'm considering it. Our chairman may be laid back, but he won't allow students to be mistreated. Especially graduate students."

The gloating look was replaced by a sick expression. "Get out."

"Gladly."

Joyce was making him pay a high price, but Clare was worth every penny.

~ ~ ~

The Nutcracker rehearsal had been long, and Clare was more than ready to go home. But first she needed to comfort Denise, who'd just been bumped from a first cast solo by a minor ankle strain.

Lisa swept by Clare and Denise in the changing room then stopped and turned. "Gee, Ross. Too bad about the ankle. A word to the wise. If I were you, I'd start planning on doing something else next year."

Clare usually ignored Lisa's nasty comments, but it was one thing to choose not to fight back on her own account, another to see a friend being hurt.

She took a breath and tried to keep her tone casual. "Actually, you're the one who should be planning a new career."

"Oh? And why is that?"

"I'm sorry to say you've failed to make the progress we've expected and hoped for." It was the kind of kiss-off line artistic directors employed when letting a dancer go. And Lisa knew it.

Her eyes widened, and her lips curled. "And what progress is that?"

"Why, we've been hoping you'd turn out to be human. Unfortunately, it doesn't seem to be happening."

"It eats, it sleeps, it dances, it showers, but it's still a robo bitch," another dancer intoned. Applause greeted the line.

"You, you are..." Lisa grabbed her dance bag, whirled, and pushed her way into one of the shower cubicles.

The water was still running when Denise and Clare left the changing room ten minutes later.

"You know she might be right about me," Denise said.

"No, she's not. She's picking on you because you're good. She never wastes her jabs on someone who isn't a threat."

"Well, I'm no threat at the moment."

"But you will be after you go home and get out the Tiger Balm and wrap that ankle in plastic wrap and elevate. You'll come back stronger than ever. And she knows it. That's why she's taking her shot now."

"I don't know how much longer I can hang on. If Justin doesn't promote me this year..."

"You can't control what Justin does. All you can do is your best."

"But, I'm not like you, Clare. Dance isn't everything to me. Sometimes I get so tired of fighting it. The injuries, the disappointments, and when was the last time you didn't wince when you looked at your feet? Maybe it is time."

"You're a wonderful dancer. You can't listen to Lisa. After all, you know what happens when you let a Vulcan get to you."

"Haven't a clue."

"Sure you do. Your ears grow points but you can't open your mouth without saying something pointless."

"Like Lisa."

"Exactly like Lisa. Look at it this way. You and I have been making first cast regularly while Lisa's been stuck in second."

"That's because you're better than she is."

"Not entirely. Lisa's a terrific dancer with excellent technical skills, but she has no heart. And everyone knows it."

~ ~ ~

"Have you heard the news about Zachary Showalter?" Lisa sidled to a *barre* position near Clare, but she directed the comment to the dancer next to Clare who was stretching in preparation for company class.

"He said he'd never had a more intuitive and talented partner than Belinda Schwarz. They just won this year's Pritzcovich Medal. Can you imagine if you were his partner and he bounced you? It would be like being given the boot by Nureyev."

It was clearly a blatant attempt on Lisa's part to push Clare's buttons. Unfortunately for Lisa, it didn't work. Not a single button had moved even slightly, and when had that happened—that Clare could think about Zach without any accompanying twinges of regret?

She stifled the impulse to give Lisa a hug.

~ ~ ~

The intercom buzzed and woke Rob from a feverish dream. He peered at the clock—four forty-five—but whether it was a.m. or p.m. was open to question.

No. Afternoon. Had to be, although it was dark out. He sat on the edge of the bed waiting for the dizziness to ease before going to answer the intercom. The buzzer went off again, sending pain shooting through his head.

"Who is it?" His voice was gruff with both congestion and irritation.

"Rob, it's me. Clare. Can I come up? Please?"

What was she doing here? He'd called her, first thing this morning to tell her their Christmas Eve, and probably Christmas Day, plans had to be canceled.

"I don't want you to get my bug."

"I'll be careful."

After hitting the lock release for the main door and leaving his front door ajar so she could get in, he went back to the bedroom and pulled on jeans and a sweater. He washed his face and brushed his teeth, but little could be done about his hair, which stuck up at odd angles as if licked into place by a manic cat. He wet it and tried smoothing it, but that only made it worse. Giving up, he went looking for Clare. She was in his kitchen, frowning at the contents of his refrigerator.

"You shouldn't be here." Keeping her from his apartment had been a major priority. It wasn't that it was so bad exactly, and it did have a great view of the Christian Science Mother Church and surrounding plaza. But the furnishings were leftovers from his last student apartment and the word "elegant" definitely need not apply. Even a word like "utilitarian" would be overly kind.

At the moment, though, he was too sick to worry about that. "I don't want to give you the flu for Christmas."

"I've had my shot. Boy, you sure don't have much food here." She closed the refrigerator and opened a cupboard. "Oh, good. Tea. But if I want to eat, it looks like I need to go shopping. And I definitely want to eat. I'm starving."

Of course. Nearly five o'clock on Christmas Eve. She had just danced in *The Nutcracker* matinee. He made his way out of the kitchen and plopped on a chair, desperately wishing he didn't feel so lousy.

"You okay?" Clare's face swam in front of his, then there was a strong push on the back of his head. "Here we go. Don't want you passing out on me, babe."

The buzzing in his ears gradually decreased. He sat up slowly, still feeling dizzy.

Clare stared at him for a moment. "You okay?"

He nodded. Although claiming to be okay was highly inflated optimism.

"I think you need to get back to bed."

She walked him down the hall. By the time they reached the bedroom his head was spinning again, and he was glad to lie down. Clare pulled off his jeans, straightened the covers over him, and plumped a pillow for his head.

Her lips were cool on his forehead. "Sleep tight, Rob."

She left the room, and he slipped into a feverish doze, awakening some indeterminate time later to a cool hand on his brow.

"How are you feeling?"

"Like I've been stomped by something large and hairy."

"Well, I think it's a good sign you still have your sense of humor. Can you sit up? I've got acetaminophen and tea here."

He struggled upright, and Clare turned on the lamp. He peered at the clock. Six thirty. It meant he'd been sleeping an hour and a half while Clare had been...?

She handed him water and two tablets, and he downed both.

"Now, tea while I finish fixing dinner?"

He accepted the warm mug. "Dinner?" His voice was a croak.

"Lucky you have a Star Market so close. It was a madhouse, what with it being Christmas Eve. But I managed to find the makings for chicken noodle soup and a salad, and I snagged the last loaf of French bread. I was totally ruthless. Pulled it away from a little old lady. She gave me a dirty look, but when I told her I needed it for a sick friend, she caved."

While Clare chattered, Rob sipped tea, surprised afterward to discover he was both hungry and clearheaded enough to make it to the dining room without difficulty. Once there, he discovered more of what Clare had been doing while he slept. She'd tuned the radio to a station playing Christmas carols and transformed his dinner table with a poinsettia plant and a cluster of candles. With the only light coming from the candles, the worst of his decorating defects were invisible.

"It's nice. Really nice, Clare." Great, so along with clear sinuses, the virus had deprived him of the power to put a coherent compliment together?

He took a seat, and Clare went into the kitchen, emerging shortly with steaming bowls of noodle soup that even to his stuffy nose smelled wonderful. Then came the purloined bread followed by plates of salad, another cup of tea for him, and a glass of white wine for her.

"Not exactly how I pictured spending Christmas Eve. The soup is delicious, by the way."

"Old family recipe. Always dispensed in times of ill health."

"I'm sorry about this."

"What? Getting sick? Well, you didn't do it on purpose, did you? You know, in the cause of scientific inquiry or something?"

He shuddered. "Absolutely not."

"That's what I thought. Besides, you'd do the same for me if I'd been the one who was sick."

"What? You mean show up, decorate, and cook you homemade chicken soup?"

"Well, maybe not all that, but you wouldn't have left me alone on Christmas Eve."

She was right about that.

When they finished eating, she hopped up and cleared the dishes. When she returned, she brought a large package with her. "The other reason I had to see you was I wanted to give you your gifts."

"Just a minute, I need to get yours." Good thing he'd figured out what to get her in time to wrap them before the flu felled him. He returned to the dining room, pleased the trip down the hall hadn't left him dizzy this time.

"Ladies first." He handed her the larger of the two packages.

She shook it and checked its heft before beginning to carefully dismantle his awkward taping.

"Are you trying to save the wrapping paper?" he asked.

"Of course not. I'm merely trying to appear sophisticated and mature."

"Count me convinced."

Meeting his eyes, she ripped the paper off and opened the lid of the box. "Oh, Rob, this is too, too funny."

She left what he'd given her in its wrappings, picked up one of the presents she had for him, and thrust it in his hands. "Go on, open it. And none of that prissy stuff. I want it open. Now."

He did as ordered, finally lifting out of its nest of tissue paper a purple panama hat with a green and yellow parrot perched on top.

"Here, allow me." Clare took the hat from his hands and set it on his head.

"Guaranteed to impress small children and frighten elderly ladies."

She chuckled. "No really, it's very becoming."

"Your turn." He placed his gift to her, a pink baseball cap with a perched parrot, on her head. "And please note how much more tasteful my selection is." He'd chosen a parrot a third the size of the one she'd picked.

She shook her head, making the parrot bob.

"You realize there's only one place we can wear these," he said.

"Behind locked doors?"

"We'll have to attend a Jimmy Buffett concert."

She shuddered, making him chuckle.

"I have something else for you." She handed him a long, narrow package. "It's something you won't have to hide in the back of your closet. And don't think I can't see that's what you're planning."

"Never." He accepted the second package. It was heavy and whatever was in it shifted slightly when he shook it. "A length of pipe? A long narrow brick?"

"Not even close."

He removed the paper, opened the box, and examined the contents.

"It's a kaleidoscope. You always notice colors, so I thought you'd like it. Well, I hoped you would."

Smiling, he lifted the tube to his eye and rotated the *barrel*. Colors cascaded, the effect intensified by the flickering of the candles.

"It's amazing. Here, take a look." He handed her the tube, resisting, in the interest of hygiene, the impulse to lean over and kiss her. When she finally set the kaleidoscope down, he gave her his second gift, a small square box.

Clare accepted it, looking hesitant. She glanced at him before beginning to pick at the wrapping tape. In his debilitated condition, it took him longer than it should have to realize she was worried it might be a ring. He gently removed the partially unwrapped box from her hands. "Let me help you with that."

He glanced at her to find her eyes riveted on the box as he finished removing the paper. He snapped open the lid, gauging her reaction as he did so. He'd be willing to bet a great deal her expression was one of relief, not disappointment, as he placed the gift back in her hands. He filed what he thought about that away for later.

"It's lovely, Rob."

She looked at him with a question in her eyes.

"It was my grandmother's."

"Oh. Are you sure?"

"That I want you to have it? Absolutely sure."

She pinned the brooch, a bisque porcelain rose, to the neckline of the dress she was wearing, then jumped up to check how it looked in the mirror. She came back smiling, and leaned over and kissed him on the cheek. "I'll treasure it. Thank you, Rob."

~ ~ ~

On New Year's Eve, a mostly recovered Rob escorted Clare and Denise to a party attended by most of the Danse Classique company. When they arrived at the apartment where the party was taking place, Clare took their coats upstairs to the loft-style bedroom leaving Rob and Denise below in the large living area. All the furniture was pushed to the edges of the room and forties band music accompanied the loud hum of voices. In one corner couples were dancing.

"That's our host, over there," Denise told Rob, nodding toward a man Rob recognized as Clare's dance partner.

Rob leaned over to speak in her ear. "Should we say hello?"

Denise tucked her hand in his arm and stood on tiptoe. "That's an outstanding idea."

They made their way to Stephan, and Denise performed the introductions, referring to Rob as a good friend.

"Glad you're here," Stephan said. "Any friend of Denise's and all that. Beer's on the deck, wine's in the kitchen."

As Denise started to say something else, Stephan's attention was pulled away by a petite blonde who came up to him and slipped her arm through his.

"Ah. Lisa, good to see you."

Rob shrugged at Denise. "We're obviously dismissed. What will it be? Wine or beer?"

"I don't care. Wine, I guess."

"Hey, why so glum?"

"Her." Denise tipped her chin, indicating the blonde who appeared to be hanging on to Stephan for dear life.

"I think he wants to ditch her," Rob said, whispering back.

"Really?"

Just then, Stephan pulled free of Lisa and pushed past Denise and Rob. "Clare. My party is now complete. Come, dance with me."

Clare shrugged, meeting Rob's eyes, but she went with Stephan to the area set aside for dancing. Without letting go of Clare's hand, Stephan leaned over and spoke to the man running the record player. The man nodded, lifted the arm from the current record, and flipped another into place.

The music that floated out was soft and seductive. As Stephan pulled Clare into his arms, Rob became aware of Denise's fingers digging into his arm. He shifted, and she removed her hand with a quick apology.

He looked from Denise to Clare to Stephan, a distinct picture beginning to form. "Shall we dance?" he said.

Denise's head jerked in what he took to be an affirmative. He led her toward the other dancers, silently thanking his mother for insisting he take lessons.

When the first slow tune segued into a second, Rob steered Denise over next to Clare and Stephan, and tapped Stephan on the shoulder. "Mind if I cut in?"

With an annoyed look, Stephan switched partners. Rob pulled Clare close so he could whisper in her ear. "Is that what I think it is?" He nodded toward Stephan and Denise.

"Depends on what you think it is."

"My guess is she's in love with him, but he's got his eye on you."

"You're right about the first part. I hope you're wrong about the second."

"Kiss me."

"What?"

"Do it."

Clare rolled her eyes but then lifted her face to his. He brushed her lips with his.

"What was that about?" Clare asked, leaning back.

"Making sure he isn't confused about who's here with whom."

"You are so bad."

"Well, if you want him to see someone other than you, the simplest way is to send a definite message. You can kiss me again, if you like."

Clare laughed and laid her cheek against his. "You know, you're actually pretty good at this."

"What? Dancing or kissing."

"Both, as a matter of fact."

"You could sound a little less surprised."

"I like that you're full of surprises."

He shuddered, pulling her closer. "You're making me nervous, love."

"Just keeping you on your toes."

"Oh well," he said. "Better my toes than yours."

Chapter Seven

Plié
An exercise involving bending of the knees in order
to develop balance and make joints and muscles
pliable and tendons flexible

As winter began to give way to a tentative spring, rehearsals for *Swan Lake* finally started. It was what Clare had been waiting for with barely contained impatience.

Despite that impatience, she hadn't questioned Justin's judgment at leaving this ballet until the end of the season. The best for last, wasn't that what he'd told Lynne? But now, she wondered. She could see the company was tired, and more dancers were nursing minor injuries than would be true at the season's beginning. Even Lisa seemed to have succumbed to the general fatigue, sniping only rarely at Clare and then with little heat.

Clare was tired as well, and instead of approaching each rehearsal with anticipation, she frequently felt...blah. Although, at least part of the blame for her malaise could be shifted to Stephan, who was dancing these days with a rote-like precision.

She winced as he squeezed too hard on a lift. It was something she'd rarely known him to do. Usually, his hands felt firm, the pressure controlled, comfortable.

Justin clapped, the sharp sound snapping Clare out of her reverie.

"What is it with you two? You're dancing like two old people having an anniversary waltz together. Take a break and when you return, I expect your full attention. Both of you."

As Justin spoke, Stephan's hand came to rest on Clare's shoulder. She walked out from under that touch and kept going until she reached one of the benches set at intervals along the length of the hallway. Stephan stalked off in the opposite direction.

She had no idea how to fix what was going on between them, although perhaps Stephan's moods had nothing to do with her. Hard to tell since he'd became abruptly uncommunicative after the holidays.

Denise, coming out of the adjacent studio, spotted Clare and came over. "Hey, how're you doing?"

"Not so good. Justin told us we're dancing like a couple of old people."

"Are you?"

"Pretty much."

"What's going on?"

"Darned if I know. If he were a woman I'd say it was PMS."

"You do realize he's in love with you?"

"No. He can't be. Besides, he knows I'm dating Rob."

"Well, sure. But the heart still wants what it wants." Lisa dipped her head but not before Clare saw the expression on her friend's face.

"Oh, sweetie. You're probably wrong, you know. There are all sorts of things it could be."

"I can always hope, I guess. Like I keep hoping Justin will promote me."

"Have you tried...I don't know, talking to Stephan?"

"And what do I say? Look at *me*? Notice *me*?"

"Maybe." Clare put her arms around Denise, gave her a brief hug, then released her. "I'll see if I can get him to talk."

~ ~ ~

Two hours later, the rehearsal finally staggered to a halt. Clare skipped a shower and dressed quickly, then took up her post near the exit to the men's locker room. When Stephan came out, she heaved her dance bag on her shoulder. "Buy me coffee?" she said.

He glanced at her. "That's it? Coffee?"

"Not exactly."

"Hmmph. Okay. Where do you want to go?"

"There's that place in Harvard Square?"

"Fine."

They walked to the trolley and then rode in silence, a silence that continued until they were sitting at a table in the back of the café with coffees in front of them.

Clare took a sip, glancing at Stephan. "We stunk up the place today."

"Not a completely original observation."

"Lisa and Ramon may end up first cast."

"Is that all you care about?" he asked.

"If it was, I'd be asking to switch partners."

"Why don't you?"

"Because you have élan. Or at least you used to."

He looked down at his cup as though seeking answers floating on its surface. "This guy you're dating. Is he the one, do you think?"

"I can't answer that."

"Can't or won't?" He looked up to give her a searching look. "How long have you been seeing him?"

"Almost a year."

"Don't you think you should know by now?"

"I don't know if that's how it happens, that one day you wake up knowing."

"If he broke up with you, how would you feel?"

"Sad. I'd miss him."

"But you'd turn the page? Keep on dancing?"

"Of course. I wouldn't have much choice, after all."

"If that happened, would you go out with me?"

"Do you have a best friend, Stephan?"

He frowned. "Sure."

"Say your best friend loved a girl. Would you go out with that girl, if you knew it would hurt your friend?"

"Probably not. What's that got to do with us?"

"I just wondered, that's all." She reached out a tentative hand and laid it on his arm. "It's a dream come true for me, you know. Dancing this role. But I can't do it alone. I need you to...just dance with me. The way we danced together last year."

He scrubbed his hands through his hair until it stood up in spikes. It made him look young and vulnerable. A reminder also of the five-year gap in their ages, their careers.

"Just friends, that's how you see me." He sounded glum.

She wished for a spell whose casting would ease his obvious longing. "Friend isn't such a shabby label." She took another sip of coffee to stop herself from saying anything more. He'd get over his crush. A relationship required tending, and although they spent a large portion of each day with each other, they weren't working to build anything together. A fact Stephan would grasp eventually.

"You're the best partner I've ever had," she said, the words her atonement for capturing his heart without allowing hers to be engaged.

"Except lately."

"After you've forgotten all about me, you'll still remember the dancing."

"Yeah, right. Don't lose my phone number, though. Deal?"

"Deal."

~ ~ ~

"You talked to him, right?" Denise asked the next day as she and Clare walked to the trolley.

"I did."

"And?"

"He said he's been in a funk. Probably it's the end-of-the-season letdown, I'll grant you a bit premature. I gave him the old rah-rah about not wanting to let Lisa and Ramon edge us out for first cast. He promised he'd try harder. And today was good, actually."

"That's it? A funk. An unspecified funk."

"Pretty much." Clare hated lying, although she'd done it out of kindness. But what if the kindest thing was to tell Denise she needed to give up on Stephan?

No. Wouldn't work. Denise was a terrier, after all. Besides, Stephan might eventually notice Denise. Who was Clare to dictate their fates.

~ ~ ~

With the détente with Stephan holding, and some extra rest made possible by Rob's involvement with a grant renewal, what followed were the most satisfying days of dancing Clare could remember. Everything felt effortless. Stephan's hands were once again steady and strong, and they were both quickly mastering even the most complex bits.

As the opening drew ever nearer, excitement fizzed through Clare, and the fatigue that had weighed her down lifted.

~ ~ ~

Stephan had regained most of his old form, until today when he was obviously once again distracted. Justin, who had little patience with dancers complaining on either their own account or about a partner, was pushing harder than he usually did. Clare kept biting her lip to hold in her irritation.

Finally during a break, she confronted Stephan. "Hey, I thought we had a deal. Check the personal stuff at the door?"

He stomped away without answering, but after the break, he apologized. He still wasn't completely focused, though. No longer was he giving her the clear, subtle signals in his breath and touch that allowed her to move confidently in sync with him. As a result she moved more tentatively, something Justin noticed immediately.

He clapped to stop the music. "You're dancing as if you've just met." He narrowed his eyes and tented his hands under his chin. "Try it again, this time as if you've done it before."

Clare closed her eyes briefly, then moved into the opening position. Stephan took his position and Justin motioned for the music to begin.

This time, it felt good. The two of them breathing together, moving together. Right up to the moment when Stephan's grip shifted, causing Clare's leg to twist as she landed.

She knew immediately it was bad. They all danced with pain at one time or another, but not with pain like this. Pain that overrode everything with a blinding flash of white that blanked her vision.

"God, Clare, I'm sorry."

Tentatively, holding her breath and steadied by Stephan, Clare tried to put weight on the leg. A fresh bolt of agony spiked from ankle to knee.

It couldn't be. It had been only a slight twist. The tiniest break in form. Rest, ice, she'd be fine. Had to be fine. She pulled in a careful breath, struggling to overcome a wave of nausea and dizziness. Without a word, Stephan picked her up and carried her to the locker room. Clare clenched her fists to keep from beating them against his chest.

Ice and ibuprofen were brought. Other dancers hovered before leaving to continue rehearsals while arrangements were made for her to see an orthopedic surgeon. Stephan and Denise were excused to accompany her.

Through the next hours, Clare kept her mind blank as technicians took x-rays, did tests. Finally, the surgeon arrived and checked the x-rays before sitting on a stool and bending over her leg. He probed the knee and moved the leg, as two residents and a nurse looked on. Then he did the same with the ankle.

"I'm afraid you've torn your ACL. We can fix that quite easily. I'm more concerned about your Achilles tendon which you've ruptured. With surgery and aggressive physical therapy, you'll be able to function, but you need to prepare for a long convalescence."

She'd already resigned herself to missing a few days of rehearsal, but there was no coping with this. Not just the loss of *Swan Lake*. For although the surgeon wasn't saying it, she knew that an Achilles rupture meant it was unlikely she'd ever dance *en pointe* again. She struggled to swallow, but her throat was too dry and tight.

He stood and patted her shoulder. "I'm sorry I don't have better news for you."

Clare clamped her hand across her mouth. She didn't dare let even a single sob escape. The medical entourage moved on except for a nurse who stayed behind to take Clare to be fitted with a temporary brace. Then she was returned to Stephan's repentant care.

"Stephan and I discussed it," Denise said as they helped her into the car. "There's no way you can manage all the stairs at your place. You need to stay with me."

"What about Margo?"

"Not to worry." Stephan said. "As soon as we get you settled, we'll get Margo."

"Do I have a choice?"

"Nope. You know you'd do the same for me," Denise said. "So no more fussing."

Was that what they thought she was doing? Fussing?

When they arrived at Denise's, after stops to pick up hydrocodone and a walker, Stephan swooped Clare up to carry her into the apartment. Damn him! How could he have been so clumsy? So careless.

Stephan deposited her gently on the couch, and Denise dug out a notepad and a pen. "Why don't you make a list of what you want us to pick up from your place?"

A list. She could manage a list. It gave her an excuse to ignore Stephan, whose Achilles and ACLs were all intact and functioning perfectly.

Denise left the room, and Stephan sat down, across from Clare. "You know how sorry I am." He reached out to touch her.

"Being sorry doesn't fix it."

He retracted the hand as if he'd been stung. "Yeah. I know."

"I don't want to see you again."

"I figured that, too."

She bent over her list, and Stephan finally took the hint and went outside to wait for Denise.

~ ~ ~

After Denise left with Stephan, the color slowly leached out of the room, and the quiet hum of the refrigerator was the only sound. No longer were there any distractions from the reality of her loss. Her career. The dance—the focus of her life as far back as she could remember...

Clarey, stop jumping around so I can comb your hair. Her mother.

Clare Eliason, if you don't sit still, I'm going to speak to your parents. Her teacher.

Eventually she'd discovered nobody else heard music in their head the way she did. Music she couldn't ignore.

"We really can't afford it, Clarey," her mom said, when Clare brought home the announcement about a ballet class being offered after school.

Clare pleaded until her mom agreed to use money she would have spent on other gifts for two lessons. After those lessons, Clare was better able to control the movement of her body in response to the music in her head.

"So that froufrou stuff has some value," her dad said.

Clare continued to practice the little she'd learned, until, finally, her mother spoke to the dance instructor and arranged a trade. Clare, with her mother's help, would clean the dance studio in return for lessons.

From the first, she worked as long as it took to perfect each movement. And she began to dream of being someone other than ordinary Clare Eliason from Salina, Kansas.

And now? How did one recover from a loss like this? One instant, one quick movement, and afterward everything changed to an unrecognizable shape. Bone and sinew, gut and heart, scraped, torn, roaring with a pain the hydrocodone didn't begin to ease. Hard to breathe even, as if the air had solidified. Still, as long as she didn't move, the injury seemed as insubstantial as the twilight. As unbelievable as an evil enchantment.

Her whole career she'd cast protective spells—starting on the same side of the *barre* for warm-up, lacing the left slipper before the right, seeking out her dancing partner before a performance to press the tips of her fingers to his in affirmation of the connection that would continue onstage. All of it leading up to that exactitude of movement, that still point at the heart of every performance. That moment, an ecstasy of sorts.

She wasn't ready for it to be over. It should be years before she had to face this. Years, compressed to minutes, seconds, now gone. Gone.

The second dose of hydrocodone finally kicked in, and a blessed darkness rolled over her. At some point, Denise returned, snapping on lights, talking, dumping Margo on the sofa. The little dog licked Clare's face and whined, forcing her out of her protective slumber.

"I found out why Stephan was so distracted today." Denise placed a bowl of soup in front of Clare. "His grandmother died last night. She was the one who convinced his dad to let him dance."

So the person who made it possible for Stephan to dance had ended her career? Where was the fairness in that? But no. This wasn't the end. She mustn't think that way. Negative thoughts were powerful. She needed to be positive. Upbeat. The surgery would be a success. She would make amazing progress. *You're my miracle patient, Ms. Eliason.*

"He feels awful."

Stephan had no idea what awful felt like.

"Wasn't it lucky the surgeon was able to fit you in right away?"

"Sure. My lucky day all around." She stirred the soup but didn't lift a spoonful to her mouth. "I'm feeling really tired."

"Can't you at least eat something?"

Clare stared at the soup, and nausea nudged at her. She shook her head and tried to stand.

"Wait. Let me help you." Denise jumped up and handed her the walker.

Clare gritted her teeth and accepted the help. She'd dealt with injuries before. Except, every other time, recovery had been a matter of strict adherence to therapy instructions. This time she'd been given no such guarantees.

You'll see, Clare. Without me, you're nothing.

The surge of bile in the back of her throat nearly choked her.

Chapter Eight

Ballon
A jump which has a light, elastic quality
like the bouncing of a ball

The phone rang as Rob was leaving for the university, and he answered to find Denise on the other end. "Stephan screwed up a lift at rehearsal yesterday, and Clare landed wrong. Ruptured her Achilles."

He pulled in a breath, trying to wrap his mind around what Denise was saying. Failing miserably. "Why didn't she call me?"

"It was pretty hectic, getting her in to see the surgeon. By the time we brought her back to my place and she took a hydrocodone, she was wiped."

"Is she okay, though?

"She needs surgery. It's scheduled for Monday."

"I want to see her."

"That's why I called, actually. She needs someone to convince her to eat."

"I have a class at nine, but I'll go right after that."

"I doubt Clare will open the door. I'll call my landlady and tell her to let you in."

~ ~ ~

After knocking didn't work, Rob got the landlady to open the door. He stepped into an apartment filled with an eclectic mix of furniture sharing space with several bushy plants. A cat

76

sunned itself on the only available window sill.

"Clare? It's Rob."

There was no sound except for the scrabble of toenails on the wood floor—Margo, moving much faster than he'd ever seen her move. She gave his hand a quick lick then trotted back the way she'd come, stopping to look at him and whining as if to say, "This way. And please hurry." He left the bag of takeout on the kitchen counter and followed Margo down the short hall to the bedroom. Clare was lying with her arm above her head, apparently sleeping.

He spoke softly, not wanting to startle her. "Clare. Love? Are you okay?"

When she didn't move, he knelt beside the bed, and took her hand in his. "Clare?"

"Rob? Wh-what are you doing here?"

Swallowing the lump in his throat, he rubbed her shoulder. "Denise was worried. She asked me to check on you."

She pushed free of him. "I'm fine. I don't need to be coddled."

He stood, struggling not to feel hurt at her tone. She swung her legs over the side of the bed. Her right leg was in a brace. It looked fine. It obviously wasn't, though.

"I brought something to eat. I'll let you get dressed."

He reheated the food, then returned to the bedroom to get her. She was back in bed, turned toward the wall, asleep, or pretending to be. He sat on the edge of the bed and rested his hand on her shoulder. Margo whined. He picked up the small animal and placed her on the bed. Margo maneuvered around Clare's feet to snuggle near her face.

"I'm so sorry you're hurt. I know it's terrible for you, but please don't shut me out. Let me help." He felt her body shaking before he heard the nearly silent sobs. He lay next to her and pulled her spoon-fashion against him.

"I d-don't know what I'm going to do, Rob."

"We'll figure it out."

He held her, murmuring it was going to be all right even though he had no idea if it would be, until her sobs eased.

"I have one small suggestion. Come have something to eat."

"I'm sick to my stomach."

"Probably because you haven't eaten. How about tea and toast?"

After a moment, she nodded. He moved out of her way so she could scoot over and ease her leg onto the floor. He handed her the walker and she stumped down the hall. In the kitchen, he rummaged until he found tea bags and a loaf of bread.

Clare sat on a chair with her leg propped on a low stool, sipping the tea and nibbling a piece of toast.

"You're looking better," he said.

She lifted the cup and hid behind it. "I still feel lousy."

"I am sorry about this."

"I know."

"What happens now?"

"Rest and elevate. Ice. Surgery."

He shook his head.

"I don't know. Is that what you want me to say? I don't know. And can we please not talk about it?"

"That's not what I meant." He captured her restless hands and held on. "Come stay with me, Clare. Let me take care of you."

"My mom is coming, and Denise said I can stay here as long as I need to."

He let it go, for the moment, and for the rest of the visit coaxed her into a gentle back and forth on unimportant subjects. It was the only thing he could think to do.

~ ~ ~

Rob read the details about Clare's injury in an article in the *Boston Globe* that labeled it career-ending.

"Is the reporter right, Clare?"

"The surgeon is pleased with my progress."

Not an answer to his question but he took the hint and backed off. Since meeting Clare, he'd read everything he could about the ballet, so he knew that although Clare was at the height of her powers as a dancer, she was also nearing the end of her career, even if she'd not been injured.

In the days that followed, watching Clare's faltering progress with the walker, her elegance and lightness extinguished, Rob felt helpless. This woman who had danced with the fluid grace of a flame, reduced to moving ponderously. It broke his heart. Clare's heart was obviously broken as well.

~ ~ ~

Her mother stayed the first week after the surgery, sleeping on Denise's couch, but now she'd gone back to Salina. It meant

Clare was on her own all day until Denise came home from rehearsals, something she never talked about.

"You can tell me how your day went, you know," Clare finally said. "Has Justin named my replacement yet?"

Denise walked over and picked up the cat. So she could avoid Clare's eyes? Then she turned, and Clare knew.

"Would you believe? He promoted me. And, I'm dancing with Stephan. Lisa and Ramon will be first cast, of course, but still."

Clare had to swallow the bitterness of her own loss before she was able to speak normally. "I'm so glad to hear Justin finally saw how good you are. You deserve the chance." She stretched her arms toward Denise who set the cat down and bent over to accept a hug.

"Hey," Denise said. "Don't you need to get ready for Rob?"

"I suppose."

"You better hurry. Isn't he usually here by now? What kind of food do you think he'll bring tonight?"

"We'll have to wait and see. He didn't consult me."

"He's a terrific guy, Clare."

Denise was right. Rob was a terrific guy. And how much longer was he going to hang around someone who spent her days feeling sorry for herself?

Clare needed to get a grip. If only she could figure out how.

~ ~ ~

"Clare, it's good to see you up and about." Justin stood and motioned her to take a seat, then he closed the door and returned to his chair behind the desk. "I hear the surgery went well?"

Her last formal meeting with Justin had been March a year ago, when he'd not only renewed her contract, but given her a substantial raise and told her she would be dancing the lead in *Swan Lake*. The best annual review she'd ever had.

Today, he looked at her, hands steepled. Trying to ignore the ominous body language, Clare concentrated on sounding upbeat. "The surgeon says I'm making excellent progress. Better than he anticipated. And I'm working really hard on my physical therapy."

Justin shifted and cleared his throat. "The report we have of your injury. We're devastated for you, of course. But at your age...it's not likely you'll achieve top form again." He picked up a pencil and fiddled with it as he began to outline the grim financial details of her severance from Danse Classique, a decision he'd been forced to make, "for artistic reasons." As he spoke, he was unable to look her in the eye.

Clare sat, her face frozen, as his words piled up like blackened slush in front of a snowplow. Her gaze wandered, taking in the bookshelves behind him—messy and stuffed with books and papers except for the one shelf holding a pair of worn pointe shoes, rumor claimed had belonged to Suzanne Farrell.

When the words finally stopped, she focused on Justin's forehead and spoke carefully. "Thank you for spelling out the situation so clearly."

"Well, don't be a stranger, Clare."

And how, exactly, did he expect her to manage that? She stood abruptly, needing to escape. Not easy, though, to make either a rapid or a dignified retreat with a walker.

Leaving the Center, she longed for somewhere she could quietly fall apart with no one to see. But this neighborhood, with its tired storefronts and triple-decker houses, had no parks, no benches, not even a small café where she might sit and cup her hands around a mug of coffee for comfort.

She made her way slowly to the trolley stop. With her contract ending in June and no possibility of renewal, she could no longer afford a cab. Nor could she afford the Marblehead house. Even food would soon tax her limited resources. A sob caught in her throat. No. She couldn't fall apart. Not yet. If she let any of it...no she couldn't. She mustn't.

She barely noticed the stabs of pain as she boarded the trolley. At Denise's stop, she stepped carefully down. As she stood catching her breath, her gaze snagged on the small shopping center in front of her. In addition to a realtor, a Chinese restaurant, and a combination deli-grocery store, there was a beauty shop.

A beauty shop. Perfect. Exactly what was needed to mark the day that formally ended her career as a dancer.

A middle-aged woman with big hair greeted her. "My, aren't you the lucky one. Mariela's eleven o'clock just called to cancel." She pointed Clare toward a young Hispanic woman with, thankfully, a more subdued hairstyle.

Mariela fastened a cape around Clare's shoulders and loosened the French braid she'd worn for the appointment with Justin.

"My, you have lovely hair." Mariela fluffed her fingers through long strands that had been trimmed only occasionally since Clare had decided to be a dancer.

When the hair lay in a smooth fall down her back, Mariela met her eyes in the mirror. "What were you thinking of doing?"

"Cut it off. All of it."

Mariela shook her head, looking shocked. "You can't mean it."

"If you won't cut it, I'll go elsewhere."

"You're sure?"

"I am." But she nearly choked on the words.

"Perhaps you'd like to donate your hair? To make a wig for someone who has cancer?"

Clare nodded assent and Mariela went to work. When she finished, Clare had short, feathery curls that made her look young enough to challenge Justin's inference she was too old to come back from her injury. Mariela spun the chair, insisting Clare look at the back. She did, blinking at tears, and she almost cried a second time at the shock in Rob's eyes when he arrived to take her to dinner.

"Your hair." He reached out to touch her head, his hand stopping halfway. "Why?"

She couldn't say the words. That she'd met with Justin. That she was no longer a member of Danse Classique. That Justin's assessment, more than the surgeon's, had forced her to accept that she would never dance again.

Instead, she attempted a smile. "It was too big a hassle." Good. Her voice sounded normal.

"I'll miss it," he said.

He always ran his fingers through her hair after they made love.

She would miss that, too.

~ ~ ~

"About tomorrow night." Denise's voice skittered into a higher register. "I have tickets for you and Rob." For her debut with Stephan in *Swan Lake*—the T. rex that had been taking up the extra space in the apartment for the last week as the opening approached.

It was a relief to acknowledge it, finally, although Clare still felt like the breath had been knocked out of her.

"You know, you're part of the reason I made it." Denise clapped a hand to her mouth. "Oh, my God. No, I didn't mean because you...I meant you've always helped me to improve. And you kept me going when I was ready to give up. I thought...and I'm just making it worse, aren't I." Denise sagged onto the sofa.

Clare closed her eyes and willed her voice to work. "I want to come. But it's so awkward with the brace." And how much lamer could she get? She sucked in a breath and forced herself to say the words. "But just try to keep me away." Although she had no idea how she was going to survive it.

Denise threw her arms around her. "Oh, Clare, this means so much to me. Thank you. If it were me, I'd be a basket case."

She was a basket case. The only surprise was that Denise hadn't noticed.

~ ~ ~

Denise arranged for Clare and Rob to be seated where Clare could stretch out her leg, and Clare made it through the first act, looking, but not thinking about what she was watching, gripping Rob's hand.

"Are you all right, love?" Rob leaned toward her as the audience began filing out for the intermission.

"I'm tired, and my leg hurts."

"Come on, I'll take you home. Denise will understand."

"No, I need to see this through." But it was one of the most difficult feats she'd ever accomplished.

Chapter Nine

Assemblé et soutenu
A firm step with a slight stop

"You have got to be joking." Rob steered the yacht with one hand and turned toward Clare with an appalled expression on his face.

It had taken her a week after *Swan Lake* to muster the courage to tell him about her meeting with Justin. She still hadn't told either Denise or her mom. "No. No joke."

But it was a joke. A cosmic joke.

For, while uplifting to the observer, the ballet was, in truth, a dark master, but one Clare had served with all her heart, through good times as well as through pain and difficulties. All for the exhilaration of the performance.

And she'd go back, in an instant, if she could. Even though what she created as a dancer was as fleeting, as insubstantial, as a rainbow.

But a dancer was who she was. If she wasn't that...she swallowed as panic rose in a sour wave into her throat. Pulling away from the whirling darkness of her thoughts, she focused on Rob, who was the only bright spot in these dark days. For added comfort, her hand rested on Margo, who lay next to her on the cockpit's bench, sleeping.

"I need to start looking for work."

"Do you have something in mind?"

The ballet had been such an overwhelming presence in her life, all she qualified for in the real world was a minimum-wage job. Unless she did the obvious and tried to find a non-dancing position with a ballet company. She'd always thought that was how she'd spend her life after she could no longer perform. But now, with even walking a struggle, the idea of watching others doing what she wanted most to do was unbearable. She might eventually resign herself, but the grief was still too raw.

She shifted to ease the position of her leg. Both knee and ankle were improving, although, on board the boat, she had to stay put.

"Clare?" Rob put the engine in neutral and came to sit beside her on the bench. "Are you okay?"

"Sorry. I was thinking."

"You want to share?"

"It's such a big muddle. I hardly know where to start. Every time I try to think about what to do, my mind goes blank." Except for the vision of herself behind a counter asking some faceless person if they wanted large fries with that. "I need to do something, though. I can't impose on Denise any longer."

"You can always impose on me."

"I already do."

"I love helping you. Actually..." He took her hands in his. "There's something I've been wanting to ask you. This isn't how I planned it, but I...that is, do you think you might..." He stopped and gave her a rueful look. "Sorry, I've never done this before. What I'm trying to say is, please marry me, Clare."

She froze in surprise.

"That wasn't very romantic was it? But I want you to know you don't have to worry about insurance, or where to live, or...anything."

She closed her eyes and took a deep breath. A pity proposal. A new low, even in the midst of an avalanche of them. "Rob, I don't—"

"No. Don't answer. Not yet. I know it's a surprise."

"You're feeling sorry for me."

"Well, of course I'm sorry you were injured. But that's not the reason I want to marry you."

"Why then?"

"Because I love you. With all my heart. And when I'm with you everything feels right with the world. Even when it's not." He held her hands, his gaze steady on her face.

She felt as if she were floating in a dream with the rocking of the sailboat adding to the unreality. So easy to just say yes and let him take care of her. Such a relief to no longer worry about what to do, where to live, how to manage until her leg healed.

Because despite what everyone thought, it was going to heal and she was going to dance again. But, it wasn't fair to marry

Rob only because she desperately needed the safety net his proposal represented.

Carefully, so she didn't disturb Margo or her leg, she leaned toward Rob, took his face between her hands, and kissed him, testing, tasting the idea.

He was a man who appreciated kissing and was willing to participate without quickly losing interest and pushing for sex. It was one of the many things she appreciated about him.

His lips fitted against hers in a give and take both firm and gentle. After a time, he pulled away, his hand still cupping the back of her head. "Was that a yes, a no, or a maybe?"

"I think...a maybe."

"I want you to be sure, Clare."

She wanted that as well.

~ ~ ~

When Rob dropped her at Denise's that evening, Clare finally made the call to her folks she had been putting off. "I met with Justin last week. They aren't renewing my contract."

"Oh, Clare. Oh, hon, I'm so sorry." Her mom's voice was tearful. "You need to come home, sweetie. You did promise to spend time with us while you were recovering."

"I know. I'm sorry. But I'm still having trouble walking."

"I thought you were healing really well."

"I am. But the brace makes it awkward." She heard her mother sniffing. Funny, she didn't feel like crying. "Rob asked me to marry him today."

"Oh, my goodness, he did? Well that's marvelous." The sniffs stopped abruptly, and Clare pictured her mother giving her eyes a last swipe and beginning to smile.

"I told him I needed to think about it."

"But, hon, you love Rob. Don't you? He's a wonderful man."

"He is. It's just..." How to explain when she didn't understand her hesitation herself.

"What is it, Clare?"

"It feels like I'd be taking advantage of him."

"Not if he loves you and you love him. You do love him, don't you?"

"Yes."

"Seems simple to me then."

But it wasn't.

She finally made a list of pros and cons. There were more pros than cons. But the certainty she craved eluded her.

~ ~ ~

"You are going to be the most beautiful bride," Rob's mother gushed when they announced their engagement at a family dinner in the senior Chapins' home. The house, a spacious pseudo-Tudor in Newton was decorated, in Lynne's words, within an inch of its life.

Mrs. Chapin frowned at Clare. "It really is too bad you had your hair cut. Oh, well. We don't want you two waiting until it grows back, do we, George." She tapped Rob's father on the knee.

Mr. Chapin sat in the only comfortable chair in the room, a recliner. Given all the other furnishings were stiffly ornate, the chair had to represent a major victory for Rob's dad.

"Now, since your mother is so far away, I hope you'll let me stand *in loco parentis* to help you plan the wedding, dear."

In loco parentis, indeed.

"There's not much to plan," Rob said. "We're having a small, private ceremony. As soon as possible."

Mrs. Chapin started to speak, then hesitated, and Clare knew exactly what she was thinking. That Clare was pregnant. Well, let her stew.

"But we have so many close friends and family. They'll want to see you marry, Rob."

"That will be difficult since we're having a small, private ceremony."

Clare gave silent thanks her parents had not had any objection to the wedding plans.

"Well, attendants. I expect you'll choose friends from the ballet?"

"Denise Ross will be my maid of honor."

"And the other attendants?"

She shook her head. "Just Denise." She'd thought about asking Lynne, until Rob decided on his sister as his best person.

"But, my dear, you must have at least three."

"Not for a small, private ceremony." Rob stared his mother down, his arm around Clare.

"Well, we'll just plan the reception for you. As our wedding gift." Mrs. Chapin's voice held a note of triumph.

For the sake of her relationship with her future mother-in-law, Clare reluctantly accepted the reception offer.

"When do you want to go shopping for your dress?" Mrs. Chapin asked.

No way. "I'm going home for a visit so my mom can help me choose."

"But I thought Filene's. I doubt Salina has any stores that comprehensive."

Clare shrugged, going for a wry look. "Probably not."

Later, when they were alone, Rob took her in his arms. "I'm sorry Mom put you on the spot. She's a born organizer."

"Indeed." Clare would have to ask Rob's father sometime how he'd managed the overstuffed chair.

"When are you going home?"

"I just said that because I don't want to go shopping with your mother. I can't afford to go home."

"Sure you can. My treat. Consider it a wedding present."

She was already uncomfortable with what Rob was doing for her, but without him, in addition to filing for unemployment, she'd likely be checking out homeless shelters and collecting food stamps.

"About the ceremony. Your mom isn't going to be satisfied with just the reception, is she."

"Probably not. But you want it to be private, so that's what we're doing."

"What do you want, Rob?"

"To be married to you. And I don't give a tinker's damn how we manage it. We can elope if you want."

It was tempting. But marriage was, after all, about more than one man and one woman. It was about the joining together of families, and what Mrs. Chapin was asking wasn't completely unreasonable, although it was the last thing Clare wanted.

~ ~ ~

"I'm getting married, Jolley." Rob's lips stretched into a wide, no doubt, silly grin as he said the words. Norman Jolliffe had been his first boss at Northeastern, and although Jolley had since moved to Stanford, they were still friends and collaborators.

"That's great, Rob. I was beginning to think you had something against it."

"Just hadn't met the right woman."

"And now you have?"

"I never realized I could be this happy. I'm hoping you and Jane will come for the wedding."

After he told Jolley the date, the sound of papers being shuffled came through the phone. "Let's see. We're going to be in France around that time, but we can arrange to stop in Boston on our way home."

Rob was pleased they were coming since Jane had given several dinner parties when she and Jolley were still living in Boston in order to introduce Rob to eligible women. She'd told him she considered him unfinished business when Jolley dragged her off to California.

"By the way," Jolley added. "I'm starting to put together another expedition. This time to Peru." Jolley's field was ethnobotany, the study of plants as potential sources of medicinals, and he'd made several trips to the Amazon region. "Two years from now."

"I'll bet Jane is thrilled."

"Resigned. I'll save you a spot."

An old line. Jolley always invited Rob, who always declined. After all, he was a chemist. He was interested in a drug only after it had been extracted from the plant. He had no interest in seeing, touching, tasting, or smelling the actual source. That was Jolley's department.

Besides, no way would he ever be parted from Clare.

~ ~ ~

The last weeks before the wedding spun by so fast they left Clare feeling dizzy. Mrs. Chapin eventually got them to agree to a larger ceremony by arguing family and close friends wouldn't understand why, with all the room in the church, they couldn't attend the wedding. Mrs. Chapin then consolidated her position by hiring a wedding planner, a young woman with the brisk manners of a matron, who arrived at every meeting with thick binders and endless lists.

"This is a terribly tight schedule," the planner fussed. "Usually I'm given nine months to a year to plan a wedding of this size and complexity."

"I'll be happy to scale back," Clare said.

"Oh, no. I'll manage, somehow. Let's see. You need to register soon, so we can include information about your gift preferences with the save-the-date notes."

"Sorry. Not doing that."

"But guests expect it."

"It's tacky."

The wedding planner huffed out a breath. "Well, you still need to register so when guests ask, and they will, you can provide the information."

"Fine."

~ ~ ~

Clare took Denise with her to Jordan Marsh where the wedding registration person, a lady of middle years and impeccable grooming, peppered her orientation talk with constant comments about "our brides."

"Most of our brides prefer to begin in our china and glassware department."

"That may be problematic." With the brace and walker, Clare pictured herself wreaking havoc among the closely spaced displays.

"Oh, of course, dear. You sit, and your friend and I can bring selections to you."

After looking at one too many white china plates with silver edges—the ones "our brides" preferred—along with glassware of every type and size, and flatware in a myriad of patterns that varied even less than the china patterns, Clare was tempted to close her eyes and point.

Except why bother when she'd already made up her mind? "These are all much too expensive."

"But this is your opportunity, dear. To choose something you might not be able to afford otherwise."

"What if we receive only one or two place settings?"

"I'm quite certain that won't be a problem with 150 guests. In fact, my recommendation is to put twelve place settings on your list."

"I'm marrying a university professor. His apartment can't hold twelve people at once."

Denise, standing behind the woman, struck a nose-in-the-air pose and Clare struggled not to laugh.

"That may be true now, dear. But you need to think about the future. The china you pick today will be what you'll eat Thanksgiving and Christmas dinners on for years to come."

Denise mimed fastidiously cutting food and lifting a bite to her mouth.

"If I receive twelve place settings, where am I supposed to store them in the meantime?"

"Some couples with large weddings rent storage units."

Clare glanced at Denise who was now giving her the shocked look of an Alice in Wonderland.

"I'm going to pass on the fine china."

The woman's lips tightened.

Clare looked around. One display held brightly colored plates that were in a variety of shapes. She pointed. "Can I please see those?"

Once again the registration lady's lips tightened, then she forced a smile. "That's part of our everyday collection. Most of our brides would never consider it for entertaining, unless possibly you went with a single shape and color."

"I think mixing colors and shapes works best for me." It had become a game, going for that lip tightening. If she worked at it, maybe she could force the woman into a full frown.

"How many settings are you thinking?"

"Eight." Clare raised her eyebrows at Denise who muffled a snicker as the woman retrieved several plates from the display and set them in front of Clare.

"Perhaps the groom should take a look before you make a final decision? Our brides usually find that's a good idea. Especially with such a distinctive choice."

"I'm sure he'll be fine with it." Rob liked bright colors, and besides, when she asked him to go with her to register, he'd given her a please-let-this-cup-pass look before suggesting she might have more fun with Denise. So, he'd just have to suck it up and live with whatever she picked.

After the plates, on a roll, she chose wineglasses and stainless steel flatware, both in simple patterns.

"Now for linens, towels, that sort of thing. What colors will coordinate with your decor?"

Clare almost did laugh at that—the thought that Rob's furnishings could be referred to as decor. Fixing up his apartment was something else she needed to think about, but it would have to wait its turn. She scanned the towel-lined wall and selected towels of rose, teal, and buttercup yellow. That, at least, appeared to be acceptable. The registration lady noted the choices on her form then directed Clare to consider sheets and quilts.

But Clare's attention was beginning to flag. The brace made walking tiring and being forced to make so many decisions in a short time added to her exhaustion.

"I'd prefer to finish another time."

The woman looked at her list and finally, finally, frowned. Clare suppressed a smile.

"But you don't have nearly enough selections for your number of guests."

"I promise to work on my avarice so we can remedy that next time."

The woman looked nonplussed. "Well, of course, dear. It's entirely up to you. It is your wedding."

"Good. Another time, then."

Denise started giggling as soon as they were out of earshot. "You are so evil, Clare. That poor woman had no idea what you were saying. She was just doing her best to steer you down the right road."

"Ah yes, the 'our brides' road.'"

"She wasn't completely wrong, you know. It is a terrific opportunity to get things you might not be able to afford otherwise."

"True. If it's stuff you want. But Rob has a small apartment. It would be a pain to try to find a place for twelve place settings we may use at best twice a year."

"Well, you could sign up for four place settings."

"But I didn't like any of them, and at those prices, I ought to adore it. Besides it's exhausting deciding what I want to sleep on, drink from, and eat off of for the rest of my life."

"Let's face it," Denise said. "You don't fit into the 'our brides' category."

"Do you?"

"More than you do, I suspect."

"Oh, Denise, honey, I'm sorry."

"It's okay. I'm happy for you, and one day I'll meet the right guy, too."

Whoever was running the universe seemed to love to throw those kinds of curves—Clare wanting more than anything to dance *Swan Lake*, and Denise wanting more than anything to be married. And neither of them being granted their heart's desire.

~ ~ ~

Clare waited out the last moments before the wedding with Denise in a small room furnished as a parlor with a fake fireplace and an old-fashioned oval mirror in a stand.

Denise reached out a hand. "Touch time, Clare."

The familiar gesture made it seem, briefly, as if she were about to step onstage. But this was real.

Denise threw her arms around Clare. "You are so lucky. Rob's a wonderful man. You're going to be happy. I know you are." She stepped back, swiping at her eyes. "Oh. I've mussed your veil. Here, let me fix it." She pulled at the veil, frowning in concentration.

"I'm scared."

Denise switched her attention from the veil to Clare's face.

"It's all happened so fast. I worry that I didn't take enough time to—"

"You love him, though, right?"

Clare nodded, but it had never been a question of whether she loved Rob. What she questioned was whether that love was enough to make the step she was taking today the right one.

A tap on the door was followed by the wedding planner's head. "Is the bride ready?"

As she had before, Clare wondered if the woman remembered her name or just the correct binder color.

"Give us a moment," Denise said. When the door closed, she gripped Clare by the arms. "Deep breath, Clare. It's okay to have the jitters. It's perfectly normal. You're going to be fine. That's a good man you're marrying."

Denise was right. Besides, it was too late to back out now. She took a breath. "Okay. Ready."

One last spasm of panic hit after Denise reached her place at the altar and the organ notes swelled. The guests surged to their feet, stirring up faint drifts of scent—a mix of candle wax and floral notes. Faces turned toward Clare, as anonymous as any audience, and she was tempted to turn and flee, but from what she couldn't have said. Perhaps the peering looks and whispers from the strangers filling the church. Perhaps from the future this ceremony initiated.

Butterflies. Jitters. Familiar and usually transitory. But not today. Today the butterflies refused to settle, even as, in response to the music, Clare and her father started down the aisle—their steps slow and careful, limited by both the solemnity of the moment and the remaining stiffness in her leg.

Clare fixed her gaze on the man waiting for her at the altar. The man who would shortly be her husband. *Oh, my God. This is so wrong. I can't...I mustn't do this.*

Despite the frantic beat of her thoughts, she continued walking toward Rob, until she was close enough to place her hand in his. Halfway through the exchange of vows, black specks obscured her vision. The priest made a quick grab, but it was Rob's arm that steadied her until the faintness receded. The priest pronounced them man and wife, and Rob kissed her on lips numbed by the words she'd just spoken.

As they walked out of the church, she stumbled and Rob steadied her, again. "Are you all right? Are you hurting?"

She shook her head, although the stumble had nearly caused her to gasp in pain.

Her new mother-in-law descended on them. "How clever of you to pair such a simple dress with an ornate veil." But the way Mrs. Chapin's lips pursed told a different story—that she found the dress too plain and the veil, Clare's grandmother's, a disappointment.

Her mother's assessment of Mrs. Chapin had been, "She's a bit of a gorgon, isn't she? But Rob's one of the good guys."

At the reception, Clare watched her gorgon mother-in-law dance with her good-guy husband. The tux fit Rob well and, unlike many men, he looked comfortable wearing it. The dancing was another battle she'd lost to the senior Mrs. Chapin.

"But there must be dancing, dear. It's expected."

"The bride can't dance."

"Well, I know you won't be returning to the ballet. But a waltz. At your wedding. Surely you can manage that."

At the casual cruelty, Clare ground her teeth.

Mrs. Chapin simply went ahead and made the plans without discussing them further, something Clare discovered when they arrived at the reception.

"I can't do it, Rob. I can't dance." She gripped his hand so tightly, he winced.

"It's okay, Clare. I'll take care of it."

And he had. When the music started, he rose and escorted his mother to the floor, announcing he didn't want to put his new bride's delicate toes at risk. Clare was so grateful that when he returned to her side she leaned over and kissed him. He gave her a startled look and blushed.

It was the best moment of the day.

~ ~ ~

When Rob suggested Vieques for their honeymoon, Clare thought it a peculiar choice since the tiny island off the east coast of Puerto Rico was periodically used by the U.S. Navy as a bombing range.

"I know it sounds weird, but Lynne and Jim said the island is peaceful. And it has a bioluminescent bay."

Could she possibly look as blank as she felt?

Rob grinned. "Living lights, in the sea. Produced by microorganisms called dinoflagellates. Marine fireflies, if you will. Lynne said it was magical."

It didn't sound magical.

"Unless you want to go somewhere else?"

He must have looked like that as a young boy, hoping for a special boon, his first bike maybe, or the chemistry set, and Clare couldn't refuse him.

It was the least she could do to make up for agreeing to marry him in spite of her doubts. "Vieques sounds...intriguing."

~ ~ ~

Except for two tiny towns, Vieques turned out to be rural and as quiet as advertised. They stayed at an inn high on a hill overlooking the ocean, and there was peace in both the view and the slow rhythms of their days. Mornings, they went swimming, often encountering a herd of wild horses near the beach. In the afternoons, they returned to the inn and made love in the bright, cool room. The rest of the time they lay under the shade trees by the pool, and Clare began to believe marrying Rob was the best decision she'd ever made.

"No moon tonight," he said, the third day. "It means conditions are perfect for dinoflagellate observations."

"You make it sound irresistible."

"All part of the plan." He waggled his eyebrows and grinned.

As the twilight deepened, she and Rob, along with twenty other people, boarded an old school bus. After a short ride, the bus turned off the paved road to rattle along a dirt track that ended on a dark beach.

There they boarded an electric-powered boat, and as the boat moved silently away from the shore, the water in the wake began to glow. The captain announced the glow was being produced by Rob's dinoflagellates, trillions of them floating in the warm salt waters of the bay. He stamped his foot, and large fish were outlined in light as they darted away from the boat.

A distance from the shore, the boat stopped so they could swim. Rob and Clare floated away from the others, who clustered near the boat, laughing and splashing. They faced each other, buoyed by the ski belts the crew had required everyone to wear.

"Lift up your arm. Like this, Clare." Rob dipped up water and let it run in a sparkling stream down his arm.

She tried it, feeling a soul-deep delight as the tiny lights flashed and winked. Again and again, she scooped up handfuls of water and watched the glitter running down her arms.

Then she twirled and lifted her arms over her head and pointed her toes, every move outlined with a pale glow. The music in her head, silent since her injury, burst into a glorious allégro. She laughed with the sheer joy of being able to move without pain or the worry she might reinjure her leg, and her dance was partnered by light.

After a time, the music slowed and stilled. She lay back in the glowing water and stared at the stars arching overhead. Rob put his arms around her, holding her gently, sprinkling diamonds onto her shoulders and breasts, then he whispered in her ear. "They're telling us we have to get back on the boat."

No. It was too soon. She needed more time in this perfect place. In Rob's arms, but freed from guilt. Suspended from grief and loss.

Chapter Ten

Capriccio
Quick, improvisational, spirited

"Damn woman. She savaged Hatsume," Rob said.

Clare handed him a glass of wine. "Who did?"

"Joyce Willette. She's trying to get back at me."

"Why would she do that?" Gradually Clare translated what they were talking about. Hatsume was one of Rob's graduate students, and she was defending her thesis—today, wasn't it? But Joyce Willette wasn't a name she remembered hearing before.

"We dated for a while." Rob frowned and took a quick sip of wine.

"Was it serious?" She picked Margo up and sat on the couch next to him.

"It might have been. I got out just in time."

"How long ago were you and she—"

"God. No, Clare. After you and I went out the first time, I broke it off."

Clare wondered what had been in her face that made Rob feel he needed to comfort her so strenuously.

~ ~ ~

Rob suggested they have a few of his favorite colleagues over for dinner. As he greeted the last two guests, Clare knew something was wrong. And when he turned to introduce the two, she understood what. The woman was Joyce Willette, who'd come as the date of one of the invitees.

After drinks were served, Clare retreated to the kitchen. She pulled the casserole from the oven, the irony of the situation hitting her—Rob, so pleased to be introducing her to the people who were important in his professional life, and who showed up but the one person he'd cross the street to avoid. And Joyce knew it. So why...? The potholder slipped and the dish slid to the floor, burning her wrist. She ran cold water over the burn, trying to clamp down on laughter that began to feel like something more.

She retrieved what she could of the casserole, a mix of chicken, pasta, walnuts, and pesto. Then she boiled more pasta and added a leftover slab of brie before mixing it all together. Feeling guilty, she watched their guests eat with gusto.

It reminded her of a story she'd read once about a Frenchman who always spat in the soup before he served the Nazi officers who came to his restaurant to eat. So it was true. People could eat anything if they didn't know what they were eating.

Once again, she felt like laughing, but if she did, they would think her mad. Instead, she ate the salad, which hadn't sojourned on the kitchen floor, and joined the conversation as needed, playing hostess, as if it were a role.

Throughout dinner, Joyce pitched frequent comments into the conversational mix. Clearly, she was intelligent, and given her lush figure and thick blonde hair, Clare understood why Rob had been attracted.

"Enough about us," Joyce said. "I want to know something about you, Clare. Didn't Robbie tell me you were a ballerina or something?"

"Clare was the prima ballerina for Danse Classique." Rob's tone had a steely edge.

"Of course. Now I remember. You were injured. Last spring, right before the end of the season, wasn't it?"

Clare tilted her head and looked at the other woman. "Yes. It was."

"Sorry. Didn't mean to step on any toes...so to speak." There was more than a hint of malice in Joyce's smile.

It reminded Clare of Lisa, which was perhaps why she decided to not let Joyce get away with it. "That was quite good, actually. You're very clever."

Joyce blushed an angry red.

Likely it was a relief to everyone, not just Joyce, when the evening ended.

~ ~ ~

"So that was Joyce Willette," she said as she and Rob cleaned up. "She's very attractive."

"She's a barracuda, and if you hadn't come along, I might not have noticed until she devoured me." He set down the stack of blue, green, and yellow plates and pulled her into his arms.

"You handled her perfectly." He rubbed his chin gently against the top of her head. "I heard a rumor she interviewed at Michigan. If we're lucky, and the stars are aligned, they'll take her off our hands."

"I bet she goes straight home and looks in her mirror, trying to figure out what you saw in me that you didn't see in her."

"Why would you think that?"

"Do you ever look at me, Rob?"

He pulled back slightly, his hands on her shoulders, frowning. "Of course I do."

"What do you see?"

"The woman I love."

"But my hair. It's going white and I'm too thin." The tears came before she could stop them.

"Clare, love, what's this about?"

"I think something's wrong with me."

"What?" He rubbed her arms, giving her a worried look. "Are you okay? I noticed you hardly ate anything."

She almost told him what happened to the casserole, but then she remembered, he'd had seconds. "I'm so tired all the time."

He snuggled her against his chest. "Maybe you better go for a checkup."

She was sorry she'd brought it up. She hated doctors. It was, after all, a doctor who kept insisting her leg would never again be strong enough for her to dance.

~ ~ ~

Rob looked up to find Greg Olson standing in his office doorway.

"Wanted to apologize," Greg said. "For Saturday night. For bringing Joyce to your place. I had no idea."

"I figured that."

"I told her she stepped over the line. She didn't like it."

"Better watch your back."

Greg frowned. "It also explains something else."

"What's that?"

"She's made comments in the Tenure and Promotions Committee that your request for promotion to full professor is premature."

"Doesn't surprise me. She told me if I didn't already have tenure, she'd do her best to ensure I didn't get it."

Greg smiled. "What did you do to her? Throw her over for Clare?"

"Exactly."

Greg's grin widened. "Damned if given the choice I wouldn't have done the same thing. Don't sweat the promotion. I'll make sure you get a fair shake."

"Appreciate it."

"And I appreciate you giving me the chance to discover the real Joyce sooner rather than later."

"Definitely my pleasure."

~ ~ ~

Pregnant. It had taken the doctor Rob nagged Clare to see only a few minutes to pinpoint the cause of her listlessness. Rob. She needed to be with him. To share what was happening to her, to them, but when she arrived at Northeastern, he was in class.

"When will he be finished?"

The assistant glanced at the clock. "Fifteen minutes. You can wait here, if you like."

"Please. Can you tell me what room he's in?"

Clare found the door to the lecture hall propped partially open. She peeked in to verify Rob was there, then she leaned against the wall to wait, listening to the flow of his voice.

"The toxicology case for Monday is that of a young female who appears to be in good health until she starts to lose significant weight. She complains of fatigue, difficulty concentrating, and shortness of breath. She walks with a slight shuffle. Nothing else remarkable shows up on physical exam. Okay, what other questions do you have?"

"Does she smoke, drink?"

"Smokes ten to twenty cigarettes a day, has an occasional glass of wine."

"Diet?"

"Vegan, when she can muster an appetite. Eats mostly apples, core and all."

"She's not a horse, is she?"

There was a ripple of laughter. The students were obviously fully engaged and enjoying the class.

"What does she do for a living?" "Where does she get her water?" The questions and Rob's answers continued, but Clare no longer listened to the words.

After several minutes, the hallway began to fill as students poured out of nearby rooms. Then Rob was there. "Clare? What are you doing here? Are you okay?"

She straightened, wincing when both ankle and knee twinged at the sudden movement. "I'm fine. I just...I was passing by." She faced Rob and made sure her expression was serious. "You know, the woman you were describing to your class? Maybe she's pregnant."

Rob froze and looked at her intently before taking a deep breath and pulling her into his arms. "Thank God. Thank God you're all right."

Only in that moment did she understand how worried he'd been about her—a woman who'd lost too much weight, had no energy or appetite, and although she might not walk with a shuffle, her gait was slow and careful. Rob leaned back and continued to examine her, as if he'd forgotten what she looked like.

"So what was wrong with the woman? The one you told the class about?"

"Oh. Cyanide poisoning."

"I thought cyanide killed you in like, five minutes."

"If you take a big enough dose. She was poisoning herself slowly, with apple seeds and cigarettes."

"On purpose?"

"Not on purpose. Clare, you're happy about this, aren't you?"

Clearly, he was. She leaned in to hug him, hoping he'd accept it in place of an actual answer, and was relieved when he took her arm and walked with her to his office.

As soon as they were inside with the door closed, he took her back in his arms. "So, when are we having this baby?"

"Late August." And impossible to imagine on this freezing cold day the heat that would be baking the city into somnolence by then.

"You're happy about it, aren't you?" Rob tipped her chin and searched her eyes.

She couldn't duck the question a second time. "It's a huge surprise. I'm...still getting used to the idea."

Rob didn't seem to be having a problem adjusting. His lips stretched into a broad grin. "Guess it's a good thing we have seven months then."

~ ~ ~

Later, Rob would decide the slow downward slide of their marriage from happiness to despair began before Clare's pregnancy, but at the time, he was certain the pregnancy alone explained her poor appetite, growing indifference to her appearance, and lack of enthusiasm.

Then she lost the baby.

He knew she needed time to recover, but now, weeks later, she still wasn't eating, was increasingly lethargic. He tried to hide his own grief from Clare, not wanting to add the weight of his sadness to her burden. Although, sometimes he wondered if she would notice if he did grieve openly.

Then came the morning he found Margo had died in her sleep. He'd knelt to give the little dog a pat. She had gone deaf and didn't always react when he came out of the bedroom. Today there was no response to his touch, no tongue swipe in greeting. The small body was no longer even warm. He wrapped Margo in a towel then went to tell Clare.

He sat on the side of the bed and laid a hand on her shoulder. "Clare?"

After a moment, she stirred and opened her eyes.

"I have bad news, love. Margo died last night."

Clare blinked, then her expression changed to comprehension and pain. "No. No. She c-can't have..."

He lay alongside her, holding her shaking body in his arms. Her tears soaked the shoulder of his shirt. She hadn't cried, at least in his presence, after she lost the baby. So perhaps these tears were for both her losses.

He made no attempt to stem his own tears, and together, in each other's arms, he and Clare wept.

"What are we going to do, Rob? We d-don't have anywhere to bury her."

"We can have her cremated, then the next time we go sailing we'll take her with us and sprinkle her on the waters. Would that be okay?"

After a moment, still clinging to him, Clare nodded her head. He continued to hold her until she moved out of his arms. He waited while she dressed, then she went with him to the vet's. Two days later, he collected the ashes, but by the time the weather was warm enough to go sailing, the rhythm of their life together had fixed into a new pattern.

Now, when he arrived home, not only was there no furry greeting from Margo, there was no scent of something delicious floating in the air. Dinner had become an endless series of frozen entrées smelling of damp cardboard as they heated in the microwave. There was also no kiss from Clare followed by her sitting with him, sipping wine, as they shared the details of their days.

He suggested she go to a therapist, something she repeatedly rejected. Finally, in desperation, he called Clare's mother.

"Rob, oh my God, is something wrong?"

The panic in her voice was understandable given the last time he'd called her was after Clare lost the baby and was admitted to the hospital.

"No, no. It's...I wanted to talk to you about Clare. Did she...that is, did you know Margo died?"

"Oh, what a shame. No, she never mentioned it."

He could hear sympathy but also relief in his mother-in-law's voice. "She does call you though, right?"

"Every Wednesday afternoon, like clockwork."

"Did she ever talk about the baby?"

"She said she feels tired and sad. Do you think it's more than that?"

"I've tried to get her to see someone. She won't go."

"Do you want me to come out?"

"Please. I'll pay your way."

"That isn't necessary. I've wanted to visit, but I didn't want to be a bother. But if Clare needs me?"

"She does." Although it hurt to admit he wasn't enough.

~ ~ ~

"Clare, it's me." The voice was Denise's. "How about lunch? I'm free any day this week. So call me. Bye."

Clare deleted Denise's message and went back to bed. She never answered the phone when it rang. Easier to ignore messages than to speak to Denise or Lynne, neither of whom would believe she was too busy to make time for them. Her only outside contact was her parents. She called them once a week in order to head off the possibility they might call her at some random time. Much easier for her to manage the conversation when she initiated it.

She tried to paint an optimistic picture for her mom and dad, but she could no longer summon the energy to move through the rest of her life. And she was hiding not only from Denise, Lynne, and her parents. She was also hiding from Rob—her thoughts, her feelings, the fact she spent most of her days sleeping. Rob made her deception easier by not expecting her to get up with him in the morning. To fool him, she had only to get up in time to heat one of the pre-packaged entrées from Star Market for dinner.

Sometimes Rob had evening meetings and didn't get home until late enough she could justify being in bed. Those were the best days.

When she was awake, time unfolded, an endless, featureless span. Asleep, dreams, when they came, flickered out of her grasp before she could catch them, like firefly flashes caught with the corner of the eye.

~ ~ ~

"Don't bother with dinner tonight, love. I'll be home early. We'll go out."

Clare clicked the answering machine off, glad she'd thought to check for messages. She pushed the hair out of her eyes and dragged herself back to the bedroom. She'd need to take a shower, then, wash her hair. Damn Rob, anyway. It wasn't their anniversary or either of their birthdays. Screw it. She was going back to bed. She could say she had cramps.

"Clare?"

Rob's voice yanked her out of a deep sleep, and left her shaking.

"Love, didn't you get my message?"

"Message?"

"About dinner."

"Oh, yeah. Sorry, I have cramps. I was trying to sleep them off."

"Your period was last week."

Damn. She didn't think he paid that much attention. "Maybe it's a stomach flu. All I know is, I feel lousy." She rolled over, rubbing her eyes. "Mom? What are you doing here?" As she sat up, Rob backed out of the room, the coward.

"My, it's so dark and fusty in here." Her mother pulled the shades open. "Now why don't you get dressed, hon. I'll make chamomile tea to help settle your stomach."

"I feel awful."

"I can see you do, sweetie." Her mother sat on the edge of the bed and scooped her into a hug. "Oh, my, Clare, you're so skinny. I'll have to make chicken soup for you."

"Oh, Mom..." Suddenly she was crying so hard, she could barely catch her breath. Through it all, her mother held her, patting gently.

~ ~ ~

After her mother's visit, Clare was too restless to sleep all the time. She began spending her days reading books she went to the library to pick out. Many she returned after reading a page or two, but in every batch at least one book was good enough to distract her. She did find it took a toll on her limited store of energy for forays into even imaginary lives, imaginary tears, but it was a distraction.

Gradually, she began to seek out books about people who had surmounted problems. But after reading several such stories, she still had no faith in her own ability to overcome.

Her restlessness continued to increase until, abruptly, reading was no longer enough. Instead, she began to leave the apartment shortly after Rob and spend her time sitting in coffee shops or wandering the aisles of busy stores or riding a trolley to the end of the line and back. All the while, she examined those around her. Listening in on conversations, watching mothers struggling with toddlers, business men and women shuffling through briefcases, students moving in response to silent music, street people going through the trash.

One day she stumbled and, when there was no pain, realized how much her leg had improved, something she hadn't consciously noticed before although she now walked miles every day and climbed on and off streetcars with ease.

It no longer mattered, though. Sometime during those weeks spent sleeping, she'd let go of her goal to dance again. In its place, she had a life as the wife of the good man who'd saved her.

Chapter Eleven

Dissonance
Harsh, discordant,
a lack of harmony

"Sorry I'm late." Rob kissed Clare, but with only the briefest touch of his lips. If he tried for more, she would simply pull away, and he couldn't bear it.

"That's okay." She sounded calm, as if she were uninterested whether he was at home or at work.

He forced himself to smile. "Did you have a good day?"

"It was fine." No smile in return.

After her mother's visit, she'd seemed better, and he'd felt hopeful, but now she'd returned to shutting him out. While he changed clothes, Clare heated the food, and after they ate, she would spend the rest of the evening reading. He'd begun to hate the sight of the books piled beside the bed.

He took his seat at the table. "What did you do today?"

"Oh, you know. The usual." She set a microwave-heated entrée down and walked over to turn on the television, another unwelcome alteration to their dinner routine.

He stood and turned the television off. Clare blinked in surprise.

"Tell me, Clare. What you did today." He spoke softly but firmly.

She chewed her lip, staring at him with wary eyes.

"Please, Clare."

"Well, I got up and showered. Dressed. Ate breakfast. Then I did my exercises, went to the grocery store. After that I...ate lunch, went to the library, read a little bit, cooked dinner."

Lots of busyness, but nothing of substance. And the cooking of dinner involved only setting the timer on the microwave.

"Are you sorry you married me, Clare?"

"What a thing to ask, Rob."

He waited, but she didn't add to her response. An answer in itself that hurt him more than a physical beating would.

"You know, we haven't done something, just the two of us, for a while. What would you like to do? If you could do anything you wanted."

She bent her head, but not before he'd seen the expression on her face. *Okay, damn it. Besides dance.* When was she finally going to accept the ballet was part of her past, not her future? Her future was with him.

"We could visit the arboretum," he said. "The lilacs are starting to bloom."

She shook her head with a sharp movement without speaking.

"Please, talk to me, Clare. It's...I'm lonely. I miss you. I'll do whatever it takes. Go to the shelter. Get another dog. See a therapist."

She shook her head without looking at him.

He threw his napkin on the table and stood, shaking.

Her head jerked, and her eyes widened in alarm.

"I need...you need...to tell me what I can do to help you." Didn't she see he was hurting, too? She wasn't the only one who'd lost something essential. He struggled every day with the fear he'd lost her.

"I can't, Rob."

"Please, Clare. Please try."

Blinking, she raised her face to his, her eyes wet. Abruptly he sat and reached out to touch her. "Tell me. How can I help."

She shook her head. "I...don't think there's anything you can do." She bent over sobbing.

He lifted her into his arms, holding her as he had after she lost the baby and again the morning Margo died.

For a while after that things were better between them. Until he noticed how much the effort was costing her.

~ ~ ~

His professional life, with his promotion to full professor approved and another grant funded, was on a roll. But his personal life was a shambles. No longer could he convince himself everything would be okay if he just gave Clare enough time.

He'd suspected he was taking a chance, asking her to marry him before she'd come to terms with her injury. But he'd wanted to be the prince riding in on the white horse, making everything right. And at first, he thought he'd succeeded, but now it was clear that even in the beginning there had been cracks—hairline fissures that over the months lengthened and deepened until nothing whole and complete was left.

He loved her so much, but he no longer believed she loved him at all.

~ ~ ~

"I thought we might go to the Cape today."

For once, Rob's suggestion appealed to Clare, perhaps because with the onset of spring, the days were longer. "How about I pack a picnic?"

"If it's not too much trouble."

"No trouble at all." She felt so guilty sometimes. She'd done nothing but let him down, let herself down. It was all she could do to muster the energy to acknowledge it. Actually doing something about it was still beyond her.

~ ~ ~

Rob drove by the turnoff to Falmouth, and a flash of disappointment darkened the day. So they weren't going sailing, after all. She waited with little enthusiasm to see where they were going as Rob followed the south coast road for several miles before turning into a narrow lane. At the end, he stopped the car.

"Are we there yet?" she said, trying to make it sound like she was teasing, although she certainly didn't feel light-hearted.

"Not quite." He came around to help her out of the car. Expression solemn, he took her by the hand and led her along a path through the scrub and stunted trees until they came out on the beach.

The ocean lay glittering before them. Shivering, she stared at that wind-whipped expanse. Rob tugged on her hand, turning her to face a small house crouched on the edge of the sand far enough from the water for safety in a storm. It was one story, except for a tower, reminiscent of a lighthouse, attached to one corner.

"What do you think?" he asked.

"About?"

"About living in that cottage for the summer?"

Dread clenched her stomach. He couldn't have. Please, let it be just an idea he had. A possibility she could modify, change. This wasn't any sort of solution. Didn't he see that? Isolating her out here with an empty sea.

She took a breath and willed herself to smile at him. "I don't know what to say."

"I know you love the Cape."

True, but she loved the part with quiet waters and harbors filled with boats and houses snugged up against each other. Not this part with its deserted beaches, icy winds, and restless surf.

"Come see."

He unlocked the door, and she stepped inside to find the cottage artfully furnished. The colors used for both walls and furniture were peaches and creams with touches of green. Perfect for a beach house.

"It...takes my breath away." Literally. She struggled to swallow.

"I knew you'd love it as soon as I saw it." He pulled her into a tight hug, obviously not hearing the panic underlying her words. "The *pièce de resistance* is this way." He grabbed her hand and led her through the bedroom, mostly decorated in cool greens, to a small alcove containing a spiral staircase.

A year ago she would have been unable to navigate those stairs, but her leg was now improved enough that she managed without difficulty. At the top, she stepped onto the plush green carpeting of a hexagonal room with six window seats. Each held plump cushions in a rainbow of colors.

She could easily love this room, if the view were something other than wind-swept beach and empty ocean.

"You stay here," Rob said. "Get acquainted with the house. I'll get the picnic."

Waiting for him to return, she wanted to weep. For him, for herself, for the pain she'd already caused and would continue to cause.

He'd added a chilled bottle of champagne to the supplies she'd packed. She watched his hands tear the foil from the top of the bottle and begin to untwist the wires holding in the cork.

"No." The word pushed out, past the tightness in her throat and the ache in her heart.

He paused, his eyebrows raised in question.

"I'm so sorry, Rob. I can't live here." She tried to find additional words to soften it, but they eluded her. Like wild birds scattered at a cry of alarm.

He set the bottle back in the ice. "It isn't working, is it?" His voice sounded raw and uneven. He cleared his throat, and for an instant, his eyes blazed with pain. Then he turned his head away. "You always seem happier when we come to the Cape. When I found this cottage, this room...you like to read. I thought..." He shook his head. "Stupid of me."

There were words to ease his pain, but they would be a lie.

He stood. "I need a few minutes before we go back." He lifted an envelope from among the things he'd brought from the car.

Clare sat unmoving, watching as his figure receded until between them lay only barren stretches of dunes being shaped and scoured by the cold wind.

~ ~ ~

After the inspiration for spending the summer at the Cape occurred to Rob, he'd spent weeks looking for the right place. He'd been certain Clare would love the cottage, especially the tower room with its wild, free view. But the whole plan turned out to be a desperate and ultimately futile attempt to reweave the connection they had somehow let unravel.

He left her in the tower room and slogged through loose sand until he reached the firmly packed area along the water. There he stopped to remove his shoes and socks before continuing barefoot along the strand.

Head down, he put one foot in front of the other until the cottage was a smudge of gray in the distance.

This is the end. The end. The end. The chant once started, kept pace. The sudden frigid touch of a wave altered that desolate rhythm, but for only an instant.

Still, that endless dirge was better than the reality it represented. Clare, her face strained, but her "no" unwavering.

It was past time he faced facts. Nothing he could say or do would make her happy. If anything, the evidence pointed to him as the problem, not the solution. Clare had been unambiguous for months, so why had he, a scientist for Pete sakes, been so obstinate about acknowledging what was before his eyes?

Love's dream.

But now he was awake.

He stopped abruptly and turned toward the water. Waves breaking far out from the shore slid in to foam at his feet. In spite of it being nearly June, the wind was fierce and cold, and his toes cramped in the chill surf. Tears piled up behind his eyes, making his head ache, then slipped unheeded, down his cheeks. He took the note for Clare he'd written with such hope, and tore it into tiny pieces, tossing them into the wind. The bits of paper swirled around him, dipping and swooping, and then they were gone.

He turned and walked slowly back to the woman he loved but was going to set free.

Chapter Twelve

Grand pas de deux - Variation for the danseuse
Dance for two - Variation for the female dancer

Rob gave her only glimpses of his pain after she rejected the idea of spending the summer at the Cape, but he returned from his walk along the beach a different man. On the drive back to Boston, he spoke only to ask if she wanted to stop for lunch. She said she didn't.

Back at the apartment, he carried the picnic up, leaving her to follow. "I'm going to the university. I'll be late so don't worry about making dinner for me."

He left and Clare stood in the living room, her arms wrapped around herself, racked with cold. Staring at a future as bleak as the view from the beach house's tower.

~ ~ ~

Clare learned about Hope House from an article in the *Boston Globe*. An ex-football player named Calvin Becker had bought an old building and was turning it into a place to teach life skills to men who no longer had dreams. According to the reporter, Becker believed lost dreams were best dealt with by practical means. It snagged her interest, the first thing to do that in months.

Still she hesitated when she saw where Hope House was located—in an inner-city neighborhood likely surrounded by dirt, disorder, and derelict buildings. A place neither pleasant nor altogether safe...and for Pete's sake, she was doing it again. Undermining herself. Talking herself out of taking a step...any step.

Whatever happened to the woman who'd leaped at the chance to fly to Madrid to dance in Balanchine's Diamonds with less than four days' notice and a couple of rushed rehearsals? That woman didn't back away from challenges.

Except, that woman had no idea life could narrow down to such, such... Blinking rapidly, she looked out the window at the bright light of a perfect spring day that mocked her dark thoughts.

Rob had already left for work, and he wouldn't be home until late. Any more, he spent only minimal time in the apartment, and during that time he avoided her. She didn't blame him. If she had a choice, she'd avoid herself as well.

She reread the article, feeling a tiny flutter of interest. Hope House needed volunteers, and an address and phone number were listed. If she called, she'd find a way to talk herself out of getting involved. Better to go, immediately, before she lost her momentum.

She grabbed a light jacket and her wallet. A short cab ride later, the driver stopped at a three-story brick row house that had once been, if not elegant, at least neat and trim. Now it had the slumped appearance of an old woman with a dowager's hump. The iron fence edging the sparse yard was rusted and dull, and tired junipers bracketed the concrete stoop. The only bright spot—the front door—was freshly painted a wildly inappropriate buttercup yellow.

Uneasy, Clare double-checked the newspaper to verify this was the address for Hope House before she dismissed the cab and walked up to that resplendent door.

It was opened by an elderly black man. "No need to knock, missy. Just walk yourself in."

"I'm here to see Calvin Becker?"

"Upstairs. Second door on your left." The man stood aside, and feeling as nervous as if she were about to step onto a stage under-rehearsed, she climbed the stairs and entered a large room apparently formed by knocking out several walls. A huge black man sorted through a drawer in a kitchen area.

"Calvin Becker?"

"Yep." He had a short, neat beard sprinkled with gray and a matching Afro. Both looked springy and soft. When he finally looked up, if he was surprised to find a white woman a third his size in his doorway, he hid it well.

"I'm here to see if I can help." She managed to make the words sound definite even though her insides wobbled like a top at the end of its spin.

"Doing what?" Becker's expression was not particularly friendly. That might have been intimidating if he hadn't reminded her of Wilson Taylor, the rehearsal pianist for Danse Classique. Wilson, a big brown teddy bear of a man, looked just as forbidding when he was first introduced.

"I saw the article in the newspaper. It said you needed help, and do you always look gift horses in the mouth?"

"But you ain't no horse." He narrowed his eyes and she lifted her chin and met his gaze.

"You expecting to be paid?" he asked.

"I expect rewards, but none that will deplete your bank account."

He shook his head. "Deplete my bank account. Oh my, oh my. You talk just like Appleseed."

"Appleseed?"

"Friend of mine. Always sounds like he's quoting one of them books he totes around." Becker continued to give her an assessing look, but she detected a glint of humor in his eyes.

"I don't mean to talk like a book. I'd just like to do something to help." If he didn't loosen up soon, she'd take it as a sign this project wasn't the right one for her, even though she badly needed something to get up for in the morning. "And no, Mr. Becker. I don't expect you to pay me."

"You can call me Beck. What's your name?"

"Clare."

"You got another name?"

"Chapin. Clare Chapin."

"Maybe we can figure something out, Clare-with-another-name. I teach good eating habits, bit of basic cooking. Other volunteers teach computers, taxes, budgets." He rubbed his cheek with a thumb. "Lavinia now, she been saying we need someone to brush the men up on their reading, writing. If she says okay, we're good."

"When can I meet Lavinia?"

"She right behind you."

Clare turned to find an ample black woman with intricately braided hair and an expression of obvious delight standing in the doorway.

"Well, now. I hear that right, beautiful. The Father sent you to help us?"

Beautiful? The Father?

Lavinia clasped her hands together. "Praise the Lord."

At least that explained who the Father was. "It's good to meet you, Lavinia."

The other woman took Clare's hand between both of hers. "Now nobody calls me that but my momma when she's upset with me and Beck when he's trying to impress somebody. Vinnie'll do fine."

"Don't get your hopes up, my sister. She ain't met the men yet. Might change her mind when she do."

Vinnie released Clare's hand and threw up her arms at Beck. "Father don't send us nobody going to quit easy."

Clare tried to decide if Vinnie's certainty was good news or bad news.

"You come with me, beautiful," Vinnie said, cutting off both debate and the possibility of escape. "Let's get you signed up and work us out a schedule."

When Vinnie took her on a tour of Hope House, Clare discovered Appleseed was Beck's nickname for the resident custodian and handyman, John Apple. They encountered Apple, a thirtyish white man with a ponytail and a guarded expression, in the break room reading a book.

After that brief introduction, Clare didn't speak to John until a few days later, when she was having lunch in the break room while he worked on a leaky faucet.

"Isn't your husband concerned about you coming here?" he asked.

Clare rubbed her thumb against her wedding ring. "He doesn't mind." The truth as far as it went. She wondered what Rob would think if she told him.

"Most husbands wouldn't want you to come here unescorted."

"It's not far, and it's good exercise." She unwrapped her sandwich, hoping to close out this particular subject.

John twisted around, a shocked expression on his face. "You walk here?"

"Easier than fighting Boston traffic and trying to find a parking place." True, she wouldn't walk in the area after dark, but during the day it was no worse than the neighborhood where the ballet center was located.

"Your husband doesn't know you're here, does he?"

"What about your family? What do they think about you working here?"

His expression might have been surprise, irritation, or something else. He bent back over the faucet. "Sorry, Clare. I didn't mean to sound overprotective, but I do think someone should walk with you. Let me know when you're ready to leave, and I'll be happy to see you have an escort."

Clare had wondered about John Apple. After that conversation she wondered even more—why was an educated man working at a menial job in one of the poorest parts of the city? The most likely explanation? He was an ex-addict or an ex-con.

~ ~ ~

"I do have one final announcement," the chairman said, winding up the faculty meeting. "Dr. Chapin has been approved for a sabbatical starting in October. He'll be going to Peru to study Amazonian plants."

"Isn't that a bit irregular?" Joyce frowned at the chairman. "To grant a sabbatical with so little notice."

"Irregular, perhaps, but not unprecedented. If you bring me a good plan like Rob's, I'll be happy to consider it."

When Rob walked out of the conference room, he found Joyce loitering in the hall, an expectant look on her face. "Wow, Robbie. Major surprise, you going on sabbatical. Didn't work out with the dancer, huh? Or are you taking your *prima* ballerina to the jungle with you?"

He'd never before been tempted to touch a woman in anger, but had the opportunity arisen at that moment, he would have struggled with his better nature not to push Joyce into traffic.

"I thank God Clare saved me from you."

Joyce's mouth gaped like a surprised fish. *Good.* He was damn tired of turning the other cheek. He walked past her to his office, closed the door, and stood rubbing his head, breathing carefully. At least Joyce's attack did have one good effect. It allowed him to substitute anger for a more essential agony.

~ ~ ~

John spoke to Beck about Clare walking home from Hope House, and Beck got on her case. "You going to come to the hood, Clare, you gots to know how to handle the brothers."

"I don't believe in violence."

"Violence don't care what you believe. Violence still there. Now what I'm going to show you, ain't no violence. It just going with the flow. So's you don't get hurt, you run up against a brother don't know you're one of us."

One of us. The words warmed her. She'd felt welcomed by Vinnie from the first moment but had remained uncertain of Beck. "Show me with Anthony," she said. "Then I'll decide."

Anthony, sixteen years old, was one of Beck's projects. Beck was working hard to keep the boy in school during the day and off the streets at night.

"Anthony. You come at me, hear," Beck said. "Like I a fat dude. Got attitude but no muscle."

Anthony, who reminded Clare of a heron picking its way through a marsh, lunged, and although Beck barely seemed to move, the boy ended up on his back, legs and arms like scattered sticks.

"You see, Clare? Anthony lying there so peaceful, he could be taking him a nap."

The boy had such a comical look of surprise, it made Clare laugh. "Are you okay, Anthony?"

"Like Beck says, I taking a nap. He somersault me. Matter a fact, felt kinda good. My back don't hurt no more."

So Clare let Beck teach her new ways to use moves once ingrained in bone, muscle, and sinew, and in the process, she learned about how to save other Anthonys one at a time.

And maybe how to save a Clare as well.

~ ~ ~

"I'm going on sabbatical to Peru."

Clare frowned. "Peru?"

"With Jolley." Looking at Clare made his heart hurt. The last two years had stripped the flesh from her face, leaving it stark, surrounded by a halo of nearly white hair. Not the injury alone causing that, but marriage to him.

She was still beautiful, though, and despite his frozen emotions, he knew he loved her. Would always love her. And if he kept his mouth shut, they could stay married. But he was no longer able to live with half-measures. It required a knack. A knack he knew at long last he didn't have.

"My salary will be deposited directly in the account. I'll go over the other financial details with you before I leave."

Clare shook her head as if to avoid a persistent gnat. "When do you go?"

"Not for another month."

"I'm so sorry, Rob. That I wasn't able to be what you wanted me to be."

"I only wanted you to be yourself."

"I can't seem to..."

"It's okay, Clare. I know you tried." It broke his heart anew to acknowledge it had been necessary for her to work at loving him, when loving her was as simple to him as breathing.

~ ~ ~

Peru. Sabbatical. Watching Rob's lips form the words, Clare knew. He'd given up on her. On their marriage. Pain blossomed, doubling her over. She straightened quickly. At the very least she owed him a dignified ending. This good man she'd pushed beyond limits he could bear. She'd left it too late...the attempt to reverse her slow drift into despair. A drift that pulled him along as well.

Not fair to try to change his mind. Dishonorable to hint she might be doing better. Better he left on his own terms. But did it have to be the jungle? Where so many things could go wrong. She ticked them off—snakebite, a host of tropical diseases, poisonous plants, accidents, contaminated water, rebels.

So easy for him not to come back at all.

At the thought, pain overwhelmed her. She barely made it to the bedroom and got the door closed before she broke down.

~ ~ ~

"Why don't you go with him, hon?" her mother asked.

"He's going to Peru. The jungle. The accommodations are extremely primitive."

"Oh. He won't be gone long, will he?"

"He'll be back for the holidays." Not exactly a lie, although her mom would interpret it to mean he'd be home for Thanksgiving and Christmas, while the holidays Clare referred to were Passover and Easter. But it simply wasn't yet possible for her to admit to anyone that Rob had left her.

Chapter Thirteen

Chassé
One foot chases the other,
done as a series

Clare walked briskly, pushed along in a swirl of leaves and trash through the gloom of an autumn afternoon. John had a cold, Anthony was at basketball practice, and Beck and Vinnie were working on something she didn't want to interrupt. Besides, Clare needed to be alone.

Tucking her hands in her pockets, she shrugged her shoulders against the chill and picked up her pace, trying not to let the hopelessness drifting in the air weigh her down any more than she already was—her heart heavy with the knowledge Rob was gone. Likely for good.

Suddenly, they were there. Two boys. Strangers. One on either side. They hemmed her in, slouching along, easily keeping pace, black sneakers silent against the pavement, almond-shaped eyes watchful in dark faces. Clare's heart slammed against her ribs and her breath caught. No one else was in sight, no traffic even. She gathered herself to run, but the larger boy grabbed her arm and pulled her toward an opening between two of the brick row houses, his fingers a tight, painful band despite the thickness of her coat.

Her only chance—to appear unafraid. That clarity eased her panicked breathing and, with that easing, she remembered what else Beck had taught her.

She leaned back, resisting the pull on her arm, looking from one boy to the other. The smaller one looked away, but the one holding her stared back with pitiless eyes. Her heart pumped rapidly but everything else slowed, and despite the grip on her arm, she felt more observer than participant, as if this were a performance.

A thought that brought both calm along with its own particular pain.

The boy holding her tossed his head, making his dreads dance. "You cooperate, we won't hurt you none, lady. We just wants your money."

So why hadn't they snatched her tote and run? She readied herself, slowing her breath, waiting for an opening. With two of them, she would have only one chance.

"This one be 'bout right size for you, Ty. Prove you got what it takes be one of us."

The boy called Ty grabbed her other arm. "Come on, lady. Ain't got all day." He nodded at Dreads, who released her.

The smaller boy jerked her toward the alley. She resisted, leaning back, digging in her heels. The pull intensified, and she leaned back further before taking a running step toward the boy, twisting to pull his arm around her, searching for the fulcrum point, as Beck had shown her. Turning smoothly now, easily. The boy and her tote flying, momentarily weightless as balloons.

Then gravity took hold and both boy and bag landed with solid thumps. Still feeling weightless herself, Clare pivoted toward the second boy, but he fled, cursing. She turned back to the one on the ground, leaning in to grab her bag, poised to run if he started to get up.

"Shit, lady. You a cop?"

The fear in his voice caused her to hesitate and take a good look at him. Not only small, but younger than she'd originally thought. A mere baby. And already lost?

She narrowed her eyes going for a Lisa-look. "What's your name?"

He rubbed the back of his head, his gaze unfocused. "Uh. Ty. Tyrese Brown."

"How old are you?"

"Tw-thirteen." He brought a hand up to shade his eyes and squinted at Clare.

He couldn't be thirteen, or even twelve. Ten, possibly. She wanted to walk away, but his fear held her more firmly than had his hand.

The decision of what to do next was so sudden and simple, she almost smiled, except she didn't dare. "I've got a choice here, Tyrese Brown." She made her tone icy and her

119

expression forbidding. "I could take you to the station. Have them book you, throw you in a cell, and forget to call anybody for a while."

His eyes widened and his head shook from side to side. His continuing fear reassured her. Not a hardened criminal yet, or he would have seen through her in two seconds. So maybe there was hope for him. Worth taking a chance, at least. "Or we can make a deal."

It was only later, when she stripped for her shower and saw the black marks on her arm, that she began to shake.

~ ~ ~

Rob left Boston for Peru with a heavy heart but with a feeling of relief. After months of emotional wheel-spinning, he was finally off dead center, moving, although it was unclear in what direction.

In Cuzco, Norman Jolliffe met him at the airport and helped load Rob's luggage into a taxi that took them to the hotel. "I'm sure you're beat," Jolley said, after helping him check in. "Rest if you like or take a look around. We'll get together at dinner. Sam will be in by then."

Rob took a nap then went for a walk around Cuzco. It was like stepping into a page from National Geographic. The narrow cobblestone streets were stuffed with buses, small trucks, and tiny cars. Sidewalks, no more than two feet wide, were filled with scurrying people do-si-do-ing around each other, the tourists with their jeans and backpacks, standing out amid the bright colors of the Indian women's skirts.

The biggest surprise was the number of school-age children who plied him with postcards. A boy of about ten had the most compelling approach. "Hey, mister. You want to see the twelve-sided Inca stone?" He laughed at Rob's puzzled look. "Come. I show you. Where you from?"

"The United States."

"Thought so. You can call me Ronnie Reagan." The boy trotted down the street with Rob following, puffing a bit from the high altitude.

Halfway down the block, "Ronnie" stopped and pointed to a huge block in the middle of a stone wall. Rob's eyes followed the boy's finger as he counted off the twelve sides. "How you like Peru, huh?"

"I don't know yet. I just arrived. Did you learn to speak English in school?"

"Naw." The boy shook his head. "I learn from tourists. Like you. Come on, I show you the puma."

The urchin led him around the corner and pointed out the image of a puma formed by more huge stones.

"You like?"

"Yes. It's very interesting."

"Then you buy postcards. Four for forty *soles*."

Rob did a quick calculation. "Whoa there, Ronnie. Ten dollars for four postcards? Bit much, isn't it?" In spite of the hustle, he was drawn to the bright intelligence and cheeky smile.

"It's for my school tuition."

"So why aren't you in school right now?"

"I go to school at night."

Right, and Rob could fit a twelve-sided multi-ton stone into a wall. "Tell you what, Ronnie. Here's two dollars. You keep the postcards."

He felt guilty later when he learned schools did have multiple sessions, and the boy might have been telling the truth about needing money for school.

~ ~ ~

"Rob, good. You're here," Jolley said, walking toward him in the hotel lobby that evening. "Like you to meet our translator, Alberto Rodriguez, and this is Sam Lewiston, our medical officer."

Sam was a tall, spare woman with a short, practical haircut.

Rob shook the hand she held out to him. "So Sam is short for Samantha rather than Samuel."

"Jolley playing fast and loose with the truth, is he?" Sam was assessing him every bit as thoroughly as he was assessing her.

"More a sin of omission."

"Is that a problem?" The question was stated calmly, but her gaze was direct and unequivocal.

"Just a surprise."

Still holding Rob's gaze, she nodded, making silver earrings, that appeared to be her only concession to femininity, dance. A good thing she didn't seem concerned about her looks. A woman who was could be a major pain.

As they ate, Jolley briefed them. "We used to come into these areas expecting the native healers to share everything they know. They're incredible naturalists and generally as friendly and willing to share as they are intelligent. But pharmaceutical companies came in and took advantage of that knowledge to develop products without compensating the natives who provided the information."

Things were changing. Now repayment was common. "That's why Sam's along," Jolley said. "To set up a clinic as our contribution."

"I'm also hoping I'll have a chance to learn about treatment modalities from the native *payés* while I'm here," Sam said.

"*Payés?*" Rob said.

"Medicine men, shamans. Payé is the term they prefer."

Jolley then summarized what he'd accomplished since arriving in Cuzco some ten days earlier. "Food, other supplies, and transportation are all set. The trickiest part was finding a small generator to run the satellite phone, but Alberto managed it. And you'll be glad to know, Sam, the last of the medical supplies arrived yesterday. It means we'll get away on schedule, a major miracle in this part of the world."

"Is lucky we can leave tomorrow or we have to wait until Monday," Alberto said.

"Why is that?" Rob asked.

"Road very narrow. Very bad we meet someone come the other way. We must start right day."

"We're looking at a total of twenty-four hours' road time to Shintuyo," Jolley said. "We'll probably overnight in Pilcopata, depending on how it goes."

"So, how many miles to Shintuyo?" Sam asked.

"Two hundred, two hundred fifty kilometers," Alberto responded.

Rob translated to miles and frowned at the number he came up with—a hundred twenty to one hundred sixty. "You're saying we'll average only five miles an hour?"

"Oh, we'll likely do better than that." Jolley cut into his llama steak. "The twenty-four hour estimate includes stops for the usual things, as well as the unexpected. Although, it's pretty much *de rigueur* that something unexpected happens on that road."

Sam grimaced. "Sounds like fun."

"Well, it can be a tough trip, but I think you'll find it fascinating."

"What's the highest altitude we'll be hitting?" Rob fought the urge to rub his head and finally gave in. He'd had a headache most of the afternoon.

"Oh, somewhere in the neighborhood of 14,000 feet."

"We'll buy coca leaves in the morning," Alberto said.

Coca leaves? As in cocaine? "Because?" Rob said.

"It help with the altitude sickness."

Rob glanced at Sam. "What does our medical officer think about that?"

"If you haven't taken Diamox ahead of time, coca is a good alternative to alleviate symptoms. You either chew the leaves or drink the tea. You won't get high, but it might help that headache."

~ ~ ~

The driver turned off the highway onto a narrow unpaved track lined with potholes and rocks, and as the van began to bump and grind, Rob took several of the coca leaves out of the recycled plastic bag they'd come in. After he'd chewed the leaves for a while, all he noticed was a slight numbness to his tongue, then he realized the headache had begun to abate and his fingers no longer had the shriveled look of something left too long under water. He didn't care for the taste of the leaves, a distinctive green flavor with an underlying bitterness, but the bad taste was a reasonable trade for the headache.

As the day progressed, the novelty of being in Peru wore off, and Rob profoundly regretted his decision to come on the expedition. Unfortunately, it was too late to back out now. He was stuck for the duration.

The only good thing? The foreignness of the surroundings and the physical discomforts of the journey distracted him, for the first time in months, from the soreness of his psyche.

Climbing above Cuzco's 10,000 feet, they passed through a stark landscape of tans and browns. The driver shifted into low gear, and Rob turned away from the sight of the sheer drop on his side of the van. They would have to wait a long time for rescue if they got stuck or slid off the road, and given the way the vehicle shimmied through the ruts, that was a distinct possibility.

Since he could do nothing to avert the possibility, he tried not to think about it. Instead, he struggled to follow the example of Jolley and Sam who were chatting in a relaxed fashion.

When they stopped to stretch their legs, Rob glanced up and was struck by the deep clear color of the sky.

"It's the high altitude and no pollution, of course," Jolley said, when Rob remarked on it.

Shivering, Rob blinked to lubricate his eyes and licked his lips, which were beginning to peel in the thin, odorless air.

Over the next few hours, the road ascended further before beginning to descend. Vegetation finally reappeared, and Rob spat out the last of the coca leaves, glad to be done with them.

Plant life became progressively more lush as the air changed. No longer was it crisp and clear. Instead it was thick and damp.

~ ~ ~

After Tyrese Brown mugged her the day Rob left for Peru, Clare told Beck about the incident and the deal she'd made with the boy to come to Hope House.

She knew by the way Beck pummeled his bread dough he was upset. "You've got to promise me, Clare. No more walking home by yourself."

She rubbed her arm where Tyrese's companion had gripped it and had no difficulty giving Beck her word.

"Don't want no gang members here."

"He isn't one. At least, not yet. And we can't just stand by and wait for him jump off a cliff before we step in. Not when we can possibly stop him from jumping in the first place." Despite arguing the point with Beck, Clare wished she'd never made the deal with Tyrese. Wished she'd simply called the police and let them handle it. But the boy was so young, so frightened.

"You think it's that easy?" Beck said.

"Of course not, but that's what you're trying to do, isn't it. Save people?"

"Only ones that wants it."

"Maybe we can help him want it."

"I'll talk with this Tyrese. If he shows up. See what he has to say for hisself. Then we'll see."

Clare felt no sense of victory at Beck's agreement. Suggesting the boy come to Hope House had been a spur of the moment thing, and now that she'd had time to think, she hoped Tyrese wouldn't show up. It would be so much easier.

She stretched her shoulders and rubbed her neck, achy from a night of being jolted awake by images of merciless eyes and dark alleys full of trash and broken glass. Her uneasiness deepening, she went looking for John Apple, knowing she needed to tell him about her encounter with Tyrese before he heard it from Beck.

He was repairing a window frame in one of the classrooms. Standing in the doorway watching him, Clare felt the way she had as a child about to confess a wrongdoing to her father. As she had then, she recited the facts of her misdeed quickly.

"You know better, Clare. If you don't want to ask me to walk you, you ask Beck or one of the men. They could've had guns or knives, and if they had, those few little moves you learned wouldn't have saved you." The screen fell with a bang, and he stooped to pick it up, swearing softly.

"It's not your job to worry about me."

He set the screen down and turned to face her. "Someone's got to, Clare Eliason."

Her heart startled into a quick rhythm.

He shifted his feet, looked away. "I saw you dance. Didn't recognize you, though. Not until we were showing you those defense moves."

"My name is Clare Chapin."

He nodded. "Clare Eliason Chapin."

"You have no right to check on me." She turned away from him, clutching her arms around herself, the only sound in the room the ragged pant of her breathing.

His hand rested lightly on her shoulder. "I'm sorry. You're right. I didn't check on you, but I had no business making personal comments. It's just that you seemed ups—"

She jerked away from his touch and ran from the room, going to the only place there was any privacy at Hope House. She closed the bathroom door behind her and locked it, then stood bracing herself on the sink, trying to still the mad churn of emotion summoned by John's words and the touch of his hand on her shoulder. *Rob. Oh, God. Rob.*

When she straightened, her gaze was caught by the image of the woman in the mirror. A woman with a small, pinched face; wide, staring eyes; and short white hair. A woman old before her time.

A woman who no longer remembered what it was like to dream.

Chapter Fourteen

Grand pas de deux - Variation for the danseur
Dance for two - Variation for the male dancer

Two days after departing from Cuzco, Rob and the others arrived in Shintuyo. As they climbed out of the van, the driver shook their hands, a broken-toothed grin on his face. "*Una buena viaje.*" A good trip.

Given they'd had two flats and one breakdown, Rob wondered what would constitute a "bad" trip, although he definitely preferred not to find out.

They completed the transfer of their supplies to open boats that Rob hoped would be more reliable than the van had been.

Travel on the river quickly became monotonous. Huge trees lined the shore like the walls of a stockade, and any flowers remained hidden, as did the wildlife, except for birds.

The river itself was several hundred feet wide and as opaque as the chocolate milk it resembled. The boatmen stuck to the middle where there was less danger of running onto a shoal or encountering debris, but it meant they had no protection from the sun. They pulled out hats and sunglasses, and Sam passed around a tube of sunscreen.

The sight of a parrot caused Rob a spasm of pain, reminding him of that first Christmas Eve with Clare. More parrots, flashing blues, reds, and greens swooped past the boats, their screeches audible over the drone of the small outboards.

When they reached the Machiguenga village that would be their home for the next six months, they found their accommodations were a grouping of four huts. Like the ten other huts that comprised the village, each was a simple raised platform with half walls of cane branches. Roofs were thatched with palm fronds.

Except for a few straggly patches of vegetation, the area where the huts were located was all hard packed dirt, with only the occasional muddy spot to remind them they were in a rainforest.

Jolley looked around, rubbing his hands in satisfaction. "Excellent. Excellent setup. We should be quite comfortable."

Rob's gut spasmed at the certainty of the discomfort in store.

The supplies were off-loaded, and the boats turned back to Boca Manu leaving them with the Machiguengas. The men, with their circular haircuts and simple serape-like tunics, resembled medieval monks—short, bowlegged, broad-chested monks. Their sturdy wives were dressed in various pieces of Western clothing—blouses or T-shirts and skirts. A cluster of children with shy smiles, large dark eyes, and straight black hair stood nearby.

As Rob lifted a duffel into the hut he and Jolley would be sharing, the full force of what he'd done hit. Here he was in a jungle, miles from everything familiar, when all he'd had to do was move to another apartment in Boston and begin a civilized dialogue with Clare about a divorce. Instead, he faced six months of primitive living that only postponed the reckoning.

It wasn't the way he usually handled problems.

~ ~ ~

Rob had been gone three days before Tyrese Brown showed up at Hope House. Beck met with him and arranged for him to come after school every day to be tutored by Clare and to spend an hour with John Apple cleaning classrooms, removing trash, and learning to do simple repair jobs.

Clare looked up as her newest student sidled into the classroom, a sullen expression on his face. "Found out you ain't no cop."

"I never said I was."

"You ain't the boss of me. Can't make me do this."

Clare hid her discomfort at his angry tone with a shrug, relieved that three men were taking practice GED tests in the back of the room. "You're right. But I can still turn you in."

"Ah, lady, why you gots to do this?"

An excellent question, and the honest answer was she had no idea. She stared at the boy, who was shifting from foot to foot, wishing she'd been able to walk away from him. Instead, with Beck now on the case, she was stuck.

"We may as well get started. I see you didn't bring any books today." She walked over to the bookcase and pulled out *Horton Hatches the Egg* by Doctor Seuss.

"Honky bitch." Tyrese had mumbled, but the words were enough for her to hear.

Dear Lord, how to handle it? What to say to a child as angry as this one? She took her time turning around, waiting until she'd managed a calming breath, but she still didn't know how to counter Tyrese's aggression.

"We'll use this today, but you need to bring your schoolbooks with you tomorrow." She gestured toward a chair, and once he sat down, she sat next to him and opened the book.

He stumbled through the first half page. "This's stupid." He slapped the book shut and glared at her.

One of the men looked over and frowned. Clare shook her head at the man. She needed to handle this herself. The certainty steadied her as she walked over to the wall phone and pretended to dial. "Sergeant Mallory, please."

"Don't have to go and do that." Tyrese jumped up and grabbed for the phone.

She held it away from him, heart pumping rapidly.

"I'll read the fucking book."

The man who'd looked up before began to stand. She motioned him to wait, but his presence reassured her. In spite of the successful outcome of her first encounter with Tyrese, she had no desire to face him down again without backup.

"We don't use language like that at Hope House."

"Fuck Hope House."

Okay, enough. "A neat trick. One I doubt you can manage."

Tyrese continued to glare at her, and she matched him look for look until he returned to his seat. He opened the book, and she sat next to him, breathing a sigh of relief her bluff had once again been successful. She nodded a thank-you to the man who had been prepared to come to her aid.

For the next hour, she worked with Tyrese, showing him how to sound out multisyllabic words, rereading some of the lines so he could hear the rhymes and rhythms, praising him every time he remembered a word he'd previously stumbled on.

At the end of the session, she was exhausted from the effort of pushing against the boy's determined resistance.

Over the next week, Tyrese made slow, contentious progress. He was still uncooperative, but she was convinced it was more and more of an act. An act that was beginning to slip. The bigger problem was Tyrese's continuing use of bad language. Then Beck overheard him asking one of the men why there was so much effing white bread at Hope House. Beck marched Tyrese to the kitchen and washed his mouth out with soap.

Amused by the story, Clare went in search of Beck. "I haven't heard of that remedy being used in years."

"Likely why there's so much trash-talking today." Beck stirred a bowl of dark batter.

"That isn't a Calvin Becker double chocolate cake by any chance?"

"Thought it might help get the taste of soap out of someone's mouth."

"You're a good man, Beck."

He stirred harder. "He don't get none till he apologizes. Told him, he don't say he's sorry, I'll let you demonstrate more of your karate moves."

Smiling at the thought, Clare left Beck to his baking. She was correcting the men's written work when Tyrese arrived for his lesson. He sidled in, eyeing her as if she were a snake coiled to strike.

"Good afternoon, Tyrese." She set the papers aside and waited while he slipped onto the chair next to her and pulled a book from inside his coat.

"Afternoon, ma'am." He ducked his head and flipped the book open. "Got something I needs to say." His eyes slid sideways, and he peered at her.

She sat still.

"I, uh, I disrespected you. Mr. Becker, he say I gots to apologize. I'm sorry."

Clare waited for more, but the boy appeared to be finished. "I accept your apology, Tyrese."

He wiggled in the seat before opening the book.

"Mr. Becker wants to see you when we're done."

"Oh. I already done seen Mr. Becker, ma'am. I don't need to see him no more."

"He won't bite."

"I surely think he might."

She wanted to laugh, but she didn't dare. Instead, she patted the boy on the arm. "I promise he won't. Now, what are we working on today?"

~ ~ ~

"Hah!"

Rob jumped as a small boy pounced at him from behind a tree at the edge of the village. Like all Machiguengan children, he was beautiful. Thick black hair stuck straight out in spikes a rock star would envy framing a face with smooth golden skin. Dark eyes danced with mischief.

Rob smiled. *"Buenas dias. Como se llama?"*

The boy giggled, his hands over his mouth.

"Me llamo Rob." He pointed to his chest, then pointed at the boy. "What's your name?"

The boy cocked his head as if considering, then danced off without speaking.

After that, the youngster shadowed Rob's every move. Eventually, Rob learned his name was Tatito, and the two of them commenced a relationship, communicating with a mix of signs and words in Spanish, English, and the Machiguengan language.

~ ~ ~

"Were you ever as angry as Tyrese?" Clare asked Beck. She wanted to believe the sullenness was a defense mechanism, but it still wore her out.

"Tyrese getting to you, is he?"

She nodded.

"Why not say you through with him?" Beck said as he wiped down a section of counter.

"I guess I'm being stubborn." She pulled up a stool and sat, resting her chin on her hands, facing Beck. "Do you think there's any hope?"

He gave her a sharp look before turning away to rinse his wiping cloth. "When I sixteen, got my first job. Fast food joint, down by the ballpark. Didn't know I was, how you say it? That thing where you can't see letters and numbers good."

"Dyslexic?" It was unclear what this had to do with Tyrese, but she settled in to listen.

130

"Yep." He turned to dig a canister of flour out of the cupboard. "This one day, we got lines a mile long when this white woman pushes into my line, saying I didn't give her enough change. Said I owed her six dollars and seventy-two cents but I only give her twenty-seven cents. Didn't even remember her. Figured she scamming me." He continued pulling ingredients and implements out of the cupboards.

"The supervisor came over, heard what she saying. Told me give the woman her change. I did it. Figured that's one smart woman. Just made six bucks for two minutes' hassle time." He stared at the items on the counter as if trying to decide what was missing, then turned to the cupboard and got out packages of yeast. "I go on working. Suddenly, same woman's in my face again. Talking about change and how I shorted her. Made me angry. She must think I'm an idiot, I don't recognize her. Only turned out she ain't complaining about me shorting her. She's giving me back six dollars. Said, when she complained, I gave her too much change. You could have laid me out with a feather. Never even had no white woman look at me like I belong to the same species before that."

He cracked eggs into a bowl and discarded the shells. Clare waited for the rest of the story, but he began to whisk the eggs into a froth without speaking.

"I don't get it. What does it have to do with Tyrese?"

"Kindness confusing him. He mugged you, now you're helping him. May take him awhile to sort that out."

~ ~ ~

After learning Beck was dyslexic, Clare stopped by a nearby grade school and asked to speak to a reading teacher.

Sally Prentice, a bouncy redhead with freckles sprinkled across her nose, didn't appear to be much older than her students, although she laughed when Clare said so. "I've been teaching fifteen years."

"I need suggestions about how to help someone with dyslexia."

"There are some studies suggesting dyslexia may be linked to difficulties in differentiating the sound of similar letters, like D and B." Sally picked up a folder and handed Clare several sheets of paper from it. "Here are some exercises that may help."

"The men I'm tutoring also struggle with writing."

"I read recently about a program in a prison," Sally said. "The prisoners were writing their memoirs, and they said it was the only thing that made them feel human." Sally paused and gave Clare a serious look that momentarily erased her gamin quality. "What you're doing, Clare, it's so important. Reading and writing can change lives."

Clare wished it were that simple.

But then she did know how simply and quickly a life could change for the worse.

Chapter Fifteen

Tournant
Turning

Vinnie looked up with a smile as Clare hung her jacket on the coat hook in Vinnie's office. "My, you're getting bad as Appleseed, beautiful. You're here all the time. Like you ain't got any other life."

Too true, although it wasn't something Clare was comfortable admitting, despite her fondness for Vinnie, who brightened the dullest day with a mile-wide smile and her standard greeting of hey there, beautiful. Clare had watched men, both fierce and mild, shuffle in embarrassed pleasure at Vinnie's enthusiasm—an enthusiasm that was slowly easing Clare's heart.

"Beck and I thank the Father every day for sending you and Appleseed to us. Good thing you two used to living on air, though."

Clare shook her head. "I don't know what you mean."

"If you needed money, we'd lose you both."

"All I'm good for is an entry-level job. As for John, I imagine it's difficult for an ex-con to find work. I think you're stuck with us."

"Appleseed an ex-con? What makes you say that?"

"Ex-con, ex-addict. He's too educated to be working as a janitor otherwise."

Vinnie shook her head. "You think that, you don't know nothing, beautiful. Appleseed's the real deal. Not saying more, he wouldn't like it, but he's no ex-con."

~ ~ ~

"I'm worried about Appleseed," Beck said.

133

"Why is that?" It seemed to be Clare's day for conversations about John Apple.

"He's gone quiet on me. Like when he first come. Ain't good." Beck added a scoop of flour to the bowl.

"Hold it. How much did you just add?" She'd offered to write out Beck's recipes and was watching him cook while she took notes.

"'Bout a quarter cup, I reckon."

"There's nothing wrong with being quiet," she said, noting the amount.

"Man a mess when he come. Thought he was through all that."

"Do you know why?" She waited, but when Beck didn't respond, she knew it would be hypocritical to push, given her reaction when John commented on her personal life.

Still, she couldn't help being curious. The discomfort from her last conversation with John had faded awhile ago, but she didn't know how to let him know he was forgiven, especially since lately she'd seen him only in passing. So was he avoiding her? But she'd been avoiding him, after all.

"There," Beck said. "When it gets like this, it's time to jump in with both hands and squeeze it good."

Maybe Appleseed was another of Beck's projects. And did Beck realize she needed Hope House as much or more than Hope House needed her? Possibly. He and Vinnie seemed to have a talent for reading troubled hearts.

With a start, she realized she'd lost track of Beck and his dough. She bent her head once again over her notes.

Beck set the bowl aside in a patch of sun with a damp cloth covering it. "Now, it rests and rises."

~ ~ ~

Clare found John working on an electrical outlet in one of the classrooms. Standing in the doorway, gathering her courage, she stared at his back—narrow compared to Beck's—and at his hair—pulled into a ponytail. Usually, she didn't care for long hair on a man, but it suited John. It was his only oddity. With a haircut and dressed in a suit, he could be...what? Professor? Doctor? Lawyer? What real deal had Vinnie been referring to?

Not wanting to startle him while he worked with bare electrical wires, she knocked softly against the door frame. "Could I speak to you, John Apple?"

He twisted from his stooped position and lifted his eyebrows. "Why so formal?"

She walked into the room and perched on the end of a table near him. "It is your name, like Clare Eliason Chapin is my name."

He stood, holding a screwdriver in one hand, and a new outlet in the other.

"I wanted to apologize," Clare said. "The last time we spoke, I was rude. I'm sorry."

"You were right. I had no business commenting on your personal life."

"Friends try to help each other. Sometimes they make mistakes. Besides, it's time I started facing up to who I am." She walked to the window and looked at the backyard, bare now that autumn was well advanced. "I decided that psychologist Beck invited in was right. 'You can't change the past, but you do have to accept it.' Wasn't that what he said? And there I was, feeling superior to everyone in the room, when they at least had the courage to admit they needed help." And what about the other thing the psychologist said? *Face your past. Look for the lessons in it. If there are amends to be made, make them. The worst thing that's happened to you can have blessings attached. Look for them.*

"You think it takes courage to ask for help?" John's voice sounded strained.

"I know it has for me."

"Are you asking me for help, Clare?"

"I know I have to do the hard part myself, but I'd like you to be my friend."

She turned from the window and found John staring at the floor. He shook himself and gave her a crooked smile. "I could use a friend, too."

"It's a deal, then."

He set the screwdriver down and took her hand in his. "Deal."

Thinking about the conversation later, Clare realized what she'd said about having to work through the hard part herself wasn't just words strung together. It was the truth.

Progress.

But she still hadn't faced everything in her past. She still hadn't examined why, after marrying Rob, she'd treated him so badly.

~ ~ ~

Once they were settled in the Machiguenga village, their scientific activities got under way, with the local payé, Soraida, leading the expeditions into the jungle. Since Rob became disoriented as soon as he stepped far enough into the trees that the village was out of sight, he was relieved as well as intrigued by how easily and confidently Soraida navigated the forest.

As he led them from place to place, the payé pointed out plants with medicinal properties, then he demonstrated how to collect the active part—leaves, roots, stems, or fruits. Back in the village, Rob watched Soraida prepare the plant materials for use, boiling some to make teas or infusions, drying others and grinding them into powders. Some powders the payé mixed into pastes with ashes collected from the burning of specific leaves. Others he placed together in complex mixtures, the exact composition of which varied depending upon the ailment to be treated.

At Soraida's urging, Rob tasted one infusion. It was bitter but not unpleasant. The payé pushed on his stomach as if it hurt then mimed drinking more. Since Rob wasn't currently having any stomach troubles, he took another careful sip before handing the gourd containing the tea back to Soraida, who finished it off with a smacking of his lips and a contented pat on his abdomen.

When Rob carried out preliminary chemical testing of Soraida's preparation, he discovered the tea tested positive for an alkaloid—no surprise given its bitter taste. The simple color tests Rob was using reminded him of how his fascination with science began—with a chemistry set when he was twelve. Now, on good days, he felt as if he'd been given a chance to start over on a fresh, blank slate after thoroughly messing up the first one.

~ ~ ~

"Love you, too. Talk to you soon." Jolley ended the call to his wife then handed the satellite phone to Rob. "I expect you want to give Clare a call."

Rob took the phone, but he didn't call Clare. Instead, he called his post-doc, Hatsume, and his sister. When he handed the phone back, Jolley accepted it with a frown. Although he'd moved away while Rob made his calls, as Rob had while Jolley talked to Jane, it wasn't possible to conceal the fact he never called Clare.

He thought about her, though. Many nights, he lay awake long after the others were asleep, thinking about her. Tracing through it all, trying to find the place where they'd begun to lose their way. Trying to convince himself that divorcing her was the right thing to do. Although neither of them had said the word, they'd both known it was where they were headed.

Other times he fell asleep immediately, only to awaken in the deepest part of the night—to the sudden snap and rustle of disturbed underbrush, the crackly sound of rain on the thatch roof, or the cacophony of insect life punctuated now and then by a screech in a different key as some wild thing located its dinner. As he lay awake, images of Clare flickered through his memory. Clare, brighter than a vision, lighting up the stage and his life; Clare, on the deck of the sailboat, her dark hair, a banner in the sunlight.

He'd loved her hair. Loved running his fingers through the long silken length of it. Now when he thought of Clare's hair, short and white, he felt a helpless grief. He missed her hair. But more, he missed the woman she'd been with that long hair. Audacious, excited to see what each day would bring.

He'd understood immediately her cropped head was a sign of her despair, and he'd waited, hoping she'd heal and let her hair grow.

But she hadn't.

~ ~ ~

Living in the jungle, what Rob missed most were hot showers and a variety of foods. Although they had brought rice, beans, and several live chickens to add to the communal pot, they ate what the Machiguenga did. Carbohydrates were obtained from the rice they'd brought and the manioc cultivated by the women in a cleared area near the village, and protein was supplied by fish caught using plant poisons, by beans and by chicken eggs.

"Their manioc growing has only a minimal impact on the rainforest," Jolley said, in response to a question from Sam. "When they move on, these small plots will fill back in within seventy-five to a hundred years. It's the areas being cleared for ranching and farming that will never recover."

On their jungle diet, it wasn't long before Rob's clothes fit more loosely, and his attitude also changed as he took more of an interest in the Machiguenga.

The villagers lived quietly, spending their days working, resting, interacting. Although Rob sought evidence of village politics or hierarchical structure, to his eyes they were invisible. Certainly there was none of the pettiness and overt maneuvering, the constant push-pull of egos, he'd faced in the academic world.

He mentioned it one evening to Sam and Jolley.

"They believe a man should live calmly, lest he disturb the balance of the universe." Jolley picked up a stick, leaned over, and drew two spirals in the dirt. "They represent that balance with this image. It's their belief that these lines hold the world in place. If they are distorted by anger or strife, they will no longer have that power, and the world will fall into chaos."

"It looks like a series of orbits," Sam said. "We consider them primitive, but their cosmology is quite sophisticated."

"What do you think they'd make of the so-called civilized world?" Rob asked.

Jolley took his pipe out of his mouth and shook his head. "I don't think we should tell them about it."

"I agree," Sam said. "Why take the chance? Their calm may be the only thing keeping the universe from disintegrating."

~ ~ ~

Rob limped into camp from a morning expedition.

"Let me take a look," Sam said. "What happened?"

"Slipped. Stupid of me."

"Not stupid. Clumsy, maybe." She made him sit, then took off his boot. She had long narrow hands. Her fingers, slender and strong, probed the ankle. "It's only a minor sprain. Too bad there's no ice." She got out an elastic bandage and wrapped it securely around his ankle and foot. "There, that will stabilize it. Ibuprofen will help if there's pain or swelling." She sat back on her heels and smiled at him. "You should be fine. Just take it easy and don't push for the next few days."

"Thanks."

"Lucky for you I was just working on the day's log. I'll be sure to give you a prominent position."

"Not exactly the way I'd choose to be featured." He stood and took a tentative step, pleased to discover if he moved carefully, he could walk with little pain. It was the first time he'd felt anything other than resigned about Sam being part of the group.

~ ~ ~

"We've certainly been getting better books lately," John said, as he and Clare unpacked the boxes donated by a West Roxbury women's group that had adopted Hope House as a service project.

"We are." Clare lifted another two books from the box, glancing at the titles. "You think we'll ever see any of the men reading Hemingway or Faulkner?"

John picked the two up and added them to one of the piles he was building. "You're the tutor. What do you teach from?"

"Mostly children's stories."

"Here, why not try them on this." He held up a book by Robert B. Parker. "Good story, snappy dialogue, and it's set in Boston."

"What kind of book is it?"

"Detective story." He handed her the book, then patted the pile he'd added the Hemingway and Faulkner volumes to. "You mind if I borrow these? I'll see you get them back."

"No problem. You're a reader?"

"Books help me survive."

Me, too, she might have said.

~ ~ ~

Clare tensed at the nasal sound of her mother-in-law's voice. It was the phone call she'd been dreading as the end of November approached.

"It's been simply ages since we've seen you," Mrs. Chapin said. "Not since Rob left. We need to do something about that. You must come for Thanksgiving, Clare." It was more command than invitation.

"I'm sorry. I'm spending Thanksgiving with friends." Beck and the men in the cooking class were planning a big do.

"Well, family trumps friends any time. You can simply tell them that, dear."

"I'm afraid I can't do that."

"Christmas then. You must come to us for Christmas. Spend the night."

"I'm planning to go home for Christmas."

"My goodness. It's harder to get on your schedule than for me to do the Sugar Plum Fairy's dance." Mrs. Chapin's chuckle was stiff with irritation. "We heard from Rob last week," she continued before Clare could reply. "He sounds good. Enjoys the work, but I expect you hear from him yourself."

Clare could think of no response to that.

"Well, you're certainly a busy young woman."

Clare steeled herself against guilt. "I hope you have a happy Thanksgiving, and I do appreciate the invitation." A huge relief, though, to be able to decline it.

Chapter Sixteen

Allégro
A term applied to steps that are performed
in a brisk and lively manner

Thanksgiving at Hope House was a roaring success. Although there was no alcohol, the adults were only slightly more sober than the children, who were delirious and noisy. Several men brought wives or girlfriends, and Tyrese and Anthony brought their moms. But the biggest surprise was Vinnie, who showed up with a shy smile and a man who grinned every time he looked at her.

After the dinner in the largest of the classrooms, they all worked together to clean up. Then they moved the tables out of the way as three of the men pulled out battered instruments—a cornet, an alto sax, and a harmonica. A fourth man moved a small table holding pans and glasses into position to serve as the percussion section.

The music they proceeded to play was happy and frolicking, with a strong beat that made it impossible for the children to sit still. Watching the little ones move with unconscious ease, Clare felt a familiar ache. Then the tempo changed and Anthony's mom began to sing "Amazing Grace" in a high sweet voice. Others joined in until the room was full to bursting with sound. Clare clenched her hands as the voices swept over and through her.

The last note faded into a moment of silence, before the stamping, whistling, and cheering urged the men into the next tune. When it started, Vinnie and her friend moved to the middle of the room and began to dance. Others joined them, pulling on the hands of those still sitting. In a panic, Clare slipped through the door into the hall, where she leaned against the wall, her eyes closed.

"You okay?" John asked.

She nodded without looking at him.

He leaned on the wall next to her. "Your husband couldn't make it today?"

"It was too far to come."

"What? Into the ghetto, you mean?"

"He's in Peru. In the jungle. Searching for the next miracle drug."

That silenced John. She glanced over to find him frowning.

"Does he know what you're doing while he's off in the jungle?"

She shook her head.

"You don't want to worry him."

"It wouldn't."

"Then he's a fool."

"No. He's not." Clare was abruptly too exhausted to stand, even with the wall propping her up. She slid into a sitting position. After a moment, John sat beside her. Close but not touching.

"Listen to them in there," she said. "All that enthusiasm, despite their difficulties. It makes me feel, I don't know...ungrateful, I suppose."

"Are you getting divorced, Clare?"

The bald question took her breath away. It was a moment before she was able to answer. "Probably."

"Then what?"

"I'll need to find a job that pays a salary."

"You might be able to stay here. That grant came through that'll pay for another staff member."

"I'm going to leave Boston. Make a clean break." It was the first time the idea had occurred to her, but it felt right.

"You know where you're going?"

She pulled her knees up under her chin and wrapped her arms around them. "Where would you go, John, if you needed a place to start over?"

"I came to Boston."

She slid him a look. "From where?"

"From Hell." He spoke without inflection, his gaze fixed, as hers had been, on the wall in front of them. His expression was the one he'd had when she asked him what his family thought about his working at Hope House.

"You want to talk about it?"

He shrugged. "Why not?" His voice sounded weary, a reminder of her fatigue whenever she thought of Rob. "My wife killed herself." John's voice was flat and emotionless, but beneath the words was a thread of agony like a bassoon playing faintly under strings. "She was depressed. For a long time. Nothing I tried seemed to help." He stopped speaking and, in spite of the thumping of the music in the room behind them, the hall seemed very quiet. "Funny. Rationally, I've accepted it wasn't my fault, but it's never made any sense emotionally. It felt like she did it to get away from me, and I didn't try hard enough to stop her."

Not long ago, Clare had been depressed and nothing Rob did had helped.

"This place saved my life," John said.

Hers as well.

For a time, they sat together without speaking, then John sighed. "How about I call a cab to take you home?"

While he went to call the cab, Clare continued to sit, listening to a foot-stomping "When the Saints Go Marching In" that was enough to wake the dead. The thought made her want to both laugh and cry.

She hugged her knees and managed, after all, to do neither.

~ ~ ~

After dialing her parents' number, Clare stared out the window of the apartment at the lights reflected in the still surface of the pool in front of the Mother Church of the Christian Scientists. The reflections shimmered slightly in the clear night air.

She was calling her parents before the effects of John Apple's story and her own admission about her marriage wore off—before denial kicked back in and made it impossible to own up to her deceit. Deceit, that made conversations with her mother like picking her way through a swamp, trying to avoid quicksand or sudden, deep pools.

"Mom?"

"Hi, honey. Happy Thanksgiving. I'm so glad you called. Did you and Rob have a good day?"

The perfect opening to confess, but thinking about doing it made her feel as though she were standing on the ledge outside the apartment, ready to take the plunge into the Mother Church's ice-cold reflecting pool.

"Actually...I spent the day at Hope House. It was great fun. Good food. Music, lots of kids. But Rob wasn't there. You see, he won't be home until April."

"Oh. I must have misunderstood you."

"No, you didn't. I'm sorry. I didn't want you to know...to worry. Rob and I. I guess you'd call this a trial separation. It's taken me awhile to...well, to admit it."

She made no attempt to fill the silence that followed.

Finally, her mother cleared her throat and spoke slowly. "So, you're saying, you and Rob—"

"Are getting a divorce." There. she'd done it. Said the damn word out loud.

"Oh, dear. I am so, so sorry to hear that, Clare. I hate to think of you alone for Christmas. Why don't you come home?"

"I doubt I can get a reservation this late, but I'll be fine, Mom. I'm used to it." Even if the years spent dancing in *The Nutcracker* hadn't accustomed her to being away from home for the holidays, it was better to be alone this year. Better than to be with people who loved her and would want to discuss and dissect her future before she'd made sense of her past. "There's going to be another party at Hope House. I'll be busier than if Rob were here." Not completely true, but enough to short-circuit feelings of guilt.

"You will tell me what's happening from now on, Clare. I want you to know you can talk to me."

"I know, Mom. Truly. I wasn't admitting it to myself before. I love you."

"I love you too, sweetie, and remember I'm always here if you need me."

Shaking but dry-eyed, Clare hung up, less weighed down than she'd been in a long time, but sadder than she'd ever been in her life.

~ ~ ~

Thanksgiving was just another day in the jungle. If it weren't for the fact he kept track of the date in his laboratory notes, Rob wouldn't have realized that was what day it was even. A retired colleague had once joked that his weeks consisted of six Saturdays and a Sunday. Rob's life had narrowed to an unending string of Tuesdays.

Jolley marked the occasion by calling Jane. Later, at Jolley's prompting, Sam said a simple grace over their usual meal of rice, fish, manioc, and vegetables. As they ate, Rob pictured his family at the big table in his parents' formal dining room. His mother had reported Clare was having dinner with friends. People from the ballet, or a made-up excuse? Either explanation was possible.

And not knowing which underscored his loneliness.

~ ~ ~

Monday morning Clare answered the phone to find Rob's sister on the line. "We missed you Thanksgiving," Lynne said.

"Yes, sorry—"

"We need to have lunch sometime, to catch up."

Clare scrambled for a response. "I...ah. I." But she couldn't fight it indefinitely. After all, Lynne was family. At least for now. She licked lips gone dry. "I'd like that."

"Name a day," Lynne said.

"Thursday?"

"Good. Is Locke-Ober's okay?"

"Fine. Sure."

~ ~ ~

Clare arrived at the restaurant to find Lynne already there. They embraced, then Lynne stepped back, smiling. "Clare. You're looking good."

"Not as good as you. You look wonderful." Clare's words were more than the polite social formula her sister-in-law had employed. Although Lynne was always perfectly groomed, today she looked especially lovely. Clare was suddenly sorry they weren't closer, but that was for the best given she and Rob were getting a divorce.

Divorce. It caught under her breastbone. She hadn't let herself think the word before John said it but, since that conversation, it had been jumping into her mind at odd moments.

The waiter came to take their drink order. When he left, Lynne opened her menu and peered at Clare over the top. "Did you have a nice Thanksgiving? Mother said you were joining friends?"

"I did and it was nice."

"Good. Let's see, I'm having a cup of clam chowder, the lobster club, and a salad." Lynne snapped her menu closed and set it aside.

"My, you are hungry."

Lynne raised her water glass and saluted Clare. "Well, I am eating for two now. Something you would have known if you'd joined us for Thanksgiving."

The meaning hit a beat behind the teasing words themselves. Clare sucked in a breath and said what she needed to. "Oh, Lynne, how wonderful. Superlative. Oh, I am so happy for you." Good thing she was sitting, because the news brought with it an unanticipated grief. Something Lynne didn't know, thank goodness, since Clare miscarried before she and Rob told his family about her pregnancy. "When is the baby due?"

"May. Rob's going to be the godfather, of course. We want you to be godmother."

Clare pulled in a breath, frantically searching for a graceful way out. "I'm honored you would ask, but I...can't."

"But you and Rob. It's perfect."

Clare shook her head, and Lynne's glow dimmed into a worried frown.

The waiter delivered their iced teas. "Are you ladies ready to order?"

Clare had never been so glad to see a waiter in her life, although it was going to be impossible to eat the salad she ordered.

The waiter left and Clare turned her attention back to Lynne. "So, have you picked out any names yet?"

"Not yet."

Clare cast about for something else to say.

Lynne leaned toward her. "I wish you'd tell me what's going on with you and Rob."

Clare closed her eyes to shut out the worried expression on her sister-in-law's face. "Nothing's going on."

"I don't believe you."

If only she could will herself somewhere else. If only she wasn't always hurting people. If only...the story of her life. "You need to ask Rob."

"Oh. I am so sorry."

"Yes. Me, too." A relief in a way to have it even partially in the open. Holding together the pretense of happy families took an enormous amount of energy.

Their food arrived, and Clare and Lynne waited silently while they were served. Then Clare raised her glass of iced tea. "Could we forget the one thing, at least today? After all, we have something really wonderful to celebrate. I am so happy for you and Jim."

They both worked hard after that to keep the conversation on general topics.

Chapter Seventeen

Demi-plié
Half bend

The jungle's pleasures were simple ones. Brightly colored birds, butterflies, the occasional blue, green, or red poison arrow frog. The light at sunset slanting through the trees in golden bars, the silvery sheen of wet forest under a full moon.

But it was a beauty accompanied by danger and discomfort. Insects of every type—ants, mosquitoes, wasps, chiggers, sand flies, cockroaches, ticks—potentially carrying malaria, yellow fever, leishmaniasis, dengue fever. Plants that, when touched, left rashes or oozing sores that healed slowly, if at all. Snakes whose venom killed quickly and painfully.

"That's the main reason the village compound is kept bare of plant growth. To eliminate hiding places for snakes," Jolley said.

"In spite of that," Sam said, "many natives do die from snake bites."

That explained why Jolley had insisted they bring protective footgear and long trousers, even though the heat and humidity made it tempting to wear less.

"The fer-de-lance, for one, has a well-earned reputation as an ankle biter, striking first and perhaps repenting later when it gets whacked," Sam said. "We're also protecting ourselves from leeches and ticks."

Sam had them check themselves after every trip into the jungle. Occasionally, despite the barriers, they found hitchhikers that had managed to get through their clothing and onto their skin.

148

~ ~ ~

Sam had brought a large carton full of paperbacks with her and Rob often noticed a faint glow from her hut when he awakened in the middle of the night.

"You read a lot."

She shrugged. "I don't need much sleep. Occupational hazard of surgeons."

"You finding any good ones?"

She smiled. "Some very good ones. Help yourself any time you'd like."

"Nights might get pretty bright around here."

"If the insomnia is too bothersome, let me know. I can give you something."

"Thanks. Appreciate it, but I think I'll try reading."

Later it hit him. He was using books to escape the same way Clare had.

~ ~ ~

Deep in their wet, green world, the main source of information about the outside world came via Jolley's calls to Jane. She always provided a summary of current events. Rob quickly discovered he didn't miss the daily litany of awful things, and not hearing about them made them recede.

The staccato rhythms of the city were here replaced by the peaceful rhythms of a slowly spinning world where day followed night followed day in roughly twelve-hour increments, and the only weather uncertainty was the timing of the daily rain showers. That rain came in degrees ranging from heavy damp to deluges that were breathtaking in their suddenness and ferocity. Being caught by one of those was like standing under a waterfall, and the heat and humidity that accompanied the rain wore them all down.

"I'm feeling irritable tonight. Best if I take myself off," Sam said, as she cleared her plate after eating dinner.

Rob watched her walk away. "Does Jane do that?"

"What?"

"Tell you when she's in a bad mood?"

Jolley chuckled. "Well, usually it's pretty obvious."

"Does it make you feel...responsible?"

"Not unless I did something to deliberately provoke her. Why? What does Clare do?"

"She doesn't mention it, but it's obvious." Also obvious was how little he'd contributed to Clare's happiness. He pushed thoughts of that world away. "I had no idea living so simply, not to mention uncomfortably, could be so restful."

Jolley got out his pipe and tamped tobacco into the bowl. "It's why I love being in the field. I miss Jane like hell, but it recharges everything. Gives me a break from all the hassle. Reminds me what I love about science."

"You ever ask Jane to go along?" Although Rob couldn't picture Jane giving up modern plumbing.

"When we were first married she thought about it, but then we had kids right away, and by the time they left home, she preferred to stay home and indulge her bad habits—eating in bed, staying up late." Jolley took a puff on his pipe, the single one he allowed himself after dinner. "Is something up with you and Clare, Rob?"

Rob sucked in a quick breath, let it out slowly. "Didn't work out."

"I'm real sorry to hear it." Jolley continued to puff on his pipe in the dark with Rob sitting silently beside him.

"Think I'll call it a day," Jolley said, standing and knocking out his pipe.

That was the good thing about Jolley. He showed his concern but he didn't force confidences. Still, his question would cause Rob a restless night.

~ ~ ~

After the lunch with Lynne, Clare returned to the apartment and stopped to look at her surroundings. Stark walls, blank uncurtained windows, and furniture that might be comfortable but looked like it had been picked up from the curb on moving-out day. Two plants were dying quietly in the corner and the kaleidoscope was collecting a coating of dust. The overall effect was more impersonal and off-putting than a cheap motel.

"It needs color," Rob had said. "Something like your Marblehead house. And new furniture, of course. Whatever you'd like."

Make it a home...our home, had been the subtext.

She'd ignored both the request and the spirit behind it. She'd simply not had the energy, at least not then. But what about now? Although she could do nothing about her major sins against Rob, she could do one thing for him—make the apartment a more pleasant place for him to return to.

~ ~ ~

Clare began the apartment makeover with Rob's study—the place he'd retreated to those last weeks whenever he was home. It featured a shabby, overstuffed chair, bookshelves full of weighty books with titles like *Organic Reactions* and *Principles of Stereochemistry*, and an old-style oak desk with a computer monitor and keyboard sitting on its marred surface. The overstuffed chair still held the imprint of Rob's body, and seeing it, she felt a wave of loneliness wash over her.

She painted the walls burgundy, then went to Rockport to search out the gallery with the painting that had caught Rob's eye on a visit last year, one of their few good days during that time. Since she didn't remember the gallery's name, she wandered the streets trying to retrace the route they'd taken. She finally located the right place, and was pleased to find it open since most places were closed with the summer season well over.

The picture Rob liked was no longer in the window, but stepping inside Clare spotted it. It was a watercolor—painted mostly in soft greens but with random hints of sunlight glancing off trees and a deep forest pool. A dreaming, peaceful scene.

"Can I help you?" A heavyset man stood in the doorway at the back of the gallery. The room behind him appeared to be a studio, which was probably why the shop was still open.

"This painting. I'd like to buy it."

"I was watching you. You didn't look at anything else. Do you mind if I ask why?"

"It's for my husband. He saw it when we were here before."

"Yet he didn't buy it for himself."

"No."

The man and Clare examined each other.

"I'm very particular about who gets my paintings."

"Oh. You're the artist?"

He nodded and extended a hand as large as Beck's. Odd to think of those huge hands painting such an ethereal scene.

"I can assure you this painting will be treasured." At least, she hoped Rob wouldn't hate it because she bought it for him.

"Do you want to take it with you today?"

"Oh yes, please."

~ ~ ~

"Christmas Eve," John Apple said. "I thought since you and I are alone...that maybe, well, you'd have dinner with me?"

"I'd like that. Very much."

John set a time, then backed out of the room, as if afraid she would change her mind if he stuck around. And maybe she would have, because, thinking about it later, she began to worry. It was, after all, one thing to develop a friendship within the walls of Hope House, quite another to take it outside to dinner.

~ ~ ~

When John picked Clare up Christmas Eve, he gave her an approving look. "I made a reservation at Tympanies. I hope that's okay?"

"Very okay." The restaurant was on Boylston Street, a five-minute walk from the Prudential Center.

"You look very nice," she told him in the restaurant, after he removed his winter jacket to reveal a perfectly ironed white shirt and blue tie.

"And you look beautiful. Green suits you."

"You don't need to patroni—"

"You don't believe that, do you. I wonder why?"

"I have eyes and a mirror. Please. Can we talk about something else?" She softened the request with a smile.

"Of course. Do you drink wine?"

After the waiter poured the wine they'd chosen, John lifted his glass. "To friendship."

She chimed her glass lightly against his, relieved at the innocuous toast. "You're full of surprises, John. Ballet. Faulkner. Wine."

"Not your usual janitor, you mean."

"I very much doubt it."

He sipped his wine, then set his glass down and stared at his clasped hands. "It helped, you know. At Thanksgiving. Telling you what happened." He stopped, cleared his throat. "First time I'd said it out loud. I wanted to thank you."

"How long has it been?" Clare spoke softly because his eyes were filled with pain.

"Three years."

His grief reached out, pulling her into its familiar terrain, and she struggled to keep her voice even. "Early times."

"Is it?"

"I think so."

"You're talking about your injury. You're reinventing yourself the same way I am."

"I'm glad you're doing better."

"Better than last week, last month." He shrugged and gave her a wry smile. "What about you, Clare Eliason Chapin? Any idea where you're going yet?"

"Not a clue."

"At least you have good options. Making it to the top of your profession. There ought to be lots you could do behind the scenes."

Clare shook her head, trying not to let the words touch her.

John took a sip of wine, assessing her. "Did you ever go to college?"

"A few courses here and there."

"Have you ever considered getting your degree?" He was obviously undeterred by her cool tone. "You could think about getting a teaching certification. You have a gift."

She was pleased the arrival of the waiter with the salads interrupted them.

When they were alone once again, she spoke firmly. "I don't think I ever thanked you for suggesting the Parker books. They've been a real hit with the men. Especially Beck."

"Beck?"

"He's dyslexic. We've been working together."

John acquiesced to talking about Beck, Vinnie, Anthony, and Tyrese as they ate their salads and main courses. While they waited for dessert, he reached into the pocket of his coat and pulled out a small, gaily wrapped package. "Merry Christmas, Clare."

She folded her hands in her lap refusing to accept the gift. "I don't have anything for you."

"Please." He held up a hand to stop her protest. "Don't deny me the pleasure of giving you something, and don't sweat it until you see what it is." He pushed the package toward her.

Reluctantly, she opened it to find a small key, hand-worked from copper wire. She looked up, a question in her eyes.

"Kenny kept picking up the odd bits of wire from my electrical jobs. When I asked him why, he brought this in to show me. Drove a hard bargain. Had to buy him a whole roll of wire in trade."

Clare fingered the tiny key. "Thank you. For being willing to part with it."

"I thought you'd like the symbolism."

He was right. She, along with everyone at Hope House, was searching for the key to the future, as well, in her case, for a key to lock away the past.

~ ~ ~

The Amazonian Christmas was as unremarkable as Thanksgiving, except for the fact Sam unearthed a can of mixed nuts and a bottle of red wine for their dinner.

"Leave it to women to be the celebrating influence," Jolley said, holding out his cup. "Never occurred to me to bring along something to mark the occasion. You got something hidden away for New Year's, Sam?"

"If I'd realized the village was going to be right by the boat landing, I would have brought more."

"No matter. Thanks for sharing with us. Merry Christmas."

Rob wondered how Clare was spending Christmas. She'd told his mother she was going home. Rob had never been to Salina, so it was impossible to envision her there. But no matter where Clare was, Salina or Boston, he couldn't be more separated from her if she'd been on Mars.

~ ~ ~

"Good morning, beautiful. How you doing?"

"Why do you do that?" Clare asked Vinnie. "Call everybody beautiful."

"You stop seeing something beautiful in a person, time you got your eyes checked." Vinnie chuckled before her expression turned serious. "The Father made everybody beautiful. Everybody. Father don't make junk."

"What about murderers? Rapists?"

Vinnie snorted. "Person forgets they're beautiful, no telling what they'll get up to."

"If somebody raped me, I'd be hard-pressed to see any beauty in them."

"Better to look for the beauty than stew in anger." Vinnie's face, usually so animate, went still. "No matter what they do, they're still God's children. But ain't easy. I give you that. Specially that person your daddy."

154

No. Vinnie couldn't mean...her father... *Oh, dear God.*

"I was fourteen, it started. Hated that man. Hated myself. Only way you get past something like that, Father's got to help."

"I am so sorry that happened to you." Clare kept her tone as calm as Vinnie's, but she laid a hand on the other woman's arm, seeking to both comfort and be comforted.

"Ah, well, I discovered it's true. What don't kill you do make you stronger." Vinnie sighed and patted Clare's hand.

Clare was uncertain what struck her more. The matter-of-fact telling, or the knowledge that sunny Vinnie had suffered such horror.

"What about you, beautiful? Maybe you know what I mean. Sometimes you got a real sad look in those eyes."

Clare blinked and shook her head. "Everybody has a bit of trouble now and then."

"Trouble shared is trouble halved. You ever want to talk, I'd be happy to listen."

But Clare wasn't yet ready to repeat words that would make her losses real—that Rob wasn't just on a sabbatical. Deep down, she knew. He didn't intend to come back to her. Her fault. All of it. *Even tiny, seemingly insignificant acts of kindness have consequences.* The psychologist said that, and she could have added, *as do acts of unkindness.* And they are never insignificant.

Amends. That was the only way to undo an unkindness, and a little bit of painting wasn't nearly enough. But how did one make amends when the person you wronged was four thousand miles away and no longer speaking to you?

~ ~ ~

"The curve of a wing allows air to move faster over the top than the bottom, producing lift," Tyrese read, the smooth flow of words proof of how far the boy had advanced in the few months he'd been coming to Hope House. With a finger holding his place, he looked up at Clare. "You ever do that? Fly."

She had, and not just in airplanes, but she understood what Tyrese was asking. "Yes, I have. One time, I flew to Europe."

"Was it cool?" Tyrese frequently engaged her in discussions as a way to avoid his homework, and she always let him get away with it, for a while.

"Very cool. I had a window seat so I was able to see the city as we landed."

"That's what I'm going to be when I grow up." He nodded his head, emphatically. "A pilot. See everything that way." His expression turned serious. "You think I can do it?"

With a swell of affection, Clare gave the boy's arm a squeeze, knowing he'd shrug off a hug. "Yes, I do. You're smart enough to learn whatever you need to know, in order to do whatever you decide to do."

Tyrese looked pleased. "Yes, sir. Going to be a pilot."

"Then you'll need to know math and science."

"No. Why I got to know that to fly a plane?"

"Well, you'll need to understand how it works, and you'll need to be able to calculate...oh, the weight and the fuel. Make sure you don't have too much of the one and not enough of the other."

"Computers do that."

"Sometimes computers don't work, so it's a good thing to know how to do it yourself."

"Okay. I see that." He bent over the book and began once again to read out loud.

Clare smiled, thinking how good it felt, this chance to encourage a child to plan his future. Although it did remind her that her own future remained in limbo, and it was past time she did something about it.

~ ~ ~

Rob watched Sam suture a bad cut one of the women got when she slipped and fell on a sharp stone. Sam's movements were quick and assured, and the woman ended up with a neat line of stitches from elbow to wrist that added weight to what Jolley had told him—that Sam was one of the finest trauma surgeons in L.A.

"So why go into the wilderness where you don't have operating facilities?"

She glanced at him, then away. "Why did you go into the wilderness where the most challenging chemistry is a color test?"

"Touché."

"I'm wondering if either of us is going to answer?" she said.

"I wanted the challenge of something different."

"Me, too." She kept her head down, concentrating on putting away her supplies.

"Clearly, something neither of us is prepared to discuss at any length." Rob spoke lightly.

She closed her medical case and turned to put it away.

Afterward, the fact they'd been open enough to admit they weren't being open, led to a greater ease between them.

~ ~ ~

Rob was walking across the village compound when Tatito jumped out in front of him. Rob made a quick grab and caught the youngster under the arms and swung him around. Tatito giggled happily. When Rob set the boy down, one of the girls was standing there, lifting her arms with a solemn expression. By the time Rob set her down, five children were standing in a respectful row, waiting their turns.

"Saw you getting some exercise this afternoon," Jolley said as they finished their evening meal.

"I fear I've created a monster." Rob rolled shoulders that were beginning to stiffen from the afternoon's game.

"It's good for you," Sam said. "And for them. You may need to set up a lottery, though. Do only a few swings a day."

"The two of you could pitch in."

"No thanks. This one's all yours." Jolley stood and stretched.

Mostly to limit the demands for swings, Rob started thinking of other things to show the children. He came up with one idea after he happened on a length of string in his duffel. A memory surfaced of his sister and a friend sitting with a string between their hands, passing it from one to the other in complicated patterns.

He went looking for Sam. "Did you ever do that string thing when you were a kid?"

"String thing?"

"You know." He pulled the string out of his pocket and slipped it over his two hands.

"Oh, you're talking about Cat's Cradle. Here, let me show you."

He held his hands out and Sam arranged the string. Then she dipped her fingers between his and transferred it from his hands to hers in a new pattern.

"Show me again."

Sam went through the two steps several times before he was certain he could do it.

When he showed Tatito, the little boy had it down pat in two tries. Rob turned the string over to the boy. The other children crowded around to see what Tatito had learned. Before long, all of them were adept. Sam eventually got involved, donating dental floss and showing Tatito the next steps, which the boy then taught to the other children.

Another idea came to Rob when his pen blotched a page and he crumpled up the ruined sheet. Rather than throw it away, he smoothed it out and folded it into an airplane. He didn't know Tatito was watching until he'd launched his creation. With shining eyes, the boy ran after it and carried it reverently back to Rob.

Rob handed a second sheet of paper to the boy, who, biting his lip in concentration, began to fold it. His first attempt was clumsy, but after Rob corrected the order of the folds and gave the boy a fresh sheet of paper, Tatito's next attempt was every bit as good as Rob's.

After that, not only did Tatito jump out at him, sometimes he remained in hiding and launched a stealth airplane at Rob.

"You've got quite a fan there," Sam said.

"He's an amazing kid. I bet he'd make a terrific an engineer." But more than teaching Tatito and seeing how rapidly he grasped new concepts, Rob enjoyed having the small boy around.

It might be as close as he would get to knowing what it felt like to be a father.

Chapter Eighteen

Elegé
A lament

After the holidays, Sally Prentice, the teacher who'd helped Clare with tutoring suggestions, called to make one of their regular coffee dates. They met in a café near Northeastern.

"You know how it is when they get carried away," Sally said, concluding a story about her husband's brief foray into woodworking that resulted in an oversupply of napkin holders she was still trying to dispose of. "Does your husband have any hobbies?"

"Being a professor seems to take all his time."

"A ballerina and a professor. It's an interesting combination. It must make for lively discussions at dinner."

Clare shook her head. "Rob knows very little about the ballet and I know nothing about chemistry." Although, in the beginning, they'd never had difficulty finding things to talk about.

"So, how did you meet?"

"At a ballet reception."

"Well, he may not know much, but he must enjoy it if he's attending receptions."

But he didn't enjoy it. He merely tolerated it for her sake. That insight had the clarity and sharp edges of broken glass.

"One of the reasons I wanted to meet is because I have a favor to ask you," Sally said. "We're having a career day next Wednesday, and you know how little girls all go through the stage where they want to be ballerinas."

Discomfort bloomed into full-blown agony.

"And I thought. That is..." Sally cocked her head and smiled tentatively. "I think it would be good for them to hear what it's really like. That it's not all about costumes and toe shoes and bright lights. The hard work behind the scenes..." Her voice trailed off, her expression uncertain.

Clare looked away, taking a deep breath. "Since the accident—"

"I put my foot in it, didn't I?" Sally bit her lip. Then she smiled brightly. "I'm sorry. Forget it, okay? Hey, you haven't updated me on Tyrese yet."

Clare went along with the change in subject, but Sally's career day request kept her company all the way home and continued poking at her through a sleepless night. In the morning, after her shower, she examined her reflection in the full-length mirror.

Although she'd gained some weight recently, she was still much too thin. She lifted her hands from her sides and clasped them in front of her, flexing her fingers. Then she moved her arms over her head, and her feet automatically shifted into position. She was no longer beautiful but she could see the elegance in the pose. She dropped her arms and let her shoulders slump. Another move she'd perfected for the dance.

But then, all of them were. Every move she made. The way she walked, held her body, moved her arms...all refined, then polished by hours of rehearsal for *Romeo and Juliet, Giselle, Nutcracker*, and a dozen other ballets. Even her facial expressions were studied, practiced, and then forgotten as it became second nature to be able to project happiness, sadness, anger, tragedy.

So, was that all there was to her? Rehearsed movement, studied emotion?

No. It couldn't be. Artists had to sacrifice for their art. She'd sacrificed her body, not her soul.

Or had she? And how did one answer such a question?

Shivering, she dressed quickly. Then, not giving herself time to change her mind, she called Sally's voice mail at the school and said she would do the career day.

~ ~ ~

"You were the star," Sally told her afterward.

160

"You said it yourself. Every little girl goes through a ballerina stage."

Sally shook her head. "No. More than that. You let them know how important it is to go after their dreams no matter what they are."

Clare had been so nervous in the beginning, she didn't remember what she'd said. As for dreams, did she have any expertise in that area?

"That bit with *Peter and the Wolf* was amazing, Clare. I loved the way you showed them that discipline and concentrated study were needed to understand a character before you can portray him or her on the stage."

She had brought a recording of *Peter and the Wolf* and used two short passages to demonstrate how facial expression and body posture helped create a character.

She could have picked something from *The Nutcracker* or *Cinderella,* or another ballet, but she wasn't yet ready for that. Baby steps.

"You have a real gift as a teacher, Clare."

It was the second time someone had told her that. Still, she shrugged it off because it was too late to do anything about it. But the interaction with Sally's class, the first time she'd played a piece of classical music since her injury, awakened a hunger in her.

Back at the apartment, she looked through Rob's albums and found amongst the country music, Jimmy Buffett, and classical jazz, the scores of the ballets she'd danced during her year and a half as a principal with Danse Classique. He also had a recording of the one ballet she hadn't danced.

She put *Swan Lake* on and sat listening to the ebb and flow of the music. What had happened to her still hurt, although the pain had receded from active roar to dull ache, but her guilt over the pain she'd inflicted on Rob, rather than diminishing, had grown.

He was such a gentle man, one who'd always put her needs before his own. Something she'd neither sufficiently valued nor reciprocated.

And time was running out for making restitution.

~ ~ ~

By the beginning of February, that cruelest of months, there were times when Clare was walking to Hope House when she suddenly realized she'd covered several blocks without any memory of waiting for lights, crossing streets, encountering people. Clearly, she needed to make some decisions about her future before she wandered into traffic. And, actually, the first decision, whether to stay in Boston, was also the easiest one. She'd already said the words out loud, to John—that a new start called for a new place.

She would miss Beck, Vinnie, John, and Tyrese terribly, of course, but leaving felt like the right thing. Both for her sake and for Rob's. But where to go and what to do once she got there were questions she still couldn't answer. They represented the same dilemma she'd faced after her injury.

Then she'd made the mistake of taking the easy way out by marrying Rob. This time, she'd do things differently.

~ ~ ~

In early February, Rob talked one of the men into taking him to visit a nearby spontaneous clearing, after learning such places were scientific enigmas. The Machiguenga believed them to be the work of supernatural beings and usually avoided them, but Javier was willing to show Rob the one nearest the village. Some of the smaller boys followed along.

Rob didn't consider himself sensitive to atmosphere, but there was something about the clearing that made him uncomfortable, or maybe he was picking up on Javier's discomfort or that of the boys, who stood in a silent cluster. As usual, the group included Javier's son, Tatito, who stood, uncharacteristically solemn-eyed with the others, the giggles and happy talk that had been the pleasant music along the way stilled.

"One theory is that the flora growing there exudes a substance that's toxic to other plants," Jolley had said. "Or it may be that the ants found in those particular plants destroy other types of plant life. If so, it's an effective relationship for both the ant and the favored plant."

Rob finished his examination of the scant vegetation and nodded to Javier that he was ready to go. The man looked relieved. The boys ran ahead, their laughter once again mingling with bird sounds and the far-off bellow of a howler monkey.

They were nearing the village when ahead of them a high-pitched animal squeal was followed by a scream of pain that was distinctly human. Rob tightened his grip on the machete he was carrying and ran behind Javier toward the sound.

The faint trail they'd been following widened into an open area caused by the loss of a large tree. A child was lying on the ground near the tree and standing over him was a wild pig, swinging its head, squealing. Several other peccaries milled around as if trying to decide what to do.

Javier charged the animal, his machete coming down in a swift chopping motion. The peccary stumbled, twisting its head as it ran past Javier straight at Rob. In desperation, Rob swung his machete in an upward motion, managing to slice the peccary's throat and cutting the animal off in mid-screech.

In the sudden quiet, the tooth clicking of the other peccaries was audible. Rob lifted the bloody machete and, with a roar, charged past the fallen child toward the cluster of animals. They scrambled away, disappearing among the trees.

He turned back to Javier and found him bent over the injured boy, his own leg bleeding profusely. Rob jerked off his shirt to make a tourniquet for Javier's leg. The other boys dropped out of the trees they'd climbed to get away from the animals.

Feeling a deep foreboding, Rob looked at the fallen child. Tatito. He felt for a pulse in the child's neck, averting his eyes from the wound in Tatito's abdomen. A pulse still beat, but it was fluttery and weak.

Rob lifted the boy into his arms, briefly meeting Javier's anguished eyes as the other man struggled to stand. Rob turned and hurried toward the village, led by one of the boys. Behind him, he heard Javier speak to the remaining boys. Then he closed his mind to everything but getting Tatito to Sam as swiftly and carefully as possible.

His arms soon ached from their burden and his lungs burned with the effort to get enough oxygen. He walked rapidly, trying not to think about how much blood the child was losing. It dripped onto Rob's arms, mingling with his own sweat. To add to his misery, flies attracted by the gore crawled on his arms and buzzed his face.

Sam, alerted by a boy who had run ahead, met Rob at the edge of the village clearing. "Here. Lay him on the table."

She pressed fingers on Tatito's neck then slipped on her stethoscope and checked before putting her hand gently on Rob's arm. "He's gone."

Rob pulled away from Sam and placed his own fingers on the spot where he'd felt that faint pulse before. Nothing. He shifted his fingers, trying another spot. Sam took his hand firmly in hers. Then Javier arrived, stumbling along, supported by two of the boys, the awful knowledge dawning in his eyes as he looked at Sam and Rob. He came and stood over Tatito, swaying, before he slipped to the ground, unconscious.

Sam knelt by Javier's side. "Help me, Rob. You need to move Tatito so we can put Javier on the table."

As if he were caught in the tangles of a nightmare, Rob moved the child to the ground and helped Sam lift Javier.

"Hand me my surgical kit." She loosened the makeshift tourniquet on Javier's leg as she spoke. Only the calm authority in her voice made it possible for Rob to respond.

~ ~ ~

"I couldn't have saved him, you know," Sam said.

The village, lately filled with the sounds of grief, was now nearly silent. Javier was back in his own hut, his leg stitched and covered with both a modern bandage and a poultice prepared by Soraida.

"You think that if you'd just been able to get Tatito here sooner it would have made a difference. But if I'd been right there when it happened, the outcome would have been the same." Sam, the physician, saying what she thought was needed to make him feel better.

She took his slack hand in hers and rubbed firmly. "Javier told me the peccaries could have done a lot more damage if you hadn't chased them off. And the tourniquet saved his life. You did well, Rob."

He had a sudden image of Tatito, peeking from behind a tree, his eyes dancing with delight. He swiped at the tears running down his face. "He was such a sweet, funny little kid."

"Yes. He was."

"How do you stand it?"

"Losing patients, you mean?"

Rob nodded.

"In the beginning, I spent hours going over every move I'd made. Second-guessing every decision. Looking for explanations. But eventually I realized that if I kept doing that, I wouldn't be able to function. So I learned to go over it once, forgive myself any mistakes I may have made, and then I try to learn from them."

She wrapped her arms around herself as if she were cold. "After I lose a patient, I go to the beach and fly a kite. When the string is all the way out, I cut it loose and watch until I can't see it anymore."

"What kind of kites?" It was just something to say.

"Different ones. Dragon kites from Chinatown, elaborate box kites, even the two-stick ones you buy in the grocery store. I fly them all the time. I only set one free when I need to let go of something."

Maybe he'd try that when he got home. Go to the Cape and set two kites free. One for Tatito and a second for his marriage.

When Sam left to go to her hut, he sat for a time, picturing an empty beach lapped by endless ocean with bright red and yellow kites soaring into the infinite blue of a clear sky. Trying to find comfort in it.

~ ~ ~

As Javier recuperated, Rob sat with him watching the village children play, remembering not only Tatito but the child he and Clare had lost. Given his pain at that memory, he knew Javier's anguish was impossible to put into words even if they had been fluent in each other's language.

~ ~ ~

"You were right," Clare told Vinnie, as she hung up her coat. "I do need to find a job that pays a salary."

"Well now, beautiful. Can't say that's a surprise. Had a feeling something's been going on with you."

"It is. I'm getting...a divorce."

"I'm sorry to hear that, Clare. Doesn't sound like that's what you want."

Clare fingered the copper key John gave her at Christmas that she now wore to remind herself she was moving toward a new life. "Whether I want it or not, it's the fair thing to do."

Vinnie looked at her for a moment with a thoughtful expression. "I think the Father's got big plans for you."

"I very much doubt that." Certainly none of the jobs she qualified for would even fall under a classification of "medium."

"Now don't you be that way, you hear me, beautiful? The Father's taking real good care of you. You got to learn to trust."

Vinnie's comfortable relationship with God never ceased to amaze Clare. The other woman talked as if He were sitting in an easy chair in the next room, and Vinnie seemed to manage whatever difficulty life handed her by saying it was in the hands of the Father. Clare teased her once that she shouldn't have to work so hard, then.

Vinnie quickly disabused Clare of that notion. "The Father expects us to do our part. Don't just hand us nothing for nothing. We got to be partners."

Clare fervently wished she had Vinnie's certainty a higher power was watching over her...and Rob. But she didn't.

~ ~ ~

Clare sat at the dining room table with a pad of paper, determined to make the decision about where she was going. Somewhere old or somewhere new? Salina maybe? There she would have family to provide backup. Which was a positive that might also be a negative if it weakened her resolve to be fully independent.

Or perhaps one of the big cities she'd spent time in—New York, Seattle, Atlanta. All would provide opportunities, although they'd be expensive, and it would take time to make new friends. Or what about Cincinnati? She'd lived there seven years which made it familiar, and the city was both large enough to provide opportunities and small enough to be comfortable and affordable. The major negative was it meant returning to the place where she'd been almost as unlucky in love as Boston. Although she should be able to avoid the bits that held bitter memories, something that could also be said of Boston.

But her Cincinnati memories no longer stung, while any thought of remaining in Boston made her chest tighten. Perhaps because running into Rob would be more than a faint possibility, given the proximity of Hope House and Northeastern.

~ ~ ~

"I'll...we'll miss you," John said when she told him her plans. He turned to pick up a tool. "When do you leave?"

"As soon as I get everything arranged."

"Here, steady this, will you?" He was building containers for the garden.

Clare took the end of the board he'd indicated and held it in place. While he nailed it into position, she looked around at the complex pattern of planters designed by John and the men, trying to picture it in bloom. "You don't belong here forever, John. You have a good brain. You need more challenge than..." She waved a hand taking in the tired house and yard.

He lifted his eyebrows.

"Remember, I've seen the kind of reading you do."

He finished nailing the board in place, set the hammer down, and ran his hand over his forehead, leaving behind a smear of dirt. He reached out and caught her hand. "You aren't wearing your wedding ring."

"It's not official yet. Rob has to sign the papers, but, well, I-I decided it was time."

"Why not stay here, Clare? Where you have friends."

"I thought you of all people would understand why I need a fresh start."

He stood for a time still holding her hand, then he sighed and let her go. "I guess I do at that."

~ ~ ~

"Cincinnati?" Lynne said.

A continuing experiment, saying aloud what she was planning.

"When are you going?"

"A couple of weeks."

"Before Rob gets back?"

"Yes."

"Don't you think you need to talk to him? Whatever problems you were having. Maybe you can work them out."

"He's better off not seeing me."

"So you get to make that decision?" Lynne was angry and making no attempt to hide it.

"I'm not the one who went away." *And I'm not the one who cut off all communication.*

"What do you call leaving Boston?"

"Getting on with my life." Clare's throat tightened. She'd been cruel but Rob was cruel as well. Not a word from him. Not in all these months.

Lynne sniffled. "He loved you so much."

Loved, Lynne said. Not *loves*. But Clare knew that. No reason, then, for her heart to squeeze in pain.

~ ~ ~

"Are you okay, Tyrese?" The boy was having trouble sitting still and he kept rubbing his hands up and down his upper arms.

"Fine. I fine." He straightened and sat stiffly as he continued to read, but when he walked out, Clare noticed he was limping. When she saw Anthony later, she asked him about Tyrese.

"He got in a fight," Anthony said. "That bad-ass, Jamal, jumped him. He hurting a bit."

"Jamal?"

"They been hassling Tyrese."

"Who has?"

"Them Bull Sharks. His old gang."

Clare mentioned it to Beck, who sighed. "I'll speak to the police. Ask them to keep an eye out, and I'll talk to Tyrese's mom. See if she's willing to move to a different neighborhood."

The next day, Tyrese walked in, ducking his head when Clare looked up at him. He slid into the seat next to her and pulled a book out of his backpack.

"What happened to your eye?" And his lip, and dear God, his hand.

"Fell."

Clare shivered with unease. "Only way you end up with a shiner like that, you fell into someone's fist."

"Nope. Just clumsy, ma'am." Tyrese shifted around in his seat looking guilty.

She caught his hand and uncurled the fingers. One was swollen twice its normal size and Tyrese jerked away when she touched it.

"You need ice and an x-ray to see if it's broken."

"No, ma'am. Don't need no x-ray. I fine." He opened the book with a definitive thump and she gave up for the moment trying to force him to accept her concern.

But if Tyrese wouldn't talk, she knew who would. "Did you see Tyrese today?" she asked Anthony as he walked her out of Hope House.

Anthony nodded. "Man, he sure be hurting."

"Do you know what happened?"

"Bull Sharks been hassling him." Anthony did a little shuffle step and pretended to shoot a basket. "They ambushed him, but he getting smart. Mostly manages to avoid them. They ain't good at hiding theyselves."

"Do they know he comes to Hope House?"

Anthony appeared to consider that. "Don't know. Tyrese, he tell me he real careful. You don't need to worry. Pretty soon they find someone else they pick on."

Clare did worry, though, especially when shortly after that, Tyrese stopped coming to Hope House.

~ ~ ~

After Sam worked on Javier's leg, the healer had come and examined the wound. He questioned Sam about the sutures before insisting she use the poultice he'd prepared.

"I worried it would lead to an infection, but it seems to be healing faster than normal," Sam told Rob and Jolley later.

That collaboration broke the ice with Soraida, who had previously avoided Sam, and the two began meeting regularly. When it wasn't raining, they sat in front of Sam's hut, Soraida talking while Sam took notes, or Sam talking while Soraida listened with an intent look on his face.

"You getting any good tips?" Jolley asked her one evening.

"More than tips. Soraida's giving me an advanced course in psychic healing."

"Psychic?" Rob said.

"He believes most physical illness is a manifestation of spirit sickness."

"That's no different from what physicians in the West say about stress," Jolley said.

"You think the chanting and his trances help?" Rob said.

Sam shrugged. "It doesn't hurt. If nothing else, it's proof someone cares about them."

Rob went to bed, still thinking about it. How he and Clare were suffering from what could be viewed as spirit sickness.

Chapter Nineteen

Assemblé penchée
A firm step using both feet
and ending in a lean

A month before they were due to leave Peru, Rob suffered a bout of stomach cramps that lasted most of the day. Such upsets weren't unusual, so he didn't bother to mention it, just went to bed hoping to sleep it off. But he awoke in the middle of the night with pain so staggering, all he could manage in the first moments was to clutch his abdomen. The only thing that eased the agony even slightly was pulling his right leg up to his chest.

He didn't realize he was moaning until Jolley spoke from across the room. "What is it, Rob?"

He tried to reply, but managed only a gasp. Then Jolley was there, flicking on a flashlight. After he looked at Rob, he left to get Sam. She might have come in a minute or an hour. In the center of the pain, time no longer had any meaning.

Her cool hand brushed the hair off his brow and her calm voice said, "Now let's see what we have here."

An indefinite time later, Jolley held Rob's arm while Sam positioned a syringe and asked him to count backwards from ten. Everything faded away.

When Rob came to, it was to Sam's voice and the touch of her hand on his wrist. "Hi there. Welcome back."

"Where've I been?" The words came out mushed together as if he'd been drinking. In fact, his head ached exactly like he imagined it would after a binge.

"Right to the edge." Sam spoke lightly, releasing his arm.

It didn't make sense, but he was in too much pain to sort it out. "Hurts. What...?" he croaked, unable to get past the cotton in his mouth.

"Acute appendix. We got it just in time." Sam lifted his arm, swabbed, and quickly jabbed. "You should start feeling that or, I should say not feeling that, in a few minutes."

He drifted off, and the next hours were a confused mix of light and dark, Jolley and Sam's voices, and pain. Eventually, things began to clear up.

"Lucky for you, Sam was with us. She wasn't, you and I wouldn't be having this conversation."

"She operated on me?"

Jolley grinned. "And you've got the zipper to prove it."

"But how?"

"Like one of those movies where they boil water, clean off the kitchen table, and sharpen the best butcher knife. Nicest little piece of dissection I've ever had the chance to observe."

"Jolley's exaggerating," Sam said, stepping into the hut. "Every first-year resident can do that operation with her eyes closed."

"Doubt it, Sam. Nice work."

"And I didn't use a butcher knife," she continued, ignoring Jolley. "You've been laying around enough already. Time you got up, got moving."

"You can see why we don't use chloroform any longer," Jolley said.

"You used chloroform?" Rob shuddered, remembering a graduate school experiment in which they'd used chloroform to knock rats out before surgery. And , it had been so easy to knock them all the way to kingdom come.

"Jolley's teasing you," Sam said. "I used something more modern. Now, up you go." With that, he was on his feet, leaning on the two of them, as limp and useless as one of those rats he'd inadvertently dispatched to the great beyond.

After a trip to the privy, they lowered him back onto an air mattress since there was no way he could manage the cooler hammock. Sam allowed him to sip tea, then she gave him another pain shot.

He awoke the next day to find the camp in its usual morning bustle. Jolley showed up with a cup of tea and a bowl of rice and sat next to him while he ate.

"We need to talk about this." Jolley gestured at his bandage. "Sam says you should be fine. But if you want us to call in a boat from Boca Manu, we will. You can fly from there to Cuzco."

"I'd rather stay."

Jolley patted his arm. "Hoped you'd say that. Sam says by the time we leave, you should be good to go. Although you'll still probably feel like shit."

Rob grimaced at the memory of the rough trip from Cuzco and almost changed his mind about flying back.

~ ~ ~

During the days that followed his operation, the camp slipped back into its regular routines. The healer played his part in Rob's recovery, preparing poultices and a tea he said aided digestion and sleep. Since Rob was having no difficulty with either, the tea could have been the reason.

Two days after the operation, Jolley told him the story of that night as he sat next to Rob while enjoying his evening pipe. Alberto, who had just helped Rob back from the privy, sat nearby.

"We rigged a double layer of mosquito netting to give Sam an operating field clear of bugs, and Soraida and Alberto held flashlights to give her the light she needed. I assisted. You should have seen us scurrying to get it set. Damn close, you ask me."

"We thought you a goner for sure, Dr. Rob," Alberto said as Sam walked up to the hut.

"Thank you for my life," Rob told her.

"You have the whole village to thank," Sam said. "They all pitched in, and they're feeling pretty good about it." She bent over and lifted the bandage to check his incision. "Jolley tells me you've elected to stay. You need to know that's not ideal."

"What would you do? If it was your appendix?"

"If all I had were you guys taking care of me, I'd be for Cuzco in a heartbeat, but you seem to be healing and there's no sign of infection. That was my greatest concern." She sat back on her heels and pulled a new bandage from her kit. Soraida appeared behind her, holding a fresh poultice. She smiled her thanks and took the poultice and began securing it with the bandage.

"East meets West," Jolley murmured.

"More like South meets North," Sam said.

Rob raised a hand in thanks to Soraida.

She finished replacing the bandage. "How's the pain?"

"Bearable."

"Good thing you didn't have any nausea afterwards."

The thought made him wince. "That would have been a real topper."

"Maybe that healing service really worked," Jolley said.

"Healing service?"

"Soraida went the whole nine yards for you. Smoked his pipe, went into a trance, danced and chanted. Said he saw a woman with short white hair standing on her toes right in the middle of your chest."

"You're joking."

"Not at all. Sounded like he was describing a ballerina, although it couldn't be Clare, not with white hair."

~ ~ ~

One of the men told Clare she was needed in the office. When she arrived, Beck introduced her to a short pudgy man with colorless thinning hair. One Morrie Rabinowitz. A homicide detective with the Boston Police Department.

"We're waiting for Appleseed, then we'll get started," Beck told Clare as she took a seat next to Vinnie.

The door opened, and John walked in. Rabinowitz straightened from his slouch against the wall. "J.B.?" The detective looked puzzled.

"Rabbit." John Apple's tone was flat. "It's been awhile."

"At least three years, maybe more."

"What's this about?" John asked.

"We got us a Jamal Hicks. Stabbed to death last night."

Rabbit—Rabinowitz— looked from Clare to Beck to Vinnie. "Any of you know him?"

Clare shook her head as did Beck and Vinnie, until with a lurch of her stomach, Clare realized Jamal was the name of the Bull Shark Anthony said was hassling Tyrese.

"Why do you think we might know Jamal?" she asked.

Rabinowitz looked at John before replying. "Gang member. A Bull Shark. I understand an ex-Bull Shark comes here for tutoring. Tyrese Brown. He's the one I want to talk to."

"Why Tyrese?" John said.

"We have a witness. He claims Tyrese ambushed Jamal. Stabbed him."

"Who's the witness?"

"Another Bull Shark."

"Convenient," John said.

173

"Could be a setup. Could be true. So, about Tyrese?"

"He hasn't been here this week," Clare said.

Rabinowitz stared at her for a moment, then pushed himself out from the wall. "He wasn't at home either. Guess we'll have to figure out where else he might be. Good to see you, J.B." He nodded at the rest of them.

Odd how intimidating a man in an ill-fitting suit and indifferent tie could be when he had the power to arrest and incarcerate, even if his nickname was Rabbit.

"Anthony told me someone named Jamal has been hassling Tyrese," she said.

Beck shook his head. "Knew I shoulda got Tyrese and Nellie moved."

"Too bad someone decided to play witness," John said. "Means they'll have to go ahead and charge Tyrese."

"They have to find him first," Clare said. "Do you think he's hiding, Beck?" She refused to even consider Tyrese might be missing because he was dead.

"No way to know, but don't look good."

"Police have been cracking down on gangs," John said. "Unlikely they'll give Tyrese the benefit of the doubt."

"We can help," Clare said. "The fact he comes here for tutoring and is doing well in school."

"What if the judge asks how you managed to convince Tyrese to come for tutoring?" John said.

She winced. "We can't just let them charge him with murder."

"Even if he did it?"

She shook her head. "I don't believe he did. Tyrese's smart. He wants to make something of himself. He was trying to avoid the gang. If he did stab Jamal, it had to be self-defense."

"I agree with Clare," Vinnie said. "That boy was working hard, doing good."

"We can't stop the police from charging him," John said. "All we can do is try to help him when they do."

~ ~ ~

"So how do you know Detective Rabinowitz?" Clare asked, as John walked her over to Huntington Avenue that evening.

"Paths crossed a few times."

"You've crossed paths with a homicide detective?"

"I was a cop."

"Oh." Oh, indeed. Real deal, indeed.

"Incidentally, not something I'd like bandied about Hope House."

"Of course not. So why does he let you call him Rabbit?"

"I think he enjoys being underestimated."

"And you're J.B., huh? What does the B stand for?"

"If I tell you, I'll have to make you disappear."

"It couldn't be any worse than Rabbit."

"Yes. It could."

"Bertie? Barnie?"

"Worse."

"I can't think of any other bad B names."

"Would you believe Boniface? My mother thought it sounded classy."

"Ouch. So were you ever called Bonnie?"

"Not if I had anything to say about it." His tone was a near growl.

Clare laughed. Then she sobered. "I'm worried about Tyrese."

"With good reason."

Not the reassurance she hoped for.

~ ~ ~

"Rabbit located Tyrese," John said when Clare arrived at Hope House the next morning. "He's at Children's Hospital."

"How is—?" Her throat closed on the rest of the words.

"We don't know. Beck and I are going to visit."

"I want to come with you."

"We figured you would."

At the hospital, she and John waited while Beck went to Tyrese's room. When Beck returned, he looked somber. "It ain't good. He's been beat, real bad, and he's awful sick."

"Can we see him?"

"Ain't much use. They got him drugged."

"I'd still like to see him," Clare said.

John went with her. When they reached Tyrese's room, they found a policeman on guard outside the door. After calling Rabinowitz to get them approved, he let them enter. Clare laid her hand on the shoulder of the woman seated by the bed, then looked at the boy lying there.

Tyrese's eyes were swollen shut and he had cuts and bruising on his face and a heavy dressing on one arm. The middle finger on one hand was splinted.

"My poor, poor baby."

Clare patted Nellie's shoulder.

"They surely near to kilt him."

While Clare reached out to touch Tyrese's good hand, John took Nellie's hands in his.

"Oh my, oh my." Nellie moaned, rocking back and forth in her chair. "They think my baby stabbed that Jamal."

"You've got to be strong for him." John continued to hold her hands. "You need to tell us what happened."

"Don't know nothing. Only know my boy, hurt. Hurt bad."

"How did that happen?" John asked.

Nellie continued to rock, unable or unwilling to say more.

John stood and motioned to Clare. "You try," he whispered.

She pulled a chair next to Nellie, sat down, and took one of Nellie's hands in hers. "Would you mind if we said a prayer for Tyrese?" It had to be Vinnie's influence rubbing off on her.

"Oh, that would be real nice. Me and my boy would surely appreciate that."

Remembering how Vinnie led the prayers when they'd visited one of the men in the hospital, Clare motioned to John, and the three of them made a circle, holding hands with each other and the unconscious boy.

Clare took a breath and began. "Heavenly Father, we know you are watching over your servants Nellie and Tyrese in their time of trouble. We ask you to keep them safe and to grant Tyrese a full return to health, and we ask you to lift the burden of suspicion from Tyrese. In the name of your son, Jesus, we pray."

"Amen," Nellie said. "Thank you, Clare. That were real nice. Vinnie couldn't have did any better."

Clare didn't know how to start questioning Nellie until the other woman solved that for her. "Tuesday, Tyrese was sick. He was home in his bed when that Jamal got hisself kilt."

"You were with him?" Clare asked.

"I work nights, and he was at home when I left. When I got back in the morning, he still there, sleeping. My poor baby. I got the baddest feeling I ever had."

"When did Tyrese get beat up?"

Nellie rocked and moaned. "That why he sick. Come home Monday like that." She pointed with her chin at the bed. "Wouldn't let me do nothing, though. But when I couldn't wake him Wednesday morning, I brung him here."

Nellie fell silent, and John touched Clare's shoulder and motioned it was time to go.

"What do you think?" she asked him as they rejoined Beck.

"Police are going to figure Tyrese went out Tuesday night and ambushed Jamal like the Bull Sharks are claiming, then got home before his mom did, and she's covering for him."

"Nellie said he got beat up Monday, and there's no way he could have gone out Tuesday and attacked someone bigger and stronger in that condition. Besides, he'd already broken his finger. Remember the last time he came to Hope House? It was swollen."

"I do, now that you mention it," John said.

Clare pictured Tyrese writing. "He had trouble holding a pen. So how could he hold a knife?"

John rubbed his chin. "I'll ask Rabbit if the M.E. can tell if the doer was right-handed or left-handed."

"It still don't look good," Beck said. "Look like a bunch of gangbangers beating on each other. Nobody going to have sympathy for Tyrese."

Chapter Twenty

Soubresaut
Sudden leap using both feet

"You don't look so good," Sam said, coming to sit next to Rob in the opening to the hut.

"Just tired." He gritted his teeth at a sudden pain in his gut.

Sam leaned toward him. "That wasn't just a gas pain, was it?"

"Probably it was."

"I didn't want to mention it before, but operating the way I did, there could be sequelae."

"Sequelae. What does that mean?" He tried not to give in to the urge to rub his abdomen in front of her.

"Adhesions, obstruction, strangulation."

"If you're trying to make me nervous, you're doing a fine job." He gave in and pressed on his stomach.

"You'd better let me take a look."

He hated the feeling of helplessness he'd had since the operation. And Sam giving him her doctor look didn't help. She pressed on his abdomen. "Jolley asked me to talk to you about calling your wife."

"Don't."

"She has a right to know you almost died."

"What's to be gained from telling her now? It's not like she can do anything."

"Your decision. Liver's normal." She continued pressing and moving her hands around, frowning while she did it. Then she used her stethoscope to listen for bowel sounds. Finally, she sat back on her heels and reeled off several questions about bowel habits and flatulence that would have made him cringe if he wasn't already miserable.

"Well, I don't think it's serious," she said, as he sat up and adjusted his clothing. "Just cramping, after all. Let me know if anything changes."

It sucked not being himself. The simplest tasks took more effort, proving the truth of Sam's statement that he'd been right to the edge. Although he hadn't seen any tunnels with bright lights at the ends, he now understood how easy dying could be. Understood as well how weak and vulnerable Clare must have felt after her injury.

For the first time he realized what a temptation his proposal of marriage had been.

~ ~ ~

Between rain showers, Rob and Sam took their evening constitutional around the village.

"You ever been married, Sam?"

She shook her head. "Almost. Once."

"What happened?"

"We ended up different places for our residencies. He said it didn't matter since we'd be sleepwalking through those years, anyway. Unfortunately, during a bout of sleepwalking, he got a nurse pregnant. Married her. Since then I've never had the time to get close enough to anyone else to consider making it permanent."

"You never said why you came on this expedition."

She glanced at him. "Maybe to save your life."

"You believe like the Chinese you're responsible for a life you've saved?"

"Good God no. If I did, I wouldn't be able to even think about walking into an operating room." She stopped and bent over to look at a plant. "Soraida and I talked about the responsibility of the healer." Sam sounded thoughtful. "You want to guess what he said?"

When she glanced up at him, he shook his head. "No idea."

"He said everyone, healer or not, affects everyone else. When we do a good turn we create a positive energy that goes out to the world and produces something splendid, a flower, maybe...peace, love." She straightened and they continued walking. "Whether it's true, I like the idea."

Light slanted low through the branches of the trees surrounding the village and they walked for a time in that golden light.

"As to why I came on this trip. Well, one day, it hit me. I could leave L.A., and nobody would miss me. Oh, sure. The guy who had to cover my shifts at the hospital, he'd miss me, but other than that..." She frowned, her gaze on the ground. "You believe in serendipity, Rob?"

"You mean coincidence?"

"More than coincidence. The stumbling over some piece of information right when you need it, or meeting someone who says something and you realize it's an answer to a question you hadn't asked yet but needed to."

"Like Kekulé dreaming about snakes and coming up with the structure for benzene," Rob said. "Or Fleming discovering penicillin because his cultures got contaminated. It happens all the time in science."

"I think it happens all the time in ordinary life, we just don't notice it. When I started on this trip, I was thinking about leaving medicine." Her steps slowed along with her words.

"I couldn't see the point anymore. Patching up gang members who'd been stabbed or shot, just so they could go out and stab or shoot someone else. And then I'd patch up the someone else and..." She made a circular gesture with one hand and turned onto the narrow path leading to the stream the village used for its drinking water.

"Your appendix reminded me of how I used to feel when an operation went well. I realized maybe I was making a difference, even when I couldn't see it. Funny. I had to come all this way to discover what was right in front of me."

"My appendix is pleased to be of service."

"How about you?" She pointed at his left hand.

He'd meant to leave his ring behind, but at the last minute he'd been unable to do it.

"Have you been married long?"

He shook his head. "A couple of years."

"Married before?"

He had it coming. She'd answered his questions, after all. "She was the first."

"So what happened?"

"She was a dancer. The prima ballerina in a major company. She was injured. Without dance, she wasn't sure who she was. I took advantage of that. Got her to marry me."

"She could have said no."

"I could have helped her without marrying her."

"And after that?"

"She got pregnant. Lost the baby. Pushed me away. Wouldn't let me comfort her. It was...dreadful. I kept hoping she'd get better, but she didn't. Finally, I accepted it wasn't going to work. That's when I decided to come on this trip."

They reached the small stream and stood watching the water curl by.

"Would you have regretted not marrying her as much as you appear to regret marrying her?"

He stood thinking about it. Not to answer Sam, but because it was something he ought to know. Except, it was unknowable. As unknowable as whether he'd ever loved the real Clare or a fabrication that existed only in his imagination.

"You ever had an operation?" he asked instead.

"No, thank goodness."

"It makes you vulnerable. Weak. Lets things leak out you can normally keep under wraps."

"Well, if you can't talk to the person who's seen what you're really like on the inside, who can you talk to?"

Indeed.

"You know," she continued, sounding solemn. "There are those who say we know we're becoming wise when we see value in our deepest pains."

"You manage that yet?" he asked.

"I think it takes a very long time and lots of experiences, both good and bad."

He wondered if six months in the jungle and two encounters with death would be enough for him.

~ ~ ~

Clare was surprised to hear Denise's voice on the apartment intercom since it had been months since they last spoke. Then she opened the door to find not only Denise but Stephan. Stephan, whose bad day had ended her career.

"My God, Clare, your hair. You're Odette, in the flesh. It suits you."

Clare motioned them inside, not letting Denise's comment wound. Odette. The White Swan. "It's been awhile."

"My fault. Totally," Denise said.

But it wasn't. After she lost the baby, Clare cut her ties with the past. Not that difficult to do. With the exception of Denise, as far as the company of Danse Classique was concerned, she'd as good as dropped off the planet.

Clare led them to the living room, asking if they wanted something to drink. Playing little Mary Homemaker as if it were a role.

"Nothing for us, Clare. We came because we have fantastic news." Denise pulled her down to sit next to her on the sofa while Stephan grabbed one of the dining table chairs, swung it around, and straddled it, facing them.

"Stephan had this absolutely, stupendously, fabulous idea." Denise glanced at Stephan, a proud expression on her face. "We're doing a fundraiser to help dancers transition into other careers. We've got a theater lined up and most of the company is committed to perform, and we thought, that is, Stephan and I, that you might be willing to choreograph a number for the two of us. You know. Like those dances you used to make up after rehearsals?"

"I'm sorry. I can't."

"But, Clare," Denise said. "It's a terrific chance to stick a finger in Justin's eye. We know how rotten he treated you after your injury. If you hadn't married Rob, well, you would have had a really tough time."

But she did have a tough time. Marrying Rob hadn't prevented it, just postponed it.

Stephan picked up the discussion, sounding as earnest as Denise. "What happened to you forced us to think."

"It shouldn't end the way it did for you." Denise's lip trembled and, for a moment, she stopped speaking. "We'll all need something to do, eventually."

"Yeah. Nissie's right. Not thinking about it doesn't keep it from happening."

It was all coming at Clare too fast. Denise turned philosopher and Stephan sticking his neck out with an idea Justin was sure to hate. "I'm sorry. I can't do it. I'm leaving, you see. Moving back to Cincinnati."

"When?" Denise asked.

A good question. Tyrese was still in the hospital and nobody could estimate how long his legal case might drag out, and Clare wasn't leaving until that was settled.

"Soon." She rubbed her head then found herself staring at Denise's hands. On the fourth finger of her left hand was a ring.

Clare reached out and touched it. "What's this?"

Denise blushed and looked over at Stephan. "We're getting married."

"Why, that's wonderful news."

"Yeah. Well." Stephan shifted uncomfortably. "About the benefit?"

Denise gave Clare a steady look. "Don't you dare say no. We won't accept it. We need five minutes of choreography to the music of your choice. We're getting married in June. Consider it a wedding gift."

"I can't do it."

Denise patted her hand. "It'll be such fun, working together again." She looked at Stephan, who stood and replaced the chair. Then Denise smiled at Clare, as if she had just said yes instead of no.

~ ~ ~

Clare closed the door behind Denise and Stephan and stood for a moment, clutching her arms around herself. It felt as though a cold breeze was wafting through the apartment, chilling her. She stumbled into Rob's study and huddled in his easy chair, trying to stop the shaking.

First Tyrese and now this.

All of it pushing at her, making her restless and uncertain, just when she'd started to feel normal and purposeful for the first time since her injury.

~ ~ ~

With her departure from Boston on hold because of Tyrese, Clare began to search for a temporary place to live so she could vacate the apartment before Rob returned. She shared her frustration with Sally during one of their after-school coffees. "Everything I look at is ugh!" She shuddered at the memory of dingy apartments and resident hotels smelling of cats, curry, and cabbage, and most of them far too expensive.

"I have a friend who lives in an upstairs apartment in her parents' house in West Roxbury. She's getting married, and she wants to make sure the apartment is rented to someone who will be nice to her folks and not throw wild parties."

Clare shook her head. "No way can I afford a nice apartment in West Roxbury."

"Let me take you to meet them. Maybe you can work something out."

~ ~ ~

The Rosens insisted on renting to Clare.

"It won't be for long, you know."

"Honey, you may love it so much you'll decide not to leave, after all," Mrs. Rosen said.

Next, on Vinnie's advice, Clare signed up with a temporary employment agency. They called right away with her first placement—filling in for a maternity leave in the office of the Chairman of the English department at Northeastern.

The perfect position, since she'd be near both Hope House and Children's Hospital. The only problem would be her proximity to Rob once he returned, although, luckily, his office was in a different building.

~ ~ ~

After Denise and Stephan's visit, the thought of going back to the beach where her marriage ended kept nudging at Clare. Nothing about the impulse made any sense, except perhaps as part of the overall effort she was making to understand herself and her relationship with Rob.

On Saturday, she finally gave in to the idea, although she made several wrong turns before she finally found the cottage. Stepping out of the car, she zipped her jacket against the cold fingering its way down her neck, and tucked her hands in her pockets. Sea and sky were both gray today with whitecaps and scudding clouds—weather as uncertain as her mood.

She walked around a dune, then stopped to examine the cottage, something she hadn't done the first time. Like a child's drawing, it was a simple square with a peaked roof, a door in the middle, and windows on either side. Even the tower to the one side was the fanciful kind of addition a child would make.

The blue-gray siding and rose-colored door accented with white trim gave the cottage a pleasant, welcoming demeanor. As she examined it, the steady wind keened through the grass and sea oats, producing a rattling that melded with the sough of the waves coming on shore. A percussion section of sorts to accompany the faint melody that sprang to life in her head—the first time she'd heard her music since the trip to Vieques.

She closed her eyes, concentrating on that music—a piano playing a dancing *allégro* accompanied by a single, solemn violin. She walked to the firmer footing at the edge of the surf, listening to the music, and beginning to picture choreography to complement the notes. Without conscious volition, her body moved, responding to the music.

When the notes faded, she sank into the softer sand above the tide line, feeling the pull in muscles long unused to leaps and twirls for, caught up by the dance, she had forgotten about her ankle and knee.

The sun came out, transforming the sea from navy to a sparkling royal blue with white apostrophes of foam. Odd to think that the water curling onto this beach might have once been where Rob had gone. Flowing thousands of miles from raindrop to rill to branch to tributary to the Amazon and then the ocean, to finally touch at her feet.

A cloud shadow abruptly erased the sun sparkles, but the waves continued to slide in then out in endless motion. Ebb and flow. The movement of living things. The eternal in and out, like breath, the contractions of the heart, or a man and a woman loving each other.

Tears pricked her eyes. She shook her head, trying to shake off the spell, not knowing if it was cast by the sea, her memories, or the phantom music.

Chapter Twenty-One

Balancé en avant et en arrière
A forward and back rocking step

Monday morning was cold with skiffs of spring snow. Clare walked to Northeastern, hunching against the chill, humming the melody that came to her during her visit to the Cape. It needed to be written down so she wouldn't lose it and, luckily, she knew someone who could help with that—Wilson Taylor, the rehearsal pianist for Danse Classique.

"Best way, Clare. You come in after company class," he told her when she called.

"I don't want anyone to know." Not until she was sure.

"You're working on the fundraiser." A wide smile underpinned Wilson's voice. "Good for you, Clare. Denise and Stephan told me they asked you."

"I don't know if it's any good."

"We'll find out quick enough. Tell you what. Sometimes I play after hours. You come in, we'll work on it then."

They set a time and Clare hung up, shaking. The scrap of music in her head was just that. A scrap. A minute, two minutes tops. She reached for the phone, planning to call Wilson to cancel, but remembering how pleased he'd been when she asked for his help, she couldn't bring herself to do it.

~ ~ ~

When Clare met with Wilson, it didn't take long to work out the basic melody. She hummed and he picked out the notes on the piano before transferring them to paper. After he played what

186

they had so far, the music in Clare's head continued. She hummed the next bit and Wilson played. Another bit came and more after that. At the end of an hour, they had five minutes of music.

"It's real fine, Clare. You got something in mind for the dancing part?"

"I thought I did." But the slog to get the notes on paper erased that tentative inspiration.

"How about, I play and you dance."

"Oh, I don't dance anymore."

Wilson frowned, then nodded. "Why don't you sit and listen, then. See if it comes to you. Like the music did."

When she didn't answer, Wilson turned and began to play, but even though he added chords and layers of notes making the music sound more finished, she felt no imperative to get up and move.

Three days after the session with Wilson, a tape arrived in the mail—her music, played by piano and violin. She'd told Wilson there should be a violin, playing more slowly and solemnly than the piano, and he'd run with it.

Saturday, Clare drove to the Cape, carrying a player and the tape Wilson sent. Once again, the beach worked its magic, and this time she wrote out the sequence of steps before the memory faded.

Monday she took a deep breath to quell an attack of nerves and called Denise to say she had something to show her and Stephan.

~ ~ ~

"Rabbit came by the hospital this afternoon and questioned Tyrese," John told Clare when she arrived at Hope House for an evening tutoring session.

"Is Tyrese that improved?"

"He's better, but he's still one sick little boy."

"So how did it go?"

"It's a mess." John looked worried. "Nellie lied about Tyrese getting beaten up on Monday. It happened Tuesday about the time Jamal was killed. Tyrese made his mom promise not to tell anyone he went out. She was trying to help. Unfortunately, Rabbit now knows Tyrese placed himself at or near the scene."

"Do you think Tyrese killed Jamal?"

John shook his head then shrugged. "I don't know. Seems unlikely, but this isn't going to go away."

"So how is the witness saying Tyrese did it?"

"He says Tyrese ambushed Jamal, stabbed him. Then he jumped Tyrese to fend him off."

"Tyrese wanted to avoid the Bull Sharks. Why would he attack Jamal, especially when there were other gang members there?"

"Witness is claiming Jamal was by himself when Tyrese attacked him. He just happened on the scene."

"It's bad, isn't it."

John nodded. "The prosecutor will barely need to break a sweat on this one."

~ ~ ~

Clare stopped by Hope House on her lunch hour to ask about Tyrese.

"He was assigned counsel." John spoke from under the sink in Beck's kitchen. He stood, stretched, and rubbed his neck. "Rabbit says the attorney they assigned couldn't save Mother Teresa."

She took a deep, shaky breath. "What are we going to do?"

"Unless you've got a chunk of spare change lying around, not much we can do."

Given her determination not to take anything more from Rob, she had only enough to stretch to the end of the month. She'd have to see if she could get a loan.

"The coroner did say Jamal was stabbed by someone holding a knife in his right hand," John added.

"Did you tell Rabbit that Tyrese is left-handed?"

"And I reminded him about the broken finger."

"Then why is he charging Tyrese?"

"He's got the witness. So he's playing it that Tyrese stabbed Jamal with the only hand available. His right one."

~ ~ ~

As the dates for Rob's return to Boston and her move to West Roxbury approached, Clare worked on the note she would leave for Rob. Writing it was more difficult than she anticipated. Eventually, she turned to the computer to see if that would be easier than covering page after page with disjointed words, then crumpling and tossing the sheets when she reread them.

Dear Rob... She tried to picture him, but the only image she could bring up was of him standing with his back to her, fishing off the side of the *Ariadne*. She willed him to turn around, but when he did, his face was still invisible, backlit by the sun. The memory of his voice was gone as well. But not the guilt.

She took a breath and tried to concentrate on the computer screen. Slowly her fingers moved and words began to form. As the screen filled, her eyes blurred and the words became indecipherable. Her fingers slowed, then stopped.

Nothing would make this easy for Rob. Not a note. Not her leaving without seeing him. And if she really wanted to erase herself from his life, why had she changed the apartment? Imprinting herself on every square inch. Better to have left it alone and simply removed all traces of her occupancy.

Once again, she'd been thinking only of her needs.

~ ~ ~

"What happens when you get home?" Sam asked, as she and Rob packed for their return to the States.

"I go back to my routine."

"And your wife?"

Clare's moving to Cincinnati, Lynne said the last time they talked, and his mouth went dry.

When, he'd asked.

Before you get back. And just like that, he realized he was counting on seeing Clare, hoping to find a way to salvage their marriage.

Hope. The cruelest emotion.

"Rob?" Sam was peering at him with a troubled expression.

"I'm sorry. What did you say?"

"You have to face things with her. Your wife."

His steady movements packing the supplies Sam was handing him slowed. He rubbed his forehead, realizing as he did so, his head had begun to ache.

"When you were sick you asked for her. Her name is Clare, isn't it? You're still in love with her."

"No." The word took all his effort, but lies usually did.

"You need to at least speak with her. Tell her how you feel."

"I don't think so." He shoved the filled duffel aside, struggling to hold on to some semblance of courtesy, although Sam had to know she'd stepped, and was continuing to step, way over the line.

"It's unfinished business. You can't move on, until—"

"Wrong. I've moved on." The words felt wrenched from him. He turned away and picked up an empty duffel as a distraction.

"You can't fool me, Rob. A person under the influence of drugs doesn't lie. Running away didn't solve anything for you, and chances are it didn't solve anything for her either."

"The hell it didn't. She's doing fine. Planning a new life. In Cincinnati." Oh, God. What was happening to him? Why couldn't he keep his mouth shut? Why was he standing here, letting Sam batter at the defenses he thought he'd managed to construct? Defenses that would allow him to live without Clare in his life. Defenses he now knew had all the protective power of a house of cards.

Sam reached out and touched his arm. The last straw. He vaulted off the hut's platform. The shaft of pain in his gut barely registered in the roaring desolation of what she'd forced him to accept. That when he got home, Clare would be gone.

Later, he apologized to Sam.

She gave him a long look. "You remember me telling you I never got close enough to anyone to plan any sort of future."

He made it as gentle as he could. "Don't, Sam."

"I just wanted you to know."

~ ~ ~

The trip back to Cuzco was grueling. As the van ground along, bouncing in and out of potholes and ruts, Rob held on, bracing himself against the jolting and lurching.

When they stopped for the night, every inch of his body felt pummeled. But what made him feel worse was seeing how Sam was avoiding him.

~ ~ ~

Exhausted from days of primitive travel capped by the long flight from Lima to Boston, Rob took out the key he'd not needed for months and fumbled it into the lock on the apartment door. He slid his luggage inside and went down the hall to the living room where blue walls striped with gold from the setting sun met his startled gaze. He walked into the kitchen, taking in the tangerine backsplash, dishes in the drying rack, and an African violet—a splashy purple—on the windowsill.

He turned and walked to the den. In the doorway, he stopped once again. After he'd absorbed the impact of the burgundy-colored walls, the painting caught his eye. He recognized it from a day he and Clare spent in Rockport. What was it doing here? Puzzled, he turned to the master bedroom. Here the walls were a pale silvery gray and a new bedspread in a blue, green, and black geometric design covered the bed.

Until Clare entered his life, he'd always been satisfied with the basics—a reasonable amount of cleanliness and neatness, a minimal amount of furniture, a comfortable bed. Then Clare opened his eyes to other possibilities, and he'd hoped she would make this apartment a bright and beautiful home, but she hadn't.

So what was this about?

He walked down the hall to the second bedroom where he'd slept those last months before leaving for South America. It was the only unchanged room—its walls still a sterile white and the room itself neat to the point of asceticism. He walked past the bed into the bathroom to find Clare's cosmetics on the counter.

What were they doing there? Hadn't Clare left? The end of March, Lynne said. So why were her things still here?

Leaving the bathroom, he noticed boxes lined up alongside the bed. He opened the closet door and the light scent Clare used drifted off the clothes still hanging there.

When he turned, Clare was standing in the doorway watching him, eyes wide with shock. They stared at each other for a moment before he managed to clear his throat.

But Clare spoke first. "You weren't due home until Friday."

"We finished up early. Changed our flights." He struggled to figure out what was different about her. Her hair was whiter, but that wasn't it. She wasn't as thin, but that wasn't it either. She seemed more...herself, somehow. And what was she thinking as she stood looking at him. That he'd changed too?

He'd discovered the extent of the change after they'd arrived in Cuzco. He'd showered, letting the hot water sluice over his body and ease his aching muscles. When he'd stepped out and as the mirror cleared, he'd been shocked at the sight of the man standing there. A man with shaggy hair and a thin face with sharp contours in cheek and chin. A man with none of the softness that had begun to settle around his middle, and through that now-flat middle, the red and silver track of a scar. And there were other changes. Invisible ones.

"I meant to be moved out," Clare said. "I thought it would be easier."

It would, but maybe Sam was right about them needing to talk.

"My apartment won't be ready until tomorrow. I'll go to a hotel tonight."

"You don't have to do that." The words came automatically, the thought more slowly—what apartment? Wasn't she moving to Cincinnati?

Clare bit her lip. "Thanks. I imagine you're tired."

"What's this about, Clare? Paint, pictures, plants?"

She looked away, clenching her hands together. "It's supposed to be an apology. Then I realized I shouldn't have changed it without asking you."

He thought about how warm and welcoming the apartment now looked, how walking into this one remaining white room gave him a chill. But sorting all that out would have to wait. "I'd like to take a shower, and after that I expect I'll sleep at least twenty-four hours."

"Are you hungry? I can fix something."

"That's okay. You don't need to do that."

"Really. It's no trouble."

"You're sleeping in here now?"

"I moved in here, while I was painting the other room."

She left him then, and he returned to the master bedroom. He checked the bureau and the closet to find his clothes had been returned to their original places from the spare room. A good thing, since the clothes he'd brought back from the jungle needed to be burned.

He took a shower then slipped into a pair of slacks and a sports shirt, enjoying the simple fact he had clean, pleasant-smelling clothing to wear. In the jungle, they'd had to boil their clothes so they wouldn't begin to smell and then rot.

He found Clare in the kitchen putting together a salad while two pots simmered on the stove. It represented a major change from the last meal she'd prepared for him.

He pointed at the pots. "I hope neither of those contains rice or beans."

She gave him a quizzical look.

"I've eaten enough in the past six months to last me the rest of my life."

"Oh. No. I thought spaghetti." She turned away, cutting tomatoes for the salad.

"You look good, Clare."

She ducked her head and began to shred lettuce. "Was it a good trip?"

"Depends on how you define good." So many memories, he had no idea which one to share with her. "What about you?" he said, instead. "Have you kept busy?"

She nodded and turned to add spaghetti to the one pot before she took the lid off the second and stirred its contents. Then she bent over to check the oven, and he caught a glimpse of rolls browning. He was suddenly ravenous.

While Clare finished cooking, he set the table. Then she handed him two plates of spaghetti. It smelled delicious. She sat in her usual spot, kitty-corner from him, and unfolded her napkin. "So. What else did you eat besides rice and beans?"

"Lots of manioc, fruit, fish."

As they ate, he told her a couple of stories about the trip. They weren't about anything important, but he was working hard to be polite, and the stories were adequate for that.

"We stopped talking," Clare said. "Before that day."

He looked at her in surprise. He knew exactly which day she was referring to. The day he'd taken her to the Cape to show her the cottage.

"Yes. Why do you think that was?"

She tipped her wine glass toward him. "It hurt too much."

He hadn't yet drunk enough wine to agree with her. An odd reversal of roles. Clare sharing and him backing off.

~ ~ ~

It made Rob uncomfortable, sleeping in the master bedroom while Clare slept in the guest room, but she refused to move. He stretched out in bed, and sleep—deep and dreamless—came swiftly. He awoke in the dark and turned his head to squint at the alarm clock. Only five fifteen, but he was slept out.

He pulled on a pair of jeans but didn't bother with a shirt or shoes. In the kitchen, he foraged in the refrigerator for sandwich makings and carried the resulting sandwich and a fresh cup of coffee into the living room where he sat eating and sipping coffee, watching the sky begin imperceptibly to lighten.

In spite of the coffee, his eyes grew heavy. He didn't feel like moving, so he reclined the chair and dozed where he was.

~ ~ ~

When she got up at seven, Clare found Rob asleep in the living room. With the worry lines smoothed out and the sadness in his eyes veiled, he looked younger than the day they met. God, he was thin, though. As if he were recovering from a serious illness rather than returning from six months in the jungle. Then she noticed the scar. A scar that hadn't been there when he left Boston.

She raised her eyes to his face to find he was awake and watching her. She nodded toward the scar. "What happened, Rob?"

"Acute appendix." His voice was uninflected.

"While you were in the jungle?"

"Yes."

"You had surgery in the jungle?"

"Lucky for me, we had a surgeon with us." His tone was casual, but he was obviously assessing her response.

She stood transfixed, letting the knowledge seep in—that Rob could have died. "I'm so glad he was there."

"The surgeon was a woman. She said I went right to the edge."

"The edge?"

"I almost died. Tends to focus the mind."

Sadness slipped through Clare. "When you focused, what did you see?"

"All sorts of things. I'm still thinking about them."

He stared past her, out the window.

"Would you like another cup of coffee?"

His eyes refocused on her. "No. Thank you." He went back to staring out the window.

It was too much. Rob's sudden, unexpected appearance, their awkward dance around the things they needed to say to each other, and now this announcement he'd nearly died.

She left him to his contemplation of the dawn and went to get dressed. When she stepped out of the bedroom she found Rob, dressed and obviously ready to leave for Northeastern. So why hadn't he left already?

"I'll be moving today," she said, relieved her voice was working reasonably well.

He looked puzzled.

"I found a place to stay until I leave for Cincinnati. It's available today."

He frowned, and Clare wrapped her arms around herself, trying not to shiver.

"Do you need any help?"

"I can handle it, but thank you."

"Well, be sure to ask if there's anything I can do. You know how to reach me." He picked up his briefcase.

She focused on the back of the chair she was gripping, shifting her weight from foot to foot. "I'd like to hear more about your trip."

"I guess we could have dinner sometime."

"That would be nice."

He nodded. "It's a date." But he didn't suggest a day and time.

He left, and she forced herself to eat breakfast. Then she finished filling the boxes and carried them down to the car. Luckily, she didn't have much. Clothes, records and tapes, a few books, and the heirloom dishes her mother gave them as a wedding present.

She unloaded everything at the new apartment then made a trip to the mall to buy an air mattress, linens, a pillow, and enough kitchen items to allow her to cook and eat simple meals. Next she went to a grocery store.

After unloading the car the last time, she drove back to Rob's apartment. She wrote him a note telling him the divorce papers were on his desk, and she left the note along with keys to the apartment and car on the dining room table.

Then she walked out, pulling the door shut behind her.

It was done.

Chapter Twenty-Two

One of the first things a boy learns with a chemistry set
is that he's unlikely to get another one.
Anonymous

Rob checked the spare bedroom and found the boxes gone and
the closet empty except for the parrot hat he'd given Clare that
first Christmas. It was shoved into the corner. Seeing it
brought tears to his eyes. Why did she leave it? As a final
nonverbal punctuation point to their relationship? Or did she
overlook it?

He found a note with her new address and phone number
along with keys on the dining table. The note said the
paperwork for the divorce was on his desk. And so it was,
neatly stacked to the side. He stared at the pages, his gut
clenching, then he noticed a humming noise. When he hit the
space bar, the computer screen lit up and filled with words.

Dear Rob,

I believe we truly discover ourselves only when we
face difficulties. I discovered I am less courageous
and less kind than I thought I was. Although that's
painful for me to acknowledge, I doubt it
approaches the pain I inflicted on you.

There's no way I can fully make up for hurting you,
but I have tried to make what small amends are in
my power. Since the failure of our marriage was
my fault and mine alone, I have instructed my

196

attorney to neither ask for, nor accept, any support or other payments.

You're a good man, Rob. My greatest regret is that I was unable to love you the way you deserve.

Timing is critical, my love, not only in dance, but also in life. Our timing was

He frowned at the note. It was unfinished like everything about his relationship with Clare. Still, how odd of her to leave it for him to find at some random time. He reread it, stumbling on the one sentence...*my greatest regret is that I was unable to love you the way you deserve*...and on those oddly intimate words, *my love*. Words she'd rarely used as a form of address.

He stared at the screen until the words blurred.

~ ~ ~

"Rob, dear, it's wonderful to see you." His mother hugged him then stepped back with a frown. "Clare isn't with you?"

"For Pete's sake, Alice. Let the boy get his breath." His father thumped him on the back. "It's good to have you home, son."

"Good to be home." Rob went over to hug Lynne, arching over her bulging midriff to do it. "Looks like my niece or nephew is ready to put in an appearance."

"Tomorrow would be fine with me, but the doctor says it'll be at least another month."

Pain squeezed his throat at the memory of the infant he and Clare had lost. Thank God his family didn't know about that.

"Now Rob, you never said. Is Clare joining us this evening?"

"No, Mom, she isn't."

His dad and sister glared at his mother.

"Well, we do have a right to know what's happening. We're family, after all."

"Clare and I are getting a divorce." Just words. They hurt only if he let them.

"Well, I should have guessed. After all, she refused to join us for the holidays. Not much of a family girl, that one."

He clenched his jaw, trying to let his mother's comments flow past without their sharp barbs doing any damage, something that was taking more of his energy tonight than usual.

After the obligatory cocktails, they moved to the dining table. Lynne passed him the mashed potatoes and he added a small scoop to his plate.

His mother frowned. "You need to eat more than that. You've lost a lot of weight. You haven't been sick, have you?"

He summoned a smile. "No, of course not. I've gotten used to smaller portions, I guess."

"What was it like?" Lynne asked.

About as different as something gets from this. At his family's expectant expressions, he struggled to string words together. "Primitive...but fascinating. We ate mostly rice and beans. So this is a nice change." He continued in that vein for a time—how they had chewed coca leaves for altitude sickness, the horrible road conditions to and from the river, his encounter with "Ronnie Reagan" in Cuzco—until his mother was satisfied and turned her razor attention to Lynne and the details of her pregnancy.

He forced himself to eat as his family's voices ebbed and flowed around him as if he were a stone in the middle of their conversational stream. He glanced across the table to where Clare should be sitting, remembering the first time he'd brought her home. For Thanksgiving. They'd been in silent cahoots that whole day, exchanging quick, laughing looks as the others talked.

"Rob, is something wrong?"

At his mother's sharp tone, his body jerked. "Oh, sorry. Those two days of rough road took their toll."

Lynne's expression was full of sympathy. He wasn't fooling her. She knew him too well.

When they finished eating, he pushed back his chair and stood. "Great meal, Mom. Thanks, but I'd better head home before I start having trouble keeping my eyes open."

"But, we've hardly seen you," she said.

"I'll stop by again after I get the lab squared away."

He climbed in the car and closed the door on the identically furrowed brows of his mother and sister. A relief they'd let him go with only token resistance. He should also be relieved he wouldn't have to face Clare back at his apartment. Instead, remembering her absence, a letdown that was more than simple fatigue washed over him.

~ ~ ~

Rob spent a second day slogging through his mail and meeting with his research group. By six thirty he'd had enough. As he headed across campus, he was behind a man and a woman walking together. Then the woman's quick, light way of moving registered. Clare.

She and her companion reached Huntington Avenue where they stopped and continued to talk intently. The man clasped Clare's arm briefly before turning and walking back toward Rob. Rob examined him as he approached. Good-looking he supposed, if you liked the hippie type.

As he looked back toward Clare, the southbound trolley pulled in, blocking his view of her. When it pulled out, Clare was gone.

~ ~ ~

"I'm having trouble with that one bit," Denise said.

Clare sighed. Her life had become so much more complex lately as she juggled her day job at Northeastern with evening visits to Hope House and the hospital. And now rehearsals with Denise and Stephan had been added to the mix.

"You try it." Denise sounded exasperated. "You'll see it's tricky."

Clare had no intention of putting her losses on display. "Let's focus on getting the other steps learned. We can work on the difficult parts later."

"It'll take less time if you'd show me how to do it." Denise might be sunny most of the time, but when she dug her heels in, even ballet directors walked carefully.

"Fine. Stephan, Wilson, take a break. Come back in fifteen minutes." Clare slipped off her shoes. "Okay. Let's start from the beginning." She began marking the beats, as she went through the steps with Denise. Then she played the tape she'd brought along in case Wilson wasn't available. When the piece ended, Denise turned to the door where Stephan and Wilson stood watching.

"That's it!" Stephan walked toward them, a big grin on his face. "Not a man and a woman, but the two of you."

Understanding dawned and panic set in. "Oh no you don't. I won't do it. I can't."

"You have no idea, do you, Clare?" Stephan said. "You were wonderful, and just think of the human interest. Everyone loves a comeback story. We'll prime the dance critic at the *Globe*. Attendance will skyrocket."

"To watch me fail. No. No way." Her body trembled. "I'm completely out of shape. An embarrassment."

"Okay," he said. "If that's your objection, here's what we'll do. Tomorrow, I'll video the two of you dancing. If you see anything embarrassing or flawed in your performance that can't be smoothed out with rehearsal, we'll stop bugging you. But, you've got to give it your best shot and an honest appraisal."

"You're not going to leave me alone until I agree, are you?"

"Nope."

He didn't need to sound so smug. "You have the music and the choreography. I've done what you asked."

"Call us greedy," Stephan said. "We want more. We want you, Clare."

She wondered if that had been the plan from the beginning.

~ ~ ~

"Okay, Clare, here we go." Stephan popped the tape out of the camera and prepared to play it back.

Her hands clenched as the tape began to play. On it, two women danced, one wearing pointe shoes and moving with assurance and a youthful vigor. The second dancer, who was barefoot, moved with a muted grace.

"There. You see it, don't you?" Stephan said, pointing. "There. And there again...see that. You've caught it perfectly. The dancer and her shadow self. It's going to be stunning."

Clare looked away from the video screen, biting her lip. Did they think she was a fool? It was one thing to dance as part of a practice with only the four of them present. Stephan was insane if he thought she was stepping onto a stage.

"This piece plays directly to our theme. The beauty of the dancer in her prime, stalked by the fear of age and injury," Stephan continued, oblivious.

"No."

Stephan rewound the tape. "You don't see it, do you? Look at this dancer, Clare. Forget it's you. Look at her face. At the way she moves. The point isn't to match Denise. This is a character part. Not a prima role. This role requires wisdom, Clare, and an understanding of loss."

What did he know about loss? *Damn him.*

"If Denise and I dance this, the symbolism is lost. With you and Denise, though. It's pure magic."

"Stephan's right," Wilson said. "If you won't take his word for it, take mine. You had me in tears, Clare."

"I'll make you a deal," Stephan said. "Come back Thursday. We have a full rehearsal scheduled. You and Denise dance this piece and see how the group reacts. If they don't get it, we'll leave you alone."

Denise, who had been standing silently off to the side, finally spoke. "He doesn't keep his word, he'll answer to me, Clare."

Not that it was any comfort.

~ ~ ~

Clare peeked in the doorway. Dancers milled in one corner of the room, stretching and lacing up pointe shoes or slippers. Stephan saw her and nodded to Wilson, who began playing her music. As Denise took the first steps of the dance, Clare slipped into the room to a quick flurry of whispers.

She had gone over the dance in her head and decided that as the piece progressed, her movements should gradually fall behind Denise's. Concentrating on that, she ignored the group gathered by the piano watching.

As the music ended, Denise did a quick *pirouette* then lifted her head and arms in triumph while Clare slowly completed the last turn, then stood with her head bent and her arms by her sides. For a long beat there was silence, then the other dancers surrounded them, their clapping and exuberant exclamations bouncing sharply off the mirrors. Several were wiping tears from their eyes, a reaction that had none of the tentativeness of pity. With a flare of excitement, Clare lifted her head and met Stephan's eyes. He nodded at her with a self-satisfied expression.

She'd been well and truly snookered. Vinnie would claim it was all the Father's doing.

~ ~ ~

Rob called Clare and invited her to come for dinner at the apartment, saying they needed to discuss the divorce. When Clare arrived, he seated her on the sofa in the blue living room, opened wine, and poured each of them a glass. Then he took a seat in the easy chair facing her.

"I thought I saw you on campus the other day."

"It's possible. I'm working a temporary job with Professor Molina."

"What kind of a job?"

"I'm filling in for an assistant on maternity leave."

Clare trapped behind a desk. Working at a computer, answering phones. It made him sad. But Clare didn't seem sad. "You work late. I saw you the other day. After six thirty."

"Oh. I must have been coming from Hope House."

"Hope House?"

"It's a place where people put their lives back together. I volunteer there."

"Is it on campus?"

"Back behind."

Did she mean Roxbury? "Is it safe?"

"Oh, Beck makes sure I have an escort."

"Beck?"

"The man who runs Hope House. Well, actually, Vinnie runs it, but it was Beck's idea."

While what Clare was saying made little sense, at least they were talking.

"What do you do there?"

"I teach people to read and write. If you like, I can give you a tour sometime."

"Sure. Okay." He'd like to see the place—and meet the people—who'd helped Clare lose her defeated look.

"Lovely." Clare smiled at him, in a free and open way she hadn't smiled since her injury.

As they moved to sit at the table, which he'd decorated with candles and flowers, he was reminded of the early days of their marriage—a bittersweet memory. He wondered if Clare was also remembering. Her pensive expression indicated she might be.

She took a small bite of the *coq au vin* he'd picked up at Cassat's, tipped her head, and examined him. "You got your hair cut."

The first thing the day after his return. "The hippie look never did suit me." The memory of the ponytailed man he'd seen escorting Clare popped into his mind. Not Clare's type, he would have said, but obviously someone she knew well. Beck, perhaps?

"The absentminded professor look suits you."

"Ouch."

She smiled at that, then began to tell him more about Hope House. He listened intently, sipping wine and eating slowly, as she talked about Beck and Vinnie, Anthony, Tyrese, and John Apple. Feeling, truth be told, a little jealous they'd found a way to pull her out of her depression when he couldn't.

"I'm doing all the talking," Clare said.

"You seem happy."

Clare looked surprised. "I guess I am. Or at least I'm content. How about you, Rob? What was the last six months like for you?"

"They were…" Life altering was the truest description, but he wasn't yet ready to share all that implied. "Interesting." He looked away, thinking about what to add. "We stayed in a Machiguengan village. They live simply, doing what they want when they feel like doing it. Own practically nothing. Certainly none of the things we think are essential."

Clare cocked her head. "You envy them."

"In some ways, I guess I do." Odd to admit it. An unexpected gift Clare had picked up on it.

"What was a typical day like?"

"Hot. Humid. Buggy. The payé, medicine man that is, led the expeditions. He'd point out a plant and explain how he used it. Then we'd collect samples and I'd test them."

"Did it work?" Her voice was soft.

"They were only crude qualitative tests. All we could tell was if any potentially active compounds were present."

"That's not what I meant. You went to get away from me."

For a moment their eyes met.

"Yes." His gaze skittered from blue walls to darkening sky. "And no. It didn't work."

When he looked back at her, she was staring at her plate. "Did it work for you?" he asked.

"There's no simple answer."

"Give me the complex one."

She blinked, apparently surprised, then spoke thoughtfully. "It's rather a long story."

"We've got all night, and there's more wine."

She took another sip of wine, put her glass down, and began talking, telling him the rest of the story—about the mugging and Tyrese and the deal she'd subsequently struck with the boy.

Anger built. How could Beck and the other people Clare mentioned have allowed her to step so blithely into danger? She could have been raped or killed. A dull pain in his jaw made him realize he was clenching it. Clare continued the story, telling him about the gang harassing Tyrese, who was now going to be charged with murder as soon as he recovered enough to leave the hospital.

To distract himself, he asked her the one question she hadn't addressed. "Do you know if he did it?"

"He says he didn't."

"You believe him?"

"Yes, I do."

"Why?"

She gave him a sharp glance. "Because of how we met, you mean?"

"Yes."

"Once he stopped being scared and angry, it turned out he's smart and funny and sweet and...I'm very fond of him. I want to help him."

But sometimes you couldn't help. Rob's throat tightened, remembering Tatito. "So how did you get started? Going to Hope House." Clearly, they'd both taken journeys these past six months, and it appeared hers, although extending only a few blocks from this apartment, had been every bit as difficult and complex as his.

"Last spring. After that day at the Cape." She looked down, hesitating. "I saw an article in the paper about Beck. I offered to help." Her gaze was unfocused as if she were watching a drama unfold. She shook herself and her eyes refocused. "They ended up helping me more than I helped them."

"And this?" He gestured at the blue walls and blinds. "When did you start working on it?"

"Last fall. I-I hope you don't mind."

"It's nice. I like it." It would have thrilled him if she'd done it a year ago. Now it mattered little, with her no longer sharing it. "Did you notice, Clare. We've been more open and honest with each other tonight than we've been in years?"

"*In vino veritas?*"

"Indeed."

"So what really happened out there?" she said.

He took a sip of wine. *In vino veritas*, indeed. *Well why not.* There wasn't anyone else he'd be able to share this with.

He spoke slowly, sorting out what he wanted to say. "I hated it at first. The discomfort. The heat, the bugs. Never feeling clean, nothing familiar to eat. I was angry with myself for not having the guts to get a divorce in the normal, civilized way. It was never quiet, you know. Even in the darkest part of the night, maybe especially at night." He put down the knife he'd been fiddling with.

"Gradually, though, I began to take more of an interest in the Machiguenga, how they lived, what they thought about life. And somewhere along the way, I stopped counting down the days and began instead to anticipate what I'd learn, see, do the next day." He wondered if he was boring Clare, but she didn't appear to be bored.

"When I asked one of the men how they navigated in the jungle, he showed me a partially snapped branch about three feet off the ground marking the trail we were on. They called them *quebradas*." He paused, remembering that day and how he'd wished for something as simple to show him his way.

"I spent part of my time with the healer. He believed illness in the body arises from disorders in the spirit. Even accidents happen because the spirit is distracted, in pain."

Because she was listening intently, he told her something he hadn't expected to tell anyone. "After my operation, Soraida took the sacred drug, the vine of the spirit, a hallucinogen, and chanted over me. He told me that during his trance, he saw the image of a woman with white hair emerge from my chest and stand on the tips of her toes with her arms raised to the sun."

Clare cupped her chin in her hands, watching him with an absorbed look. "Someone told him."

"No. I asked."

"So are you saying he had an authentic vision?"

"I'm a scientist. It's difficult to accept what can't be measured or verified, but I don't see how he could have known otherwise."

"Maybe his vision was correct." She picked up her wine glass and rolled it between her hands. "I hurt you. Not on purpose, but I was unkind." She continued rolling the glass while he waited.

She glanced at him, with a half smile. "A year ago you would have disagreed with that statement. So, do you think he was right? I made you sick?"

"No, of course not."

She spoke softly, watching him. "Could we have hurt each other more if we'd planned it?"

"I doubt it."

"We started out as friends. Can we still be after we end—"

"Are we at the end, Clare?" His chest was so tight he found it difficult to breathe.

Her eyes came up to meet his. "If not an end, then what?"

He was suddenly exhausted. "I don't know. I do know running away wasn't the answer."

"Maybe it was. I needed time alone...to figure things out."

"Did you? Figure them out?"

"I know what I did was wrong. Marrying you because I was too frightened to face things on my own."

"Was that the only reason, Clare?"

"You're asking if I ever loved you. Of course I did. Just not enough, maybe. Everything was too mixed up. I was too mixed up."

"Are you sure about a divorce?"

"I thought it was what you wanted."

"Is there someone else, Clare?"

She shook her head.

"Then, if you're doing it because you thought I wanted it...do you think we might wait awhile? Not rush it."

She cocked her head as if considering. When she finally nodded, he realized he was holding his breath.

Chapter Twenty-Three

Adagio
A series of slow, graceful movements of simple
or complex character, performed with fluidity
and apparent ease

Hope House was a shabby three-story brick building with a narrow strip of threadbare front yard. The overlay of poverty was as palpable as the smell of garbage. But no matter if he found it off-putting, this was the place that helped Clare bloom again.

He followed her inside, to find it clean but with no decorator enhancements. She led the way to the second floor past a room where several men were using computers or typewriters and others were reading or writing. Next door, they encountered a man large enough to play center for the Patriots.

"Beck, I'd like you to meet my husband, Rob."

Rob felt a brief spurt of pleasure at the words..."my husband."

Beck reached out a hand that engulfed Rob's. "Good to meet you." He appeared to be willing to be friendly but was clearly reserving judgment.

"The saints be praised."

Rob turned to find a stocky black woman standing in the doorway, beaming at him. "Hello there, beautiful." She stepped forward and took his hand between hers. "I'm Vinnie, and you must be Rob." She was a shrub next to Beck's oak. Oak, nothing. The man was a redwood. Old growth redwood. The thought amused Rob, and he smiled at Vinnie, who was examining him closely.

She nodded, smiling back, her face transformed to beauty. "You'll do," she said.

Rob felt absurdly pleased although he wasn't entirely certain what she meant. He chatted with Vinnie and Beck for several minutes, responding to their questions about his sojourn in South America. Then Clare escorted him around the rest of the building, introducing him to everyone they encountered. He tried to ignore the discomfort the searching appraisals he received caused, and mostly he succeeded. It was eye-opening to see how these men, whose bad choices and difficulties had etched lines in their faces, reacted to Clare. He saw affection in their expressions and heard respect in their voices.

"This is Kenny," Clare said. "He made this." She touched the small key she wore around her neck.

Rob had noticed the key and wondered about it. Kenny was almost as big as Beck and he moved with a slight limp. A scar bisected one eyebrow and continued to the corner of his left eye. Rob shook Kenny's hand, thinking that if he ran into him on a deserted street after dark, he'd be thoroughly intimidated.

Kenny fixed Rob with a baleful look. "You needs to talk to Clare. Tell her to stay here with us. No need her going off some other place."

"I am hoping she'll reconsider." It wasn't the way he planned on saying that to Clare.

"You hear that, Clare? He telling you to stay here." Kenny gave Clare a stern look.

"I'll definitely give it some thought." Clare spoke lightly, then she touched Rob's sleeve to direct him to follow her, as Kenny went off in the opposite direction.

"Oh, John, there you are."

Approaching them was the man he'd seen walking with Clare. Rob clamped down on a spurt of irrational jealousy. Or perhaps not so irrational, given the man's expression when he spotted Clare.

"This is John Apple. John, my husband, Rob."

Apple had a firm handshake and piercing blue eyes he used to dissect Rob.

He doesn't like me.

Apple turned to Clare, his fierce gaze softening.

He's in love with her. The realization hit Rob like a punch in the stomach.

When Apple left, Rob spoke quickly. "I better be going. Thank you for sharing this."

"I'm glad you came."

"So am I."

He wondered what she would say if he were to ask about her relationship with Apple. Probably something like, *Why are you asking?* And maybe he'd say what was really eating at him. You *no longer wear your wedding ring.*

He walked out of Hope House before he ruined the visit by saying something so stupid.

~ ~ ~

"You still planning to divorce that nice man?" Vinnie asked Clare when she saw her later.

"What makes you think he's nice?"

"Clear as the nose on your face, beautiful." Vinnie tapped Clare on the cheek. "That's a good man. I seen enough bad ones to know. So how about it?"

"Yes. I'm still planning on it." She gave Vinnie a steady look, daring her. She should have known better.

"Like to know why."

"You know that expression Beck uses," Clare said. "You've got to walk the talk? Well, Rob walked it all right. All the way to South America."

"And you upped the ante by planning that move to Cincinnati. That right, girl?"

"Best laid plans." Clare sighed. "I was planning to be gone before Rob got home."

Vinnie harrumphed. "And you still don't believe the Father's watching over you?"

"Are you saying the Father arranged for Jamal to be murdered?"

Vinnie looked shocked. "Course not. But the Father can take the bad, use it for good. Like making sure you're still here when that husband of yours come home. You don't think the Father had a hand in that, means you ain't paying attention. Besides, notice you ain't said you don't love him. Course love ain't only about what you feel. It's about what you do. People talk about love, really talking 'bout sex. Sex okay. Just ain't enough to build a life on. Why I got to tell you this? You know it already, beautiful."

Clare thought about Rob standing here today talking to Vinnie and Beck. He was thinner and older than the man she married, but he was also more definite. As if the jungle had done away with any softness. Had it also done away with what was left of his love for her?

If so, Vinnie was wrong, and the Father was a trickster.

~ ~ ~

"I may be dancing for the fundraiser, but I am not speaking to a reporter about it."

"What about photos?" Stephan asked.

Clare glared at him. He gave her a thoughtful look and then, as if realizing this was one time he needed to back off, did so.

Clare warmed up, using the familiar movements to calm her mind. If Stephan wanted to use her comeback as a publicity hook, he'd have to do it without her. It was one thing for her to step back on a stage, another thing entirely to have the details of her life spread out for everyone to pick over and then use as litter box liner.

Besides, there were no guarantees she'd be ready. Five minutes of performance didn't sound like much, but spending those minutes moving in precisely controlled ways required a level of fitness she'd not yet achieved. And she had to build that stamina slowly and carefully.

Dancing again was both exciting and terrifying, but when the lights dimmed after this performance she would walk away without regret. What was becoming clear, however, was that she wouldn't be walking away from her marriage and from Rob with the same ease.

~ ~ ~

After the visit to Hope House, Rob telephoned and invited Clare to a second dinner, this time at a restaurant.

"How are things progressing with Tyrese?" he asked, after they'd been served.

"Slowly. Although not much can happen until he's ready to leave the hospital."

"Is he still going to be charged?"

"It looks like it, even though Jamal was killed by someone holding a knife in his right hand. Tyrese is left-handed, and he

210

has a broken finger on that hand. The prosecutor still thinks he did it, using his right hand."

"You don't?"

She shook her head. "Jamal was big and fit. Tyrese is a lot smaller, and he was already injured. No way he would have survived if he'd taken Jamal on the way the witness says he did."

Images of Tatito flashed across Rob's mind, along with what it was like to be powerless to save the child. "You care about this kid."

Clare lifted her eyes from her plate, and nodded. "I do." She looked away. "It could be I'm making up for—" She bit her lip and stared at the table. "I was the one who made him come to Hope House, which is probably why the gang members kept harassing him."

He narrowed his eyes, watching her, thinking about what she'd left unsaid. "But if you hadn't made him come to Hope House, he'd probably be a gang member."

"I keep telling myself that. But seeing him..." She blinked rapidly. "He's so scared, and I am, too. Especially given his attorney."

"What's wrong with him?"

"The detective in charge of the case said the man couldn't save Mother Teresa."

"So why not get another attorney?"

"He was court-appointed since there's no money."

"You're still married to me."

"I already owe you more than I can repay."

"No, you don't."

She flinched.

He softened his tone. "I didn't buy you, Clare. At least, that wasn't my intention."

"I know. But I've taken enough from you." She bit her lip. "It wasn't right. Marrying you because I was scared."

"I took advantage."

She shook her head, sharply. "That doesn't excuse it."

His hand went to his forehead. He stopped it midway and returned it to the table.

She pushed her plate away. "Did you mean what you said to Kenny? About me staying. Or were you being polite?"

He lifted his eyes to rest on her. "Do you want another chance, Clare?" He waited, his heart slowing, his breath held.

"I do." She lifted her chin slightly, holding his gaze. "There's something I need to tell you, though."

211

He watched her take a breath and square her shoulders. "I'm dancing again."

He couldn't be more surprised if she'd said she'd decided to hang glide off the top of the Hancock Tower. "When? How? Isn't the season over?" He clamped his lips shut.

"It's only one time. For a fundraiser. Five minutes is all. No big deal."

But it was a big deal. A huge deal. "What about your leg?"

"It turns out the best thing was to let it all heal gradually. It isn't as good as new, but good enough for this, if I'm careful."

Clare. Dancing. It had always been between them, keeping them from seeing each other clearly. Like a sheet of titanium—thin and supple but opaque and ultimately too strong to breach. Since her injury, he'd learned to hate everything about the ballet. The physical toll it exacted, the focus on perfection that never let up, the indifference toward the injured dancer.

"I hoped you'd be happy for me."

"Of course, I am." The words merely a formula. Dancing a complication he didn't want to confront.

Clare was saying it would be only one time, but he didn't believe it. He'd seen how losing the ballet tore her apart. She'd go back if she could. Exhaustion overwhelmed him. It had been a mirage. Thinking she'd changed and they might be building something together to make the divorce unnecessary.

Once she had the ballet back, she wouldn't need him.

~ ~ ~

THE BALLERINA AND THE BULL SHARK. The headline in the *Globe* caught Rob's eye, exactly as it was designed to. The article that followed was a sensationalized recounting of Tyrese's relationship with Clare and the difficulties the boy was now facing. Only Tyrese's name was omitted, because he was a juvenile. Prominently mentioned was the name of Tyrese's public defender, who had to be the "anonymous source close to the case" the reporter used for the story.

Rob imagined Clare's reaction. A quick flash of intense anger followed by concern for the small boy caught up in the machinations of the adults who should be protecting him. The public defender was obviously an uncaring asshole, but he was a marketing genius. Win or lose the case, he'd found the perfect hook to get people to remember his name.

Rob hadn't been able to save Tatito, but maybe he could make up for that, at least in part, by helping this boy.

~ ~ ~

Rob looked across the desk at Edward Devaney, Esquire, friend and fellow faculty member at Northeastern. "I need the name of a good criminal defense attorney."

"Not for yourself, I trust?"

"There's a boy. Accused of killing the head of a local gang. It's my understanding his court-appointed attorney is incompetent."

"Who'd they appoint?"

"Frank Horzt." Rob leaned out of the way as the secretary handed Devaney a pile of folders.

"Horzt's ass," Devaney murmured. Smiling, the secretary left, and Devaney gave Rob a sharp look. "So what's your involvement with the case?"

Rob sighed. Futile to hope Devaney would give him a couple of names without the third degree. "A project of my wife's, you might say."

Devaney's face cleared. "Of course. The ballerina and the Bull Shark, right?"

Rob nodded.

"If it were my kid, I'd hire Marge Velez."

Chapter Twenty-Four

Entrechat
Interweaving or braiding step in which the
dancer rapidly crosses the legs before and behind
each other in the air

"Yes, I saw the story." Ms. Velez put her hands together and rested her index fingers against her lips. "What's your connection to the case?"

Rob went through it while Velez watched him over a pair of half glasses. A large, plain woman with astute brown eyes, she reminded him of Sam. "If you take the case, there's one requirement," he said, wrapping up.

She raised her eyebrows waiting.

"No one, particularly my wife, is to know I'm paying the bills."

Velez leaned forward, frowning. "I can say I'm being paid by a concerned philanthropist."

A concerned philanthropist. Unlikely Clare would recognize him with that description. A good thing. His paying for an attorney for Tyrese might confuse her as to his intentions. But then, hell, he was confused about his intentions.

"I need a retainer of $2,000, and you do realize, although you may be paying the bills, I'll be working for Tyrese. I'll inform you of anything that isn't confidential, but most of it will be, especially if it stays in juvenile court."

"I don't need reports. Just let me know when it's over."

"And I'll send you the bill."

"Of course."

~ ~ ~

Clare arrived at Hope House for an evening tutoring session to find John Apple waiting to speak to her.

"Frank Hortz came by this afternoon," John said. "Wanted to know what the hell we're trying to pull."

"What are you talking about?"

"The way Hortz was ranting, it was hard to figure out at first. Gist is somebody took offense at the newspaper article and used it to get the judge to remove Hortz. Marge Velez is replacing him. Paid for by a philanthropist who takes a special interest in kids like Tyrese. I called Rabbit. He says she's one of the best defense attorneys in the city, but he's never heard of a philanthropist doing that here."

"So who cares?" Clare said. "Being fired couldn't happen to a nicer guy." The whys and wherefores didn't matter. The truly important thing was Tyrese's fate no longer rested in Hortz's grasping, incompetent hands.

"First time I've seen someone's face turn purple. We worried he might stroke out."

"I wouldn't wish that on him," Clare said. "But it feels good to know he's off the case."

~ ~ ~

"Tell me about Tyrese." Marge Velez tapped a pen on her legal pad. "How you met him. Your interactions with him at Hope House."

Clare repeated the story she'd told Rob. When she got to the part about the mugging, Velez's eyes widened in surprise. "What did your husband think about you befriending a mugger?"

A John Apple kind of question. Not the kind Clare was expecting from this crisp, no-nonsense woman. "He didn't know about it until recently."

Velez looked at her notes, turning over a page and clearing her throat before asking Clare to continue. Clare then related how Tyrese changed from his tough-guy stance into an apt pupil and willing worker. When she reached the part about Tyrese showing up at Hope House with injuries, Velez slowed her down, asking detailed questions about when Tyrese was hurt, and the nature of those injuries.

"What happens next?" Clare asked when Velez finished.

"I expect Tyrese to be released from the hospital in a day or so. He'll then be transferred to juvenile detention, and there will be a hearing within forty-eight hours. The prosecutor plans to ask that Tyrese be tried as an adult."

It was what they feared.

"I intend to make sure that doesn't happen." Velez capped her pen and reached out to shake Clare's hand. "Thank you for your time, Mrs. Chapin."

Afterward, Clare compared notes with John and Beck, who'd also been interviewed by Velez. "I forgot to ask. Will we testify at the hearing?"

"Only the prosecution's case is presented," John said, "but Ms. Velez will get a crack at the witnesses. Given her rep, that may be all she needs."

~ ~ ~

Tyrese was discharged from the hospital on Monday, and Clare took Wednesday morning off to join Beck and John at the courthouse for his hearing.

"Beck, Appleseed, Clare," Nellie Brown said, walking up to them. Then she stopped speaking to pull a handkerchief out of her capacious purse and mop her eyes. "It sure good of y'all to come be with me and my boy."

"We couldn't be anywhere else, Nellie," Clare said. "We'll be right here praying."

"Y'all ain't coming into court with me?"

"The hearing is closed. Only family's allowed," John said.

Nellie looked outraged. "Well, I never. If y'all ain't family, don't know who is. I talk to that judge."

"That's okay, Nellie," Clare said.

Nellie just harrumphed and marched into the courtroom. Five minutes later, a young man in a dark suit came out and approached them. "The defendant's mother asked that you be present. If you would follow me?"

When they entered the courtroom, Nellie gave them a satisfied look. Clare sought out Tyrese. Frail and thin, he was seated at a table beside Ms. Velez. Across from them at another table sat the prosecutor, a heavyset man with an incipient comb-over. As the judge began to speak, Tyrese peeked over his shoulder, and Clare wiggled her fingers at him. His lips curved in a smile, but his eyes remained fearful.

After the preliminaries, the prosecutor called his first witness, D'Shawn Williams. The bailiff went off to fetch

D'Shawn, who turned out to be a six-foot-tall black man with bulging muscles. After being sworn in, he strutted to the witness chair and slouched into it, glaring at Tyrese.

Clare listened intently as the prosecutor led D'Shawn through his testimony describing how Tyrese stabbed Jamal and the subsequent struggle to subdue Tyrese.

"Your witness, counselor." The prosecutor smirked at Ms. Velez as he returned to his seat.

Velez stood but remained behind the table. "Mr. Williams, you're eighteen years old, is that correct?"

"Yeah."

"You look very fit. I bet you work out."

D'Shawn grinned at her, obviously pleased. "Do some."

"Bet you can bench-press, oh, a hundred, hundred and fifty pounds."

He frowned. "Three hundred more like it."

"Of course. Three hundred pounds."

"Objection." The prosecutor's tone was bored. "I fail to see how Mr. Williams's bench-pressing prowess has anything to do with this case. No bench-pressing involved, as far as I recall."

"Your Honor, this crime involved a violent confrontation," Velez said. "The fitness and strength of the participants is very much an issue."

"Overruled."

Clare clenched her hands in anticipation as the questions continued.

"Tell me, was Jamal Hicks as big and strong as you are?" Velez's tone was sugary.

Williams straightened his shoulders slightly, preening. "Sure. All us Bull Sharks big and strong."

"So Mr. Hicks could also bench-press three hundred pounds?"

"Yeah. Well, maybe bit less."

"What was your relationship with Mr. Hicks?"

"He, uh, he the head of us, and he a friend."

"A good friend?"

Williams slumped in the chair. "Sure."

"Do you own any knives, Mr. Williams?"

"Course I do. Got steak knives, butcher knife."

"Do you own a pocketknife?"

D'Shawn wiggled and looked at the judge, who reminded him he was testifying under oath.

"Sure, we all got pocketknives. They for protection."

"How big is your knife?"

D'Shawn held his fingers apart.

"Please put that into words for the court."

"'Bout six inches."

"Do you always have it with you?"

"Course."

"Do you have it today?"

"Don't bring nothing like that to court. I'm not stupid."

Velez continued asking Williams questions, looking more at her notes than at him, leading him through a discussion of how long he'd known Jamal and how much time they spent together. Occasionally, in a desultory fashion, the prosecutor objected.

"Did Jamal have a girlfriend, Mr. Williams?"

"Sure."

"What's her name?"

Once again, Williams wiggled. "Uh. Tanisha."

"Objection. Counselor has wandered around the lot on this. Does she have a point?"

"Your Honor, a very important point, which will be clear in just a moment."

"Overruled, but make your point quickly, counselor."

Velez looked directly at Williams for the first time, and Clare drew in an anticipatory breath.

"Had Tanisha and Jamal been together long?"

"While."

"A year?"

"Naw. Two, three weeks is all."

"Before that, did Tanisha have another boyfriend?"

Williams mumbled a response.

"I'm sorry. I didn't catch that. You need to speak up so the court can hear."

"Yeah. She did."

"Another Bull Shark?"

Williams shot a glare of pure hatred at Velez. "Yeah. She my woman."

"Did you and Tanisha part on good terms?"

"Didn't *part*." He stretched his neck and glared at Velez. "Jamal, he say, she don't go with him, he cut her."

Velez continued to scrutinize the witness for a moment. Watching her, Clare had a sense she was easing into position like an archer pulling back on a bow.

"So she left you." Velez spoke softly.

D'Shawn reared back as if he'd been slapped. "Didn't want to. Woman loves me. *Me*. Jamal just think he so cool. He not."

"Poetic justice," Velez murmured.

"Hmmph. Don't know nothing 'bout poetic crap, but Jamal, I give him what he deserved." he followed up with a cocky smile.

Velez gazed back at D'Shawn without speaking, and Clare felt as if they were all holding their breaths.

"What did you give Jamal?" The words were soft.

D'Shawn's cockiness morphed into outrage. "Oh, what? You think I did it? Didn't do nothing. Was that boy there." He pointed at Tyrese. "He stab Jamal. He a instrument of justice. I seen it." He nodded emphatically.

"You expect us to believe this boy," Velez raised her arm to indicate Tyrese, "with a broken finger on his dominant hand, attacked someone nearly three times his size and managed to stab him twice before you were able to stop it?"

"He sneaky."

"Are you right-handed, Mr. Williams?"

"What that got to do with anything?"

"Just answer the question."

"I right-handed."

"The person who stabbed Jamal Hicks was right-handed. So what we've established here is you had the means, the motive, and the opportunity to carry out this murder. The means? You admitted you always carry a knife. Your motive? To pay Jamal back for taking your girlfriend. The opportunity? You've placed yourself squarely at the scene."

"You can't do that." D'Shawn turned to face the judge. "She can't do that. This not about me. It about him." D'Shawn pointed at Tyrese and looked wildly around the room.

"You gave Jamal Hicks what he deserved."

"Did not. Jamal my friend. Didn't do nothing."

"Your Honor, may we approach the bench," Velez said.

It didn't take long after that. At the end, Velez gathered up her papers and hurried out of court on her way somewhere else. D'Shawn Williams left court wearing handcuffs, headed for adult detention.

The rush of relief made Clare feel like leaping to her feet, an impulse she curbed. Nellie faced no such restraint in expressing herself. The courtroom echoed with her "Praise the Lords." If she'd been a less substantial person, she would no doubt have leaped the railing to get at Tyrese. Instead, crying and laughing, she pulled him into a bear hug with the railing between them.

When Nellie finally let go, Clare gave Tyrese a hug, tears of happiness and relief rolling down both their faces.

Chapter Twenty-Five

Grand fouetté
Turning by a whipping movement
of the leg

"Rob, have you seen the *Globe* today?" Lynne asked when he answered the phone at home Friday morning.

"Not yet."

"There's a story you need to see."

"Topic? Section?"

"It's about Clare."

Damn it. He'd figured with Velez involved there'd be no more ballerina/Bull Shark bullshit.

"There's a special benefit performance. Tomorrow. To raise money to help dancers transition to other careers when they can't dance anymore. Clare's dancing."

Of course. The benefit. He'd put off thinking about it specifically, although he'd been unable to banish entirely the sinking feeling brought on by Clare's imminent return to the ballet.

"I'll call and order tickets for us," Lynne said.

"Not for me." He spoke firmly. He'd not yet decided if he was going, but if he did go, he didn't want to be with someone who would be aware of his every reaction.

He ended the call and stepped into the hall, picked up the paper, and opened it to find a picture of Clare and a story about the benefit. He stuffed the section in his briefcase. He'd deal with it later, although it was easier to put away the paper than it was thoughts of Clare.

~ ~ ~

"Great photo," one of the dancers called to Clare as she made her way through the backstage chaos the night of the benefit.

A stagehand grinned and gave her a two-thumbs-up as she walked by. "Terrific story, lovey."

"We're sold out, did Stephan tell you?" Denise greeted her with a hug. "How are you doing?"

"I'm nervous."

"Good. Me, too. Means we're ready."

"So what's with all the comments I'm getting? Something about pictures and stories?"

Denise turned and suddenly got busy, rubbing foundation onto her face, which had pinked up.

"Denise?"

"Oh, you know. The *Globe* did a story on the fundraiser and ran a picture. I'm surprised you didn't see it."

"Denise."

"We needed to do something. Ticket sales were slow."

Clare waited.

"Oh, all right. Here." Denise pulled a section of newspaper out of her bag and handed it to Clare.

The picture, three columns and in color above the fold, was of her and Denise in rehearsal clothes in their positions at the end of the dance. The headline read: "Comeback Planned for Ballet Fundraiser." Clare scanned the article, feeling more and more agitated. It was all about her. Her injury, the long recovery, her involvement in writing the music and choreographing the piece for the fundraiser, how she'd been convinced to also perform, and, of course, a last bit about the Bull Sharks. She raised her eyes to find Denise biting a fingernail, watching her. So she knew they'd gone over the line.

"I should walk out of here."

Denise's expression turned to panic.

Clare sighed. "If you ever even think about getting a divorce, you'll answer to me."

"Oh, Clare, you are such a peach." Denise stood and threw her arms around Clare.

Sure. A real peach.

~ ~ ~

Denise and Clare took positions next to each other at the

barre, going through the careful stylized movements to gradually warm their muscles. Clare's thoughts, freed by the thousands of repetitions, were of Rob. She'd peeked at the audience from the wings on her way to warm up but hadn't seen him. Distressed by his absence, even her usual pre-performance jitters were dampened. He had to be here. Though they hadn't discussed it, she'd counted on his presence tonight.

"Touch time, Clare." Denise released the *barre* and held out her hand. Clare touched fingertips with her, and they smiled at each other.

Well wishes were murmured by everyone they passed as they took their places in the wings. A lump in Clare's throat accompanied the butterflies that always preceded the first notes of the music. She'd missed this. All of it. The hard work, the aching muscles, and then the feeling like flying when she stepped on the stage.

During these last weeks of rehearsal, she'd kept her focus on her leg, planning each step before she executed it, constantly assessing how her leg was responding. But tonight, as she stepped onstage, her hesitation and fear fell away, and the music supported her like the sparkling waters of Vieques had.

The music ended, and as the applause crested over them, Denise took her hand. Together, they rode the wave. The audience on its feet, cheering, clapping, whistling.

Someone reached up from the audience holding a bouquet of flowers. Rob. *Thank God.* Vinnie was right, it was going to be okay. But it wasn't Rob. Just someone who vaguely resembled him. Clare smiled her thanks, then peered beyond the footlights, looking for Rob. Other bouquets were handed up, as the crowd continued to applaud.

Clare's arms overflowed and Denise, juggling bouquets of her own, helped by taking some.

As they left the stage, Justin approached from the wings. He greeted Clare lavishly, with kisses on both cheeks. "Clare, you were magnificent. You must come in to talk about next year."

She almost laughed in his face. Stopped herself, barely. "No."

"We need to talk. Next fall, Clare, you must come back to us."

"No."

"You can't mean it. I'll call you next week."

"Come on, Clare, we need to change for the reception," Denise said, freeing her from Justin.

Clare shook her head. "I'm going home."

"But, Clare. You were incredible. Everyone's going to want to see you, talk to you. And did I just hear Justin offering you a job?"

"When he wakes up tomorrow, he'll be glad I turned him down."

"I doubt it. He saw the audience reaction. He meant it, Clare. Come on. This is your night. Enjoy."

She gave in because it was easier than arguing. Besides it would be a distraction from the pain of knowing Rob didn't come.

It shocked her how much that hurt.

~ ~ ~

"You may not remember me, but we met at your wedding."

The man holding out his hand wasn't even vaguely familiar, but people often pretended to know her at receptions.

"I'm sorry, I don't remember your name."

"Edward Devaney. Your husband and I are colleagues. Your dancing tonight was inspired."

"Thank you."

"I hope it worked out with that kid?"

Clare frowned, feeling puzzled.

"Marge Velez?"

"You're talking about Tyrese Brown?"

"Was that his name? I told Rob Marge is a genius."

Vinnie and Beck were suddenly there wrapping Clare in bear hugs. Afterward, they stood nearby beaming, as one person after another came up to shake her hand and tell her she was wonderful.

Stephan and Denise rescued her and insisted on driving her home. She let them.

~ ~ ~

Rob almost didn't make it to the benefit. By the time he called the box office, only a few tickets were left. The theater was nearly filled as he made his way to the back of the balcony. He found his seat and opened the program, but before he read further than the opening words, the house lights dimmed and

Stephan Orsini walked onstage. The man responsible for Clare's injury. How had he done it? How had he gotten Clare to speak to him, let alone agree to dance? But she'd want to dance no matter who did the asking.

Stephan finished his introduction, and the program began. For the next ninety minutes, waiting for Clare, Rob didn't take in any of it. Finally, the curtain closed briefly and reopened to a bare stage. A piano sat off to one side. A pianist and a violinist took their positions and began to play. A ballerina, in a tutu, wandered onstage and began to dance. After several beats, Clare appeared in the background, dressed in a silvery body suit with a simple tulle skirt.

His eyes filled with tears. Clare, as lovely as she'd ever been, but so different from the woman he'd last seen dance in another lifetime. Instead of the vivid joy she'd projected in those days, tonight she appeared contemplative—the smooth, slow grace of her movements a direct contrast to Denise's athleticism.

The music ended and there was a beat of silence, then the audience surged to its feet. As if awaking from a dream, Rob looked around to find several women wiping tears from their eyes. He brushed at his own tears, as Clare and Denise stepped forward for their bow. Clare bent down to accept a bouquet. He should have done that. Bought his ticket early, so he'd be in the front row, able to hand her flowers.

At least a day late and more than a dollar short, again. His permanent position *vis-à-vis* Clare.

He'd walked this road before. Standing on the sidelines. Watching Clare in the spotlight. Knowing deep down, but refusing to admit it, that dance meant more to her than he did.

He left the theater and returned to his apartment where the moonlight pouring in the windows was so bright, he didn't bother turning on the light. He poured himself a tumbler of Crown Royal then sat in the recliner in the living room, sipping and staring out at the night sky.

He rolled the whisky in his mouth, flipping through his memories. Clare, tonight, so heartbreakingly beautiful. Clare, other times, other places. Most recently, standing in the doorway when he'd returned from Peru, looking appalled to see him.

God, was it really four years since they met? And from that first moment the simple knowing. *Yes. This is the one.*

He could manage without her, of course. He'd learned that from his time in the jungle. Life went on whether you wanted it to or not. But he would mourn her loss the rest of his life.

The phone rang and, startled, he sloshed whiskey on his wrist.

"Hi, Uncle Rob." Lynne's husband sounded ebullient.

"Jim. So the baby arrived?" He'd wondered if Lynne made it to the benefit.

"Yep. Little girl. Prettiest little miss you've ever seen. Well, Lynne says she will be in a day or two."

"Congratulations."

"Man, you've got to join us. Your folks are here, and we're going out for dinner. Celebration time."

Rob snapped on the light and looked at his watch. "It's ten thirty. Where do you think you'll find dinner at this hour?"

"Scorpio's. They serve till midnight. You've got to come."

"Okay. I'll meet you."

"Great. We're leaving the hospital now. We should be there in fifteen minutes. That work for you?"

Not really. He'd rather be alone, but he hadn't eaten before the benefit, and his stomach suddenly reminded him of that fact. "I'll be there."

~ ~ ~

Clare let herself into the West Roxbury apartment, turned on a light, then stood in the doorway leaning her head against the jamb, listening to the quiet. Remembering the small noises in Rob's apartment that let her know he was there.

She was reaping her reward for shutting him out. Something she could now admit she'd done from the beginning of their marriage. Never telling him all of what she was thinking, feeling. Her excuse had been that there was nothing positive about her thoughts in those days. Still, it was what marriage was supposed to be about. Sharing everything. Good and bad. Joys and fears.

Tonight, standing on the stage, accepting the applause, staring into the dazzle of the footlights, she'd seen clearly for the first time. She'd traded something real for something make-believe. And then the surprise of her instinctive "no" to Justin shocked her into a further certainty.

Rob, not the dance, owned her heart.

Chapter Twenty-Six

Grand battement
Raising and lowering one leg while the body remains still

Rob visited Lynne in the morning before she and the baby were sent home. She greeted him with a big smile, then turned back the blanket to show off her new daughter. He was surprised at how scrawny and red the infant was, like a wizened little monkey. Not that he'd ever say so. Hopefully, Lynne was right about her looks improving.

He reached out a finger and touched the tiny hand. It curled around his finger and eyes opened and peered sleepily at him.

His heart contracted. "Have you decided on a name yet?"

Jim had acted oddly when Rob asked that question last night and his mother had pursed her lips, a sure sign something was up.

Lynne gave him a fierce look. "I want to name her Robin Clare."

Well, that explained the pursed lips.

"Mother said it's insensitive of me. I agreed I'd wait and ask you what you thought."

"Why?"

Lynne looked at her daughter, her lips quirking into a half smile. "Because she looks like a Robin Clare."

As if responding to her name, the baby opened her eyes and stuck her tiny fist in her mouth and began sucking with a faint sibilance.

"And because I haven't lost hope."

Lynne might still have hope, but his was gone.

~ ~ ~

Clare awoke, and it took a moment before she realized she was listening for Rob. For water running, the clink of dishes and silverware, the rustle of a newspaper, footsteps. But the apartment was silent. In the kitchen, she found the message light blinking on her answering machine—Jim, saying Lynne had the baby. He was so excited, he forgot to mention if they'd had a boy or a girl.

Clare ate breakfast then went to visit Lynne in the hospital. She found her sister-in-law sleeping and the baby, wrapped in a pink blanket, in a bassinet beside the bed. She sat near the infant, looking but not touching, her heart aching in memory of the baby she and Rob lost.

"We're going to name her Robin Clare," Lynne said.

When the words sank in, Clare shook her head. "Why?"

"We had another name picked out, but once she arrived, it didn't fit, and Robin Clare does." She reached out to touch her daughter's head. "Rob was here. At seven, no less." Lynne grimaced. "Miss Robin was already awake and hungry."

Clare's heart jumped. So where was he now? Probably at the University. He'd always worked long hours, and ever since their problems set in, he'd spent his weekends working as well.

"When do you get to go home?"

"I have to be out by noon. Jim is on his way. We just have to wait until the pediatrician checks Robin. Oh, I almost forgot. How did the benefit go? I planned to be there until Robin decided to put in an early appearance."

"Fine. Really good, actually. Full house."

"Oh, I'm so glad to hear that. I was sorry to miss it."

Clare stood. "Well, I better get out of your hair."

"Would you hand Robin to me, Clare? I'm still sore."

No way out of it short of bolting for the door. She slid her hands around the well-wrapped baby and lifted her. Robin Clare opened her eyes, yawned, then blinked, looking solemn.

Clare transferred the baby to Lynne. "Well, congratulations again. She's precious." Trembling, she escaped.

It was such a bright morning, she decided to walk to Northeastern. She'd surprise Rob, but when she got to Rob's office, the door was locked, and the student working in the laboratory next door said she hadn't seen him.

~ ~ ~

After visiting Lynne and his new niece, Rob was too restless to stay indoors. He wanted to see Clare. Maybe go sailing. Out on the boat, leaning into a spring breeze was the perfect place for them to talk.

He caught a trolley back to the apartment to call Clare, but she didn't answer her phone. Frustrated, he decided a day of sailing was still a good idea.

As he left the harbor, the wind chilled him, filling his lungs with cold sea-scented air. The one unfinished statement Clare made the last time they met drifted into his mind. *I guess I was trying to make up for...* Was she going to say, "our baby?" Probably not. No doubt it was his visit to Lynne and his new niece this morning that suggested that. Robin Clare. Good grief. What did Lynne expect him to say?

Clare. She'd found her way back into her world. The ballet. The article in this morning's paper quoted the artistic director as saying he anticipated Clare's return to the company. Rob had no interest in competing with the ballet for Clare's affections. The divorce was set. The papers drawn up. Clare's signature already in place. All he had to do was sign and then get on with his life, unencumbered by expectations that were never going to be met. They didn't even need to meet again.

Go ahead, Chapin, admit it. You're wrong. Clare isn't the one.

Divorce. An ordinary, everyday event. According to statistics, half of all married couples experienced it eventually. No reason then to feel so...totally, utterly, bereft.

The boat suddenly pitched, and he looked up to find clouds blanking the sun. Lightning zigzagged and fat drops of rain hit his head, hands, and the deck. The *Ariadne* heaved restlessly, and he braced himself against the motion, relieved to turn his focus to the boat, the waves.

He reefed the mainsail, pulled on oilskins, attached a lifeline, and snapped on the weather radio to learn this was only a narrow band of storms. Enough to give him a wild ride and force him to concentrate, but not enough to be dangerous.

The drops of rain multiplied making him feel as if he were enclosed in a small space. He started the engine and used it to keep the boat turned into the strengthening wind. The shore was obliterated and when he looked sideways, he was able to see only a short distance, as if he were moving through a wall of thick fog.

In spite of the oilskins, he was quickly soaked, the water pelting his face and slipping down his neck. He opened his mouth to the deluge, drinking it in as the boat heaved and shuddered in seas growing more restless. The rain slid down his cheeks companioned by tears, and his voice, an inarticulate cry of pain, joined the sound of the storm.

Eventually, his inner storm stilled. Still, he stood at the helm of the pitching, tossing yacht, blinded by a thick curtain of gray, and yet seeing clearly. He and Clare. What he'd done. Stepping in to save her instead of letting her discover she could save herself. Making her dependent instead of providing the support for her to learn to find a new purpose, new joy.

He thought, as well, about Soraida's vision. Maybe it didn't mean he should banish Clare from his life. What if the vision were telling him he needed to free Clare to be the person she was meant to be?

Clearly that person was a dancer.

And yet, the way he'd reacted when she said she was dancing again...instead of support, he'd given her unspoken opposition. What a small man he'd become, one focused on his own needs. But realizing that, was it perhaps possible he might be able to find a different way to be with Clare? A way that left them both free?

In the midst of heaving water and roaring skies, he felt suddenly so light he was surprised to find his feet were still planted on the deck.

After a time, the curtain of rain ahead of the boat thinned to gauze and then parted to reveal clouds scudding overhead. Along the horizon, a band of pure clear lemon faded into the blue. Like last night. The bare stage with its blank backdrop, then the light changing slowly until it was like this. Light and dark. He checked his position to find the storm had blown him south and east. He set course for Falmouth, using the engine, leaving the sails furled. By the time he made harbor, the sky had burst into stars.

Exhausted he put the yacht on the haul-off and debated briefly whether to sleep aboard or drive back to Boston. But then it was always better to drive into Boston Sunday night rather than face Monday morning traffic.

He turned the car's air conditioner on high and aimed it at his face to keep from dozing off. The storm had made him forget to eat, so when he arrived home, he fried an egg. Then he stripped and rolled into bed, asleep as soon as his head hit the pillow.

~ ~ ~

Monday morning, Justin called shortly after Clare arrived at

Northeastern. "God, Clare, you sure weren't easy to track down. Had to threaten to demote Stephan and Denise to demi-soloists before they'd give me your number."

She turned away speaking softly, hoping Gwen wouldn't hear. "I'm at work right now, so I can't take a personal call." She'd learned her first day the woman was a gossip and a sneak.

"Look, Clare, I want to talk to you about a position with the company."

When she'd been forced to stop dancing, it had been painful. As painful as an amputation. But now she was used to a different rhythm to her life. "Justin, I don't think—"

"Don't think. Just tell me when we can meet. It can be anytime. Early morning. Noon. Evening. Brunch. Lunch. Dinner. You choose."

If she didn't meet with him, he'd likely keep on calling until she agreed. So why not let him feed her? She was finding cooking a chore in her new place.

"Okay. Dinner. Tomorrow evening. You can pick me up at seven."

"Better give me your address, Clare. Denise absolutely drew the line on that."

~ ~ ~

Justin took Clare to The Pier, a restaurant so expensive and exclusive, she was handed a menu without any prices.

After they ordered, Justin lifted his glass of wine and toasted her. "To new possibilities."

She lifted her glass in response.

Justin took a sip before setting his glass down. "The food here is truly superb, Clare. I'd like to lay out the deal now so we can enjoy it without any distractions."

"It's your call, but I can think and chew at the same time."

"Let me give you something to think about, then. Shera is retiring. Means we're in the market for a ballet master."

It was what George Balanchine, Nureyev, Baryshnikov, Farrell and others had done. Transformed their careers as principals into careers of helping the next generation of dancers develop. A chance Clare had lost hope would come along for her.

"I see I've left you speechless." Justin raised his eyebrows with an amused look.

"You want me to be the ballet master?"

"And more."

"Why?"

"Was that the first piece of music you ever wrote and choreographed?"

"Yes."

"And the first time you've been responsible for directing a dancer in a piece."

"Yes."

He nodded as if to himself. "You created a bit of magic, Clare. The music, the choreography. Denise's interpretation. Your dancing. Well, you saw the reaction. How many times have you had an audience react like that?"

She sat still, tamping down on a growing excitement that was overlaid with a feeling of unreality.

"It's what it's about, though." Jason continued. "The dancer in a conversation with the audience, and when the audience gets it, really gets it...well, I bet you can tell me exactly how many times it's happened to you."

In Madrid. Whenever she'd danced with Zach. Twice during her first season in Boston and three times in the second season. "There's no guarantee I'll ever write another note or choreograph another step."

"I'm not asking you to guarantee it. I'm hiring you to bring out our dancers' potential. Like you did with Denise in that number Saturday."

"I didn't do anything with Denise."

"Right." He sat back grinning at her. "You're a natural teacher, Clare."

John and Sally had said the same thing, except they'd been talking about reading and writing, not dancing.

"As for the choreography," Justin continued, "I don't believe it was a fluke, and it's icing on the cake for the company. So what's it going to be, Clare? I need to know soon."

"What are you offering as a salary?"

He named an amount that was more than acceptable. "That's only the base, of course. You'll receive extra whenever you're involved in the choreography."

"Okay. I mean, yes. I accept. Thank you." She stumbled to a stop and Justin grinned.

"Figured you'd say that, although you were beginning to make me sweat. Welcome back to the company, Clare. Come in next week and we'll work out the details." He sat back with an expansive smile as the waiter settled salads in front of them.

Eventually she would have to deal with Justin's pushiness, but not tonight. Tonight, she would savor the food and the moment.

~ ~ ~

The first person Clare told about the ballet master position was Vinnie.

"You see, beautiful, I was right, wasn't I. Father did have big plans for you." Vinnie's tone was one of deep satisfaction.

"I'll have to adjust my tutoring schedule. I won't be able to do as much." She wasn't giving it up completely, though. Never again would she allow one thing to take over her life.

Odd that it took her so long to understand the importance of balance—not just for the dance but in life.

"We'll be pleased with whatever help you can give us. Oh, it's good to see you happy, Clare."

Was she happy? For sure she was excited, and she did feel good. Alive. Pleased. Except when she thought of Rob. A good man. The best she'd ever known, and she'd treated him with both indifference and cruelty. She hadn't even known she could be cruel. Before she could suppress it, a sob escaped.

Vinnie came around the desk and gathered her into ample arms. "Now, now, Clare. Now, that's okay, baby. You tell Vinnie all about it."

But she didn't have the words for what she was feeling, nor could she face saying out loud what she'd discovered about herself, although it might be an exorcism of sorts. John claimed it worked that way for him.

Clare pulled out of Vinnie's arms and blew her nose. "Sorry about that."

"Why, that's all right, beautiful. Sometimes a good cry is just what a body needs."

Except it didn't seem to be helping this time. "I'm not the person you think I am."

"Now who you think that is?" Vinnie asked.

"I'm not a nice person, but you're right about Rob. He is a nice man, a good man, and I treated him..." Her voice trailed off, remembering the many unkindnesses she'd inflicted on Rob.

"So maybe you got some making up to do."

Vinnie was right. That little bit of paint on the apartment walls was only an excuse to not make a real apology.

Chapter Twenty-Seven

Pirouette en pointe
Whirling or spinning on the tips of the toes

Clare took a couple of hours off during the day on Tuesday to meet with Justin at the practice center. Funny, the day he forced her to face what her injury meant to her future as a dancer, she'd hated Justin. And if even a week ago, someone had predicted she'd end up working for the man and be pleased about it, she would have said they were crazy.

Change. Sometimes it was good.

"In addition to working with the dancers, I want you to begin thinking about something," Justin said. "I'm planning a program of new works for next year, using local choreographers and composers. I'd like you to choreograph something for us. Have you followed the company the past three years?"

She hesitated before deciding honesty was better than tact. "No."

"Thought that might be the case. I've put together videos. They'll give you an overview of the capabilities of our current dancers." As he spoke, he lifted a pile of tapes from the floor and balanced them on the edge of the desk.

It meant she needed to buy a television and a VCR. Perhaps she should also ask for an advance on that nice salary.

~ ~ ~

Clare arrived at Hope House Friday afternoon, expecting to spend an ordinary evening tutoring. Instead, she was greeted by balloons and banners congratulating her on her new

234

position. She was soon surrounded by laughter, hugs, and speeches. Several of the men had gifts for her: homemade cards, a feather, a snow globe of Faneuil Hall and, from Kenny, a small copper-wire model of a ballerina. When the presentations ended, the music began. This time she had no choice but to join the dance.

Beck swung her around first. Although a large man, he was graceful and easy to dance with. After Beck, she moved from partner to partner, her feet flying. John was there, but he didn't ask her to dance. They'd last spoken the day before, when she'd encountered him painting one of the classrooms.

"I've been wanting to tell you—your support, friendship this past year. They helped me a great deal."

At her awkward words, John's movements slowed and finally stopped. He turned and stared at her.

"When I came here, I was...lost. Anyway, I wanted to thank you, John Apple, for your friendship."

"I wish you well, Clare Eliason Chapin." His voice was calm, his expression remote.

She nodded at him, and he turned back to his painting.

She left him to it, her heart hurting at the loss of the camaraderie they'd shared during some of her darkest times.

~ ~ ~

On Saturday, Clare went to the Chestnut Hill Mall and bought a small television and a VCR. It took a breathtakingly short time to spend most of the money in her account. At home, she went through the videos, noting each dancer's strengths and weaknesses, thinking about how best to help them fit into the program Justin had planned for next year. She finished late in the evening and sat back sipping a cup of tea, no longer thinking about the dancers, but about how Rob had reacted when she mentioned the ballet.

Before her injury, he'd always attended her performances so he could drive her home. In those quiet midnight hours, they'd sat eating, talking, laughing. Rob helping her to relax so she could sleep. But he'd never truly enjoyed the ballet. She was certain of it. He'd endured it for her sake, and she'd neither acknowledged nor sufficiently valued his sacrifice.

What a shallow person she'd been.

~ ~ ~

On Monday, Clare returned from lunch to her office at Northeastern to find a gift bag on her desk. Her first thought was it must be from Justin, but when she peered inside she found the parrot hat Rob gave her so long ago in another life.

"Those delivery guys are getting more professional all the time," Gwen said, nodding at the bag.

"What do you mean?" She reached for the envelope accompanying the hat.

"This one was wearing a tie."

She opened the card, already knowing whose handwriting she would see.

> *Rob Chapin requests the pleasure of*
> *Clare Eliason's company*
> *Saturday at seven for dinner*

"So who's it from?"

She stared at the card. Why was he using her maiden name? And why so formal? What did it mean?

"Well, just ignore me, why don't you."

Clare grimaced. Gwen, long-time receptionist and only fly-in-the-ointment of this particular temporary position. "I'm sorry. Did you say something?"

"I said, who's it from?"

"Oh. A friend."

"Right, and my name's Demi Moore."

Gwen could be right. Clare didn't know if Rob was still her friend. If he was, wouldn't he have come to the benefit?

Thinking of the benefit, another memory surfaced. The man who came up to her at the reception and said he worked with Rob. His name was something with a D...Devin, Dover?

She pulled out a copy of the Northeastern phone book and ran a finger down the column of *D* names. Devaney. That was it. Edward Devaney, Esquire, College of Law. He'd said something about Rob and Marge Velez, who'd claimed she was being paid by a philanthropist nobody ever heard of.

Frowning, Clare went back to typing a manuscript she was determined to finish before she left to begin her position with Danse Classique.

~ ~ ~

Saturday evening, Rob arrived at her apartment precisely at seven, punctual as always. She didn't invite him in since she still had no furniture. Nor did she have anything to offer him to drink, except water. All nonessentials waiting until she was more solvent.

"This seems to be a nice, quiet neighborhood," Rob said as he helped her into the car.

"It is, and it's convenient to public transportation."

"That's great. How are you enjoying working for Professor Molina? I've heard he can be a curmudgeon."

"Only to the students. He's been very pleasant to me." And enough already with the inane pleasantries. "You know, if we'd been this awkward our first date, there never would have been a second."

He blinked rapidly, then glanced at her. "Sorry. You're right, but you see, what I was thinking..." His voice trailed off.

"What?" She turned to look at him, or at least his profile.

"I know you're supposed to get only one chance to make a first impression, but I thought you and I...well, maybe we can try backing up. As if we're at the beginning, getting to know each other. I know I've changed, and I expect you have too."

She stared at him.

"That probably sounds stupid. I guess it's better if I just sign the papers and be done with it. Shame, though. To let those years go to waste." He stopped speaking abruptly and his hands tightened on the steering wheel.

"You want us to pretend we've just met each other?"

"Yes, that's it."

The awkward suggestion was so...Rob-like. Clare began to smile, then straightened her lips. If he saw her smiling, he might think she was laughing at him, and maybe she was, a little. But mostly she was smiling in relief to know he wasn't planning to end the evening by handing her the signed divorce papers, although that would be totally unlike him.

Except. If she were to play along with his suggestion, she should keep an open mind about what he was like. He said he'd changed. It might be interesting to discover the particulars. "Okay, you've got yourself a deal."

"Good."

They didn't talk as he drove into town, but the silence was a comfortable one. Rob parked the car on St. Botolph Street near Northeastern and walked her into a restaurant that was tiny, quiet, French, and one of her favorites.

"So tell me, Rob Chapin," she said after they were served glasses of wine. "What do you like best about being a professor?"

As if to check her sincerity, he gave her a quick glance, then he leaned back, speaking thoughtfully. "Well, Miss Eliason, let's see. The freedom, I guess. Aside from a few meetings and my classes, I pretty much set my own schedule. And as long as I have grant money, I can work on whatever scientific question intrigues me the most."

"So what scientific question intrigues you?" Sad to admit that although she'd been married to him, she knew only the surface aspects of what he did at work every day.

"I'm studying plants used by native healers to see if they contain active compounds."

She tipped her head, motioning for him to continue, glad for the game.

"Most people figure it's only a coincidence when a payé, a medicine man that is, cures someone. That the patient was going to get better anyway. But I think *payés* are amazing ethnobotanists."

"What's that?"

"A person who understands plants and how to use them. It takes years to be a *payé*."

"So is that your goal. To become a *payé*?"

He shook his head, and she realized she'd never before asked him what his dreams were.

His expression turned pensive. "I just came back from Peru where I worked with a *payé* for six months. I barely scratched the surface of his knowledge of plants and healing rituals. He even used a few of them on me."

"Are you ready to order?" The waiter stood poised with a napkin over his arm, a pen and pad at the ready.

"Give us a minute, will you," Rob said.

After they'd perused their menus and placed their orders, Clare picked up the thread of the conversation. "Why did you need the services of a *payé*?"

"I had to have an emergency appendectomy in the jungle. The surgery was performed using modern methods, but then the healer performed a healing service, and he provided a poultice for my incision."

Once again, the thought of Rob having surgery in the jungle made her throat tight. He could have died so easily. Suddenly, she wanted to touch him, to reassure herself of his solidity. Instead, she circled the lip of her wine glass with a finger. "Do you think the healer helped?"

Rob looked thoughtfully at his own wine glass before taking a sip and setting it down. "The incision did heal more quickly than my surgeon expected."

"What was it like in the jungle?"

"It was...completely different from any other place I've ever been. Instead of sirens and the hum of air conditioners, we had the screech of birds, the buzz of insects. The sheer magnitude of all that green, raucous, aggressive life. Overwhelming. Claustrophobic at times. And us in the middle of it. With no filters, no barriers. Our huts didn't even have complete walls."

As Rob continued to talk, she sat back listening, trying to visualize what he was describing. Comparing it to what she'd read about the Amazon.

"One day, I was down by the river at dawn. All of a sudden, the tops of the trees exploded into the sky as thousands of macaws took off. Blue, red, green. An enormous cloud of color. And my God, the sound. As if everyone in Boston was leaning on their horns. Then they were gone, and I could hear the river again."

They sat silently as the waiter came and placed salads in front of them. Clare waited until they were alone before she spoke past the lump in her throat. "Were you happy there?"

"Happy? No. At first, I hated it. Then I made friends with the Machiguenga, the people we stayed with. The way they conducted their lives...it made me wonder how different our world would be if we lived more simply and chose the wise rather than the clever to lead us."

He stopped to take a bite of salad, chewed, swallowed, then continued. "I haven't been happy for a long time, but I did find some satisfaction being there. There was interesting work to do and no phone calls to return, no mail to open, no meetings to attend, or news to watch."

No wife to worry about. But Rob was too kind to add that.

"One of the Machiguenga men took me on as a project. He taught me to find paths through the jungle, to spot animals hidden in the shadows, to locate food and water. The peculiar thing is, it rains a great deal and there's the river, but safe drinking water is always in short supply. One day, we'd been walking for several hours, and my water ran out. The man showed me this vine. He cut the end and the clearest, most delicious water was right there, like turning on a tap."

Ann Warner

She could see it clearly. Living water coming out of the vine and Rob smiling at the native man and then taking a grateful drink. She wished she could have shared that with him.

He stopped and took a sip of wine, before looking across at her. "What about you? Do you have a career?"

"I'm finishing a temporary job typing a manuscript for an English professor. Next week, though, I'm starting a new job. One I'm very excited about." She paused, then took the plunge, watching him closely. "I'm going to be the ballet master for Danse Classique."

He was bringing a bite of salad to his mouth, and the fork stopped in midair. His lips tightened. "Does that mean you're a dancer?"

She struggled to continue speaking. "Most ballet masters used to be dancers, which I was. A long time ago. I'm not anymore."

"How come?"

She glanced at him, but saw nothing in his expression to indicate he was deliberately baiting her. "I was injured and was no longer able to dance. For a long time, I let it paralyze me. You know that phrase, 'stop the world I want to get off'? That was me. Only I couldn't get off."

"What did you do?"

"I didn't handle it well."

"You're obviously better now, though?"

"Once I finally got out of bed and started tutoring men and boys with real problems. Compared to what they face, my being unable to dance is a minor difficulty."

"Not to you."

"True, but I made it worse than it needed to be."

"You learned something from the experience, though."

"Yes. I did."

Their eyes met and her heart contracted. Rob had lines at the corners of his eyes she'd not noticed before, and his temples were brushed with silver.

The waiter placed their entrées in front of them, and they ate slowly, continuing to talk. Clare asked Rob to explain how he studied the plants the *payé* told them about. She listened carefully to his answers, then asked more questions, and although Rob's work was complex, she could understand it when she made the effort to do so.

What an odd suggestion on Rob's part—to pretend they'd just met. It was working, though. Such a huge relief to let go of the past, for even one night.

240

After dinner, Rob drove her home and walked her to the door. She unlocked it, then turned to thank him.

"My sister and her husband own a boat. Would you like to go sailing with me?"

"Yes. I would."

"Good. Are you free tomorrow?"

She nodded.

He set a time, leaned in and kissed her cheek, then turned and walked to his car. Bemused, she climbed the stairs to her bare apartment.

~ ~ ~

Sunday dawned with clear skies, warm temperatures, and brisk breezes—perfect sailing weather. During the drive to the Cape and the loading of supplies aboard the yacht, Rob and Clare continued to play the getting-to-know-you game.

When they cleared the harbor, Rob turned to her. "Would you like to steer?"

She jumped up and took her place at the helm while he moved around the boat, turning cranks to extend the sails, then he came and stood beside her. After a moment, he pointed. "Try to keep us lined up with that spit of land."

She wondered if he'd deliberately echoed what he'd said and done the first time they'd gone sailing.

Possibly.

She was reminded of other sails with Rob. Days when the wind thrummed in the rigging and the sun turned the bow wave to crystal. After her injury, sailing had been the only activity that eased her heart. "I used to sail." She watched him out of the corner of her eye. "I've missed it."

"Why did you stop?"

"The man who took me had to go away...to save himself."

His lips tightened. He balanced on the balls of his feet as the boat heeled from the swell. "Save himself from what?"

"From me."

Rob's eyes were invisible behind dark glasses, but his mouth was tight. For a time after that, neither of them spoke.

~ ~ ~

When they returned to Falmouth in the late afternoon, Rob suggested driving to Provincetown for dinner, which was how they'd often ended such a day in the past.

In the Provincetown café, Clare slid into the booth across from Rob, noticing how clear and calm the day on the water left his eyes. It had worked that way for her as well, leaving her with a pleasant lassitude, due in part, perhaps, to the game.

But as relaxing as it was to leave the past behind, it had to be faced eventually.

Chapter Twenty-Eight

Grand pas de deux - Coda
Last movement of the grand dance for two

"I believe I owe you one," Clare said, after the waitress dropped off coffees and the dessert menu.

He raised his eyebrows in question. "For what?"

"Marge Velez."

Damn. His hands tightened on his cup. So the woman hadn't kept her mouth shut. Or was Clare simply fishing for information?

She stirred her coffee, looking at him. "I ran into Edward Devaney, and he said the most curious thing to me about telling you Marge Velez was the best."

She stopped speaking. He kept his head down, focused on his mug.

"Why did you do it?" Clare's voice was soft, but clearly she wasn't going to buy any half-assed attempts to say he didn't know what she was talking about.

A mistake not to ask Devaney to keep quiet, but he never expected Clare and Devaney's paths to cross. In honor of their new openness, he decided to tell her the simple truth. "I met a young boy in Peru. The son of the Machiguengan man who was teaching me about the jungle. One day, Tatito was attacked by a wild pig. His father was also injured. I had to carry the boy back to the village. He died in my arms."

Swamped by memory, he stopped to reorder his thoughts. "When you told me about Tyrese, it reminded me of what it was like not being able to save Tatito. I'm glad it worked out."

Clare laid a hand on his arm. "It was a wonderful thing to do."

"Please don't say anything to anyone else."

"Why didn't you want me to know?"

That was the rub. "I didn't want you to think...well, that I had no faith you could solve your own problems."

"Even though, in this particular instance, I couldn't."

"You'd already turned me down, but when I read that ballerina/Bull Shark piece, I wanted to stick a spoke in Hortz's wheel. Selfish impulse. I didn't expect you'd ever find out."

"I don't believe it was selfish. Did you ever meet Hortz?"

"Devaney said his nickname is Hortz's ass."

Clare laughed. "Thank you for that. It's perfect."

~ ~ ~

"I have another question. I want to know if you like the ballet?" She'd asked Rob that question before, the first time they'd gone out. Then, he'd smiled and said with her help, he was working on it. This time he didn't smile.

"I used to. I don't anymore."

"Why not?"

He gazed at her steadily before looking away. "I once knew a principal dancer. I saw how the ballet treated her after she was injured. I hated it after that." His voice held a deep undertone of anger, but he wasn't angry with her. Or maybe he was. For going back.

"You weren't there." The words pushed their way out.

"I wasn't where?"

"At the benefit." She sucked in a breath. "I was afraid...that my ankle might give out in the middle, or that it wouldn't, but my dancing would be...that people would pity me. Then I realized if you weren't there, nothing else mattered."

"I was there."

Her head came up and she stared at him.

"I'll never forget it. You were... Your performance...it..." He stopped, took a deep breath, raised his face to hers. "It made me cry."

For a time they met each other's gaze across a short gap of table.

"You always took care of me, and I took it for granted. As if it were my due. I don't think I ever thanked you, at least not properly."

He reached out and touched her under the chin, then smoothed the corners of her eyes with his thumbs, wiping away the wetness. "It was never a hardship doing anything for you, and you showed me in all kinds of ways you were grateful."

"But when I was injured, I kept kicking and screaming instead of buckling down and dealing with it. Until you said 'enough' and went away."

"I...I couldn't stay." His voice was flat, his face shuttered. "It wasn't my finest hour either."

"I understood. Your leaving was necessary. It forced me to stop hiding from life, you know."

"You must hate me."

"Oh, no, Rob. I've never hated you. How could I?" She looked down at her plate. "After I started going to Hope House, I realized everyone has problems, some large, some small. Some huge. What matters is how a person deals with them, and I made a mess of it."

"You're being too hard on yourself."

"No. No, I'm not. I had a chance. To be courageous. I blew it."

"It took awhile, but you figured it out."

She shook her head.

"It took courage to dance for the benefit."

She ducked her head, looking away from the blaze in his eyes. "No. It was—"

"Admirable. Difficult. Brave."

"I'm glad you came."

"I would have hated to miss it. I'll never forget it."

They sat staring at each other.

"You folks decide on dessert yet? We've got fresh cherry pie."

"Sure. Bring us one piece, two forks." When the waitress left, Rob smiled at her. "We've been working hard. We deserve a treat."

~ ~ ~

Driving back to Boston, they didn't talk much. Clare tuned the radio to a country music station then sat back and dozed, occasionally waking enough to visualize combinations of steps to fit the music. When they got to her apartment, Rob walked her to the door. He bent his head and kissed her briefly on the mouth. She wanted more than that fleeting contact. She wanted his arms around her, holding her tight against him. She wanted...she took a breath and curbed her desire.

It was good Rob wasn't forcing the pace. The work they were doing, sorting through the past, explaining, asking forgiveness, forgiving, was complex. Best to finish before they took any other step.

~ ~ ~

Tuesday evening, Rob took Clare to dinner at Legal Seafoods in Chestnut Hill.

"I don't have any furniture yet," she said, as they finished eating. "How would you like to spend a few minutes window-shopping with me?"

Of course. It was what he should have done when they first married. Gone with her to choose things for the apartment. Instead, he'd handed her a checkbook.

In that way, he'd been merely following his father's example, but he now understood that a home should reflect both people living there.

In the furniture store, Clare indicated a table with an intricate, gilded design. "What do you think of that?"

"It would make excellent kindling."

"You like it that much?"

"Actually, I believe I'd chop that up first." He pointed at a sofa. Its sibling sat in his parents' living room. With sudden clarity, he realized how much he disliked it.

Clare was obviously trying not to smile. "I take it French Provincial isn't your favorite."

He shuddered. "If that's what this is."

"Why don't you like it?"

"Where to start." He rubbed his chin. "Well, it's fussy and pretentious. It looks like it expects to be dusted frequently but aside from that you can bloody well leave it alone, and for God's sake don't even think about sitting on it."

Clare laughed. "So what do you like?"

"The opposite of this, I guess. I have no idea what you'd call it. How about you?"

"I agree. This is too fussy."

The offerings of the second furniture store were equally unacceptable. "Looks like it's going to take more work than I thought it would," Clare said. "Although, I can't really afford to buy anything yet."

He found himself almost saying not to worry, he'd pay for it, then stifled the impulse, realizing it was part of the pattern he was determined to alter.

The shopping trip did accomplish one thing. He and Clare learned more about each other's home decor likes and dislikes in a couple of hours than they had during their years of marriage.

~ ~ ~

Although Clare arrived at the Danse Classique practice center early, she found Justin already halfway through a pot of coffee.

She'd awakened excited and happy. Easily explained, of course. A new job. Back in the world she loved. And the progress she and Rob were making was adding to her feeling of well-being. She broke off thoughts about Rob to pour herself a cup of coffee.

Justin leaned back and breathed in the steam from his own cup. "Have you watched the videos?"

"I have."

"Any ideas yet about a new piece? Not that I'm expecting it, of course."

"Actually, I do." Clare sipped her coffee, smiling to herself. She hadn't planned to think about the program until she'd settled back in, but then Rob had given her the perfect idea. "What I'm thinking is a dance based upon the third act of a classical French farce. With its careful timings of entrances and exits, a farce is very like ballet, pulled into a different shape. It would provide multiple opportunities for brief pas de deux in various combinations. I'm also thinking that throughout the dance, pieces of fussy furniture would collapse and, for the finale, the wronged men would bond as they gather up the debris and toss it into the fireplace." She waited while Justin sat, obviously thinking.

"We have several people who could handle the comedic aspects of such a program." He named four dancers, the same four she'd decided would be the best choices for the two intertwined and mismatched lovers. "It's unconventional. Interesting." Justin rubbed his hand back and forth across his lips. "I like it."

Excitement bubbled inside Clare and threatened to overflow. It was the best first day she could ever remember.

~ ~ ~

"How did it go today?" Rob asked when he picked her up for dinner.

"Amazingly well. It's good to be back."

"Well, it looks like it agrees with you. Guess that means I better suck it up and get used to it."

"You're also going to have to suck it up and share creative credit with me when I choreograph the inspiration you gave me."

"What inspiration is that?"

"Justin wants me to come up with a short piece for a program of new works for next year. You're responsible for giving me the idea to do a dance based on a French farce involving hoity-toity furniture. Justin loved it."

"So a professor and a dancer isn't such an odd combination after all."

"Not odd at all."

~ ~ ~

"You need to bring your parrot hat with you." Rob said when she opened the door to him the next Sunday.

"You're not kidnapping me to go off to a Jimmy Buffett sing-along are you? Because I'd rather go sailing."

"No sing-alongs. But I have a surprise, and it definitely requires a parrot hat."

Intrigued but uneasy, she retrieved the hat from her bedroom. The last time Rob tried to surprise her, when he'd rented the beach cottage, it ended badly.

"Do I get any hints at all?"

"Nope. You'll just have to wait until we get there."

When he took the usual turnoff to Falmouth, she sighed in relief that the surprise wasn't replacing the sail he'd promised her. They arrived at the yacht, and Rob transferred on board bags of provisions along with a large carton. She stored the food then sat in the shade of the cockpit watching as he prepared to get under way. Once they did, he set course to sail along the south coast of the Cape. It finally hit her where they were going, after Rob pulled out binoculars and scanned the beach. She waited to see if she was right.

Finally, Rob turned and handed her the binoculars and pointed. It was difficult to focus given the movement of the boat, but she didn't need the binoculars to know where they were—about a hundred yards out from the cottage.

Rob reefed the sails and set the anchor. "Okay. Time to get out your parrot hat."

She pulled it out of her tote, and he took it from her and settled it on her head. Then he reached into the box he'd carried aboard and took out the panama with the disgruntled-looking parrot she'd chosen for him. He handed it to her and she, in turn, placed it on his head.

Next he lifted a portable tape player out of the box, placed it on the bench, and hit the Start button. The first notes of "Margaritaville" began to play, transporting her back to that wonderful, silly day before Rob and she knew each other well, but had already learned to laugh together. Tears filled her eyes, although it wasn't exactly sadness she was feeling.

Next, Rob reached into the box and pulled out several sheets of paper. "Now that I've set the proper mood, I'm hoping you'll help me dispose of these. That is, if you agree they aren't needed any longer?" He looked at her intently as he handed her the pages. She knew what they had to be. The divorce agreement with her signature affixed to the last page. Rob's signature was still missing, thank God, and what a near thing that had been.

She handed him back half the sheets, keeping the last page for herself, and while the song continued to play, they each tore their respective pages into tiny pieces. The fragments of their mistakes swirled around them like miniature seagulls, until a gust of wind swooped them up and over the rail to skim along the water. A whitecap broke over them, and in an instant, they were gone, leaving only the crisscrossing pattern of the waves behind.

The notes of the song ended, and Rob pulled her into his arms, holding her as if he had no intention of letting her go again.

Chapter Twenty-Nine

*And let the winds of the heavens
dance between you.*
Kahlil Gibran

Clare sat on the bench in the sailboat's cockpit, watching Rob fish lazily off the side. It seemed incredible that for once this wasn't a dream. Whenever she'd tried to remember him while he was in Peru, this was the image that came to her. Rob, either turned away from her, or facing her but backlit by the sun so she'd been unable to see his face.

"Did either of us have a clue?" she said.

He turned his head and gave her a steady look, then he reeled in his line. "Doesn't seem like it."

She looked at his dear face as he came and sat on the bench next to her.

"While I was in the jungle, I thought about us. Did you do that, Clare? Think about us?"

She nodded, meeting his gaze. How odd to be able to live in physical intimacy with a person and yet hold back so much of yourself you remained strangers. Her heart felt like it was swelling, and after a moment, she recognized the feeling for what it was. Love. She loved Rob.

She'd first felt this way the night of the benefit. Since then, the feeling had grown until it filled her whole consciousness. She loved this man. Loved him passionately and wholeheartedly.

But without the abrupt demarcation of his leaving, she might never have known. "You make everyone else seem...insubstantial." Wonder filled her. "But I have so little to offer you."

"Yourself. That's enough."

They sat without touching, looking in each other's eyes. She leaned toward him and cupped his cheek with her hand. "It's really quite simple. Isn't it?

"What, Clare?" His voice was soft, although she heard a faint tremor in his words.

"Rob. I..." She closed her eyes for a moment seeking courage, then opened them and met his clear gaze. "I love you. I think I always have, and I didn't know it. How could I not have known?"

"You were hurt, uncertain."

"I wasted so much time."

"It's all right now, Clare." He reached out to lay his hand on her head, as if in benediction.

~ ~ ~

The sun traversed overhead, and the yacht lying at anchor bobbed gently in the swell. The two people joined together in the small cabin moved in their own rhythm. Touching and blending. Discovering. Forgiving. Asking silent questions neither was any longer afraid to answer. Transcending the hurt they'd done each other.

After they joined, they slept, rocked in the arms of a quiet sea.

<<<>>>

About the Author

The books Ann loved most as a child were those about horses. After reading Mary O'Hara's Wyoming ranch stories, she decided she would one day marry a rancher and own a racehorse—not necessarily in that order. Since it was abundantly clear to Ann, after reading *My Friend Flicka* and *Green Grass of Wyoming*, that money could be a sore point between husbands and wives, not to mention racehorses don't come cheap, she decided appropriate planning was needed. Thus she appended a "rich" to the rancher requirement.

But when she started dating, there were no ranchers in the offing, rich or otherwise. Instead, Ann fell in love with a fellow graduate student at the University of Kansas. Not only does her husband not share her love of horses, he doesn't even particularly like them, given that one stepped on him with deliberate intent when he was ten.

After years in academia, Ann took a turn down another road and began writing fiction. Her first novel, *Dreams for Stones*, was published by Samhain Publishing in 2007. The protagonist is both a university professor and part-time rancher—proof perhaps that dreams never truly go away, but continue to exert their influence in unexpected ways.

Those unexpected influences have continued to play a role in Ann's succeeding books, including this one.

Visit Ann at:

http://AnnWarner.net

or

On Facebook

Ann Warner Author of Emotionally Engaging Fiction

A Note to Readers

Thank you so much for reading *Counterpointe*. This novel is one of the *five thousand* or so books being published *each day*, so I'm thrilled you found it. And I hope you'll want to participate in the book's success by bringing it to the attention of other readers.

Things you can do not only for me but for other authors you enjoy:

Write a review and post it to whatever site(s) you prefer: Amazon, B&N, Kobo, Goodreads, etc.

Make a point of telling friends and family about *Counterpointe*.

Post information on your Facebook or Tsu pages.

Something else I hope you will do:

Go to my website and sign up for my mailing list:
http://AnnWarner.net/mailing-list

In return you will receive a monthly electronic newsletter containing insider information about the stories behind the stories, my writing process, and suggestions of other books you might enjoy, as well as early notifications of new releases and special offers.

I love hearing from readers.
You can contact me through the form on my website

http://AnnWarner.net/contact

Thank You!

Acknowledgements

Thank you to all the readers who have enjoyed my novels and let me know it, and a special thank you to Kari Brunson for ballet details and to fellow writer Judy Carpenter for valuable suggestions.

And my gratitude, as always, to my wonderful editor, Pam Berehulke. Pam is responsible for everything that is correct in this novel. Any errors are due to my obsessive revising after Pam has worked her perfection magic.

Also by Ann Warner

Absence of Grace

The memory of an act committed when she was nineteen weaves a dark thread through Clen McClendon's life. It is a darkness Clen ignores until the discovery of her husband's infidelity propels her on a quest for her own redemption and forgiveness. At first, her journeying provides few answers and peace remains elusive. Then Clen makes a decision that is both desperate and random to go to Wrangell, Alaska. There she will meet Gerrum Kirsey and learn choices are never truly random and they always have consequences.

This book is available as a free download from
www.AnnWarner.net

Doubtful

Doubtful Sound, New Zealand

For Dr. Van Peters, Doubtful is a retreat after a false accusation all but ends her scientific career. For David Christianson, Doubtful is a place of respite after a personal tragedy is followed by an unwelcome notoriety.

Neither is looking for love or even friendship. Each wants only to make it through another day. But when violence comes to Doubtful, Van and David's only chance of survival will be each other.

Love and Other Acts of Courage

Water is everywhere in *Love and Other Acts of Courage*. Maritime attorney Max Gildea sees it flowing under the Golden Gate bridge from his office window and also sees it from the terrace of the house he has built on a jut of land overlooking the Pacific. Near New Zealand, in the Tasman Sea, a vast deep tide of it overwhelms and sinks the yacht, *Sylph*. Off Australia, turquoise waters hide what has happened to a couple left behind on a dive trip. And in Sydney harbor, more water passes under Harbor Bridge and on past the Opera House. *Love and Other Acts of Courage* takes place in all of these settings.

A number of years ago, I read a story about a freighter colliding with a yacht and then sailing away, without attempting a rescue. Of the two adults and two children on the yacht that night, only one, a woman, survived.

I subsequently learned about the limited options available to that survivor to make the freighter crew pay for their incompetence in hitting the yacht and their inhumanity in leaving the scene without attempting a rescue. In real life a suit was filed, and there was, eventually, some sort of settlement. But the crew members were never held accountable for their inhumanity.

I felt a similar outrage, mixed with astonishment, at a report about that same time of a dive boat taking a group out to the Great Barrier Reef and returning to the harbor minus two of the passengers. The boat crew failed to notice or react to the extra shoes and bags left behind. Nor did the bus driver remark on the fact he had two fewer passengers at the end of the day than at the beginning. Having been on such boats, if I were reading about this event purely as a piece of fiction, I would question its believability. This only goes to show that fact truly is often more strange than fiction is allowed to be.

In *Love and Other Acts of Courage*, I take these events and weave them into a story replete with heroes, heroines, and villains, and because it's my story, the bad guys are dealt with.

Memory Lessons

Glenna Girard has passed through the agony and utter darkness of an unimaginable loss. It is only in planning her escape, from her marriage and her current circumstances, that she manages to start moving again, toward a place where she can live in anonymity and atone for the unforgivable mistake she has made.

As she takes tentative steps into the new life she is so carefully shaping, she has no desire to connect with other people. But fate has other ideas, bringing her a family who can benefit from her help if only she will give it. And a man, Jack Ralston, who is everything she needs to live fully again, if Glenna will just let herself see it.

Dreams for Stones
Indie Next Generation Book Award Finalist
Scheduled for re-release 2015

Poignant and haunting, a love story of loss and second chances.

It takes courage to be human. And it especially takes courage to love, knowing that love inevitably opens the door to loss. But what is fascinating about this human conundrum is the hopefulness with which most of us manage it.

But we also live with the possibility of wonderful new beginnings. As an author, that's what pulls me in for closer examination. Come with me then and meet Alan, a man who has given up on love, and Kathy, a woman who has learned to let go of love too easily. It will take all the magic of serendipity, old diaries, and a children's story to heal these two.

Sign up for my newsletter in order to be notified when *Dreams for Stones* is re-released in 2015.

All my novels are available in electronic and print versions from Create Space, Amazon, and other retailers.

Made in the USA
San Bernardino, CA
29 January 2016